THE ENVOYS IN THE MULTIVERSE

TWO

A WORLD AT RISK

TAYLOR SORENSEN

innovo
PUBLISHING

Published by Innovo Publishing, LLC
www.innovopublishing.com
1-888-546-2111

Publishing quality books, eBooks, audiobooks, music, screenplays &
courses for the Christian & wholesome markets since 2008.

A World at Risk
Volume 2 in The Envoys in the Multiverse Series

Library of Congress Control Number: 2024911039
ISBN: 979-8-88928-021-7

Cover Design & Interior Layout: Innovo Publishing, LLC

Printed in the United States of America
U.S. Printing History
First Edition: 2024

Has God called you to create a Christ-centered or wholesome book, eBook,
audiobook, music album, screenplay, or online course? Visit Innovo's
educational center (cpportal.com) to learn how to accomplish your calling
with excellence.

ACKNOWLEDGMENTS

First and foremost, none of these stories would exist on paper without You, Jesus. Thank You for continuing to enable me and embolden me to write these parables. Thank You for showing me Your truth, patiently teaching and shepherding me, and being faithful even when I'm not. Any and all glory justly goes to You, God, and I pray that You expand Your kingdom and deepen relationships through this book!

I would also like to thank everyone God has put in my life who has taught me more about Him and challenged me to grow in my faith and guide others in doing the same. Thank you, Mom, Dad, Derek Wilkerson, Keith Burkhart, Drew Ray, Daniel and Carol Ray, Jimmy Patterson, Colton Seamans, Ryleigh Andrews, and so many others I could name! Thank you all for selflessly pouring into me and several others as we walk with Christ together. He has produced much fruit in each of you!

Thank you also to my amazing brothers, Brett, Scott, Todd, and Jack. Each of your walks and passions for Christ and His church inspires and pushes me to go deeper with mine. He's got amazing plans in store for each of you, and I can't wait to see them play out, Lord willing.

A huge thank you to my Aunt Leah, who has been one of my strongest advocates and unofficial advertisers for my previous book. Your support and encouragement is thoroughly appreciated.

I also want to thank Sharon Pierce and Gillson and Sophia Keller, probably my biggest fans outside of family. Thank you all for wanting to read the last book together and desiring to go through this adventure with me! Sharon specifically, thank you for each and every encouragement you've given as the last book was published and as I wrote this one. It has not gone unnoticed.

Finally, I would like to thank Dr. Bart Dahmer and Rachael Carrington for their guidance and support in the publishing of my books. I am extremely thankful for how clear, prompt, and authentic you both have been, and I'm grateful to get to work with you again. Here's to many more parables being made accessible wherever God leads!

"We are human, but we don't wage war as humans do. We use God's mighty weapons, not worldly weapons, to knock down the strongholds of human reasoning and to destroy false arguments. We destroy every proud obstacle that keeps people from knowing God. We capture their rebellious thoughts and teach them to obey Christ. And after you have become fully obedient, we will punish everyone who remains disobedient."
—2 Corinthians 10:3-6

"And all of this is a gift from God, who brought us back to himself through Christ. And God has given us this task of reconciling people to him. For God was in Christ, reconciling the world to himself, no longer counting people's sins against them. And he gave us this wonderful message of reconciliation. So we are Christ's ambassadors; God is making his appeal through us. We speak for Christ when we plead, 'Come back to God!' For God made Christ, who never sinned, to be the offering for our sin, so that we could be made right with God through Christ."
—2 Corinthians 5:18-21

PROLOGUE

D arkness crowded the unlit room as it lay unoccupied, thriving in the stillness and silence. Soon the silence was broken as a creature entered on what sounded like four hooved legs. Clanking metal—sheathed weapons tapping armor—could also be heard as the creature approached a lantern in the nearest corner. It was lit with a self-lighting torch, a device known only to more technologically advanced species. The being did this with every lantern along the wall, then continued to the next one until all five walls were finished. Then, it flew up and lit a few overhanging lamps that hovered several yards above the ground. Even though the room still seemed half dark, one could now tell that this room was a personal training ground filled with wooden targets and dummies, even some hanging with the lanterns above. One could also recognize the creature in the room: Maewing.

The renowned and well-revered leader of the Self-Worthy, Maewing was an independent comrade whose only aim was to guide everyone to realizing their own individual potentials through public, political, and even militant means. Maewing was a winged ponytaur, a relatively small centaur blessed with the gift of wings—and passion. She was very proud of her army, her friends as she liked to call them, and was so sure of and determined in her purpose. She wore her usual silver breastplate and white chain mail, plus dark red horse armor, a new gift from the elf Ives, whom they'd rescued from the Elven Kingdom of Liberdane shortly after they had lost that kingdom to the Vine, Nazir, and his Envoys.

That was two whole years ago, Maewing said to herself. *There is no need to dwell on those thoughts anymore.*

But she did. Those Envoys had done barely any of the fighting or work, yet they were the ones who managed to steal the kingdom from them, all because her team didn't have the crown and Nazir (*who did he think he was anyway?*) appointed a random couple to be its king and queen. This cost the Self-Worthy dearly in time and numbers, and they were even now recovering from that loss.

Maewing finally stopped in her thoughts. She'd gotten cross enough. She unbuckled the sheath containing the Sword of *Chârâsh*, the weapon she received from one of her troops that could take one across the multiverse—*Rôb Tĕbêl*—supposedly without going through Nazir.

Maewing placed the Sword on a table near the room's entrance and trotted intently toward one of the wooden dummies, grasping her mortal, dual-bladed sword in its holster (a sheath would never work for that weapon). Without warning, she drew the sword and began slashing angrily and skillfully at the dummy, taking chunks out of it with every strike. She then swirled around to a target behind her, delivering several kill moves muffled out by her shouts. She did this passionately with every mannequin in that room, wielding her sword so quickly it was but a blur. Then, Maewing took off into the air and slashed at the overhanging targets, circling and weaving through them multiple times and swooping for shots at the targets below. She did this for almost an hour (for ponytaurs also have great endurance) before alighting in the middle of the room, every dummy around her in tatters. She would have to ask one of her friends to help her replace these later.

Taking several heaving breaths, Maewing glanced at the Sword of *Chârâsh* sitting on the table. She decided to practice a little with that too. She walked slowly toward it and picked it up without a second thought.

That is a fine blade, there.

Maewing turned instantly and swung the Sword around her. There was no one there, but she plainly heard that voice the instant she'd grabbed the blade. Perhaps it was a thought, only that thought was not hers. That voice was not hers; it was male—beautiful and subtle, yet potently clear at the same time.

That Sword is the key.

"Who are you?" Maewing asked sharply. "What do you mean?"

The key to your dream's realization. The Sword has the capability to unite the worlds, to unite them physically. And you have the power to unite them under one purpose: their individual purposes.

"How do you know this? Tell me who you are!"

You may consider me a voice to guide you to your true self. A voice you can trust.

"I have trusted many in vain. Show yourself worthy of my confidence."

I know your deepest thoughts, the ones you never let anyone know. You've been in doubt—doubt that your mission can truly succeed across every realm, with every person. You've let thoughts creep into your resilient mind that this purpose of yours can't be done. That it's all for naught.

Maewing was in awe. "And?"

And the Sword of Chârâsh can ensure its success. However, I must warn you: you will never have an opportunity to use its full power.

Maewing gripped the Sword tighter. "How do you know this?"

What kept the Self-Worthy from applying its power in Liberdane? What stopped them from getting to use it beyond going to and from that world?

"The Envoys."

The Envoys. The voice in her head had a disgusted echo in saying this. *The servants of Nazir, the meddling Vine who reaps where he has not sown. Just as they did before, the Envoys will keep you from using the Sword at its full potential—from attaining your full potential.*

Maewing stood silently for a moment, teeth clenched. "Something must be done to prevent this."

What can be done?

"The answer to the first question is the answer to the second question: the Envoys. If they are the ones who can stop me, then their existence is a barrier that must be overcome. The Envoys must be snuffed out if the multiverse is ever to be free."

Maewing heard no more. She waited for a second to see if the voice would return, but it didn't. She looked down at the Sword in her hand, and, holding it up in front of her, she gripped it even tighter, watching the glow enhance more and more as she did so. She left the room, almost galloping, ready to prepare for the execution of her newfound resolve.

PART I

THE FIRE IS STOKED

1

A NEW FOCUS

It was a cool, autumn Friday night, which consistently promised more bustle than freedom. Clive's Steakhouse was packed and loud, even though it wasn't the finest eatery in Philadelphia by any means. It seemed like a good date place for Amory and Bernice, though they often had to speak up to hear each other.

"I'm starting to think we should've done fast food," Bernice shouted.

"Nah, not after a half-hour wait. We just sat down anyway, so we made it," said Amory twice, having to repeat himself.

"How was work?" asked Bernice.

"It was good. I got to fix the transmission on a Corvette, so that was fun! Other than that, it was pretty normal. How about you?"

"It was OK. I never really liked the work of a receptionist, but it's not all that bad. No rude callers today, thankfully."

"Have you gotten any responses from either application yet?" Amory asked.

"One said their HR position is now taken, and the other hasn't said anything," said Bernice in a monotonous tone, which was followed by a sigh.

"Dang it. I'm sorry. You've been pursuing this for a long time, and still nothing."

"I've talked to Nazir about it and asked him why he won't let me get into HR when I know that's an area I'm gifted in. He just said that he's working these things out according to *his* plan and that I need to trust him and be dependable with what he's given me now—with the people I'm with now. I wish he'd just say straight up whether I'll eventually get to work in that or not, because this waiting is frustrating."

"I can imagine," said Amory. "He's given me that talk a couple of times too. Once more recently, I asked him about that prophecy about him using us to bring awakening to the multiverse. I asked him what that even means, and how that's going to happen, and if we've even made progress. All he's really said is that we know all that we're supposed to know right now, and we just need to trust him that he'll work it out. He did say, though, that we are making progress, so that was encouraging."

"Yeah," Bernice said. "After the advice he gave us about communication in our relationship, you'd think he'd do the same thing."

"Well, maybe there are some things that we don't need to know or tell yet. Maybe the time really isn't right. Think about it. If I told you everything about my life from the get-go, would you have still wanted me, or would you have taken off running?"

Bernice chuckled. "Um, probably the latter. But it's been two years since we started dating, so you can feel free to tell me whatever you need to. I won't leave you at this point."

"Thanks," said Amory. "Wait, do you think I'm hiding something that I need to share?"

"I don't know. You just made it seem like something made you think of what Nazir's reasoning might be for withholding things, and it seemed like you were speaking from experience."

"Bernice, I'm serious. I'm not hiding anything from you."

"You sure?" Bernice asked with furrowed eyebrows, looking straight into Amory's eyes, not at all certain he was telling the truth.

"Ahem," the waitress interrupted. "Do you two know what you would like to drink this evening?" Her voice was all too familiar.

Amory broke eye contact with Bernice and looked at the table, smiling. "This isn't the section you usually wait on, is it, Twyla?"

The young elf grinned shyly, careful not to move her red hair to reveal her pointed ears. "Nay, but I never get to wait on you whenever you are here. I thought I might just this once."

"I've got to say, I'm more used to seeing you decked in your armor and knives, not a button-down shirt and apron," Bernice said to Twyla. "How is this job suiting you? And how are you liking Earth so far?"

Twyla sighed. "It has been a year and half a year since I began living in this world, and I still do not feel used to it. The culture, the technology, the people, and their general behaviors . . . they are all so strange to me—almost wrong. You have advanced far as a species over the millennia, yet I have never encountered a more self-centered and entitled race, including many Envoys. Plus, the expectations they have placed on me as a waitress—both employers and customers—have also taken me aback."

"Well, that's humans for you, especially in America," Bernice said. "I'm sorry we're like this, and I promise at least the two of us are personally trying to overcome that. I hope it gets easier for you."

"Nazir has given me the strength and kindness to endure and still reflect him," Twyla smiled. "And I honestly desire that more than the burden lightening. Whatever gives him the most glory, that is what I want."

Amory and Bernice said nothing for a moment and just grinned. Then Amory finally said, "Hey, speaking of, don't forget about our team's meeting at the Dinhs' tomorrow. You'll be off work for that, right?"

"Of course!" Twyla said. "I would not miss it! Now, have you decided what you want to drink?"

"Ah yes, I'll just take water, please," Amory answered.

"And I'll have raspberry lemonade," said Bernice. "Thanks, Twyla!"

––––––

The next day, Amory's Envoy team, consisting of Bernice, Twyla, Leona, Edna, and the dwarfish siblings Nels and Neisha, met at Edna and her parents' house over lunch. The dining room and kitchen were filled with the scents of beef and ginger, which were used in the pho they were now enjoying. The entire house (which was relatively small) was decorated with items with either American or Vietnamese flare. Everyone, with Edna's parents at either end, was seated together at the short, wooden dining table.

"So how's everyone doing?" Amory began. "How've your relationships with the Vine been lately?"

"Overall, it's going well," Bernice said, telling everyone else as Amory already knew. "But I'm having trouble finding patience and trust in waiting for an HR job to open up. I've been working toward it, and I've been putting in the time and effort, but still no results. I'm struggling to trust that Nazir has it all worked out and has my best interests in mind."

"Of course he does," said Nels. "It just might not be what you expect or want. But it will definitely be what you'll ultimately need, and you'll find more fulfillment and be closer to him as a result."

"I guess," Bernice replied. "It's just hard to see right now."

"My relationship with Nazir is going OK, I think," said Edna. "I've been struggling with a bit of loneliness, but it's nothing major, and I'll get over it I'm sure. Other than that, I'm doing well. Not much to report."

Neisha then spoke up. "Nels and I have been doing all right with Nazir, but it's still been a struggle trying to cope with this new culture. There are differences that we didn't think were possible, like how our mindsets are. For dwarves it's always been, 'If it works, let's keep doing that.' But with you humans, it seems to be, 'There must be a better, easier way.' I still don't understand, and I don't expect to, but it's still been hard to find a balance regardless."

"The same is true for me," Twyla said.

"That actually isn't true for all humans," said Mr. Dinh. "There are many cultures on Earth that have a similar mindset as you three. But you're right about it in America. There is nothing wrong with either way of thinking, but one does have to alter their own way if they're somewhere else, whether it's America or Hertengard or a completely different world. My wife and I had to learn this when we first moved to this country."

"What about you, Leona?" asked Amory. "You seem quiet over there."

"Dude, I've always been quieter than most everyone," Leona grinned. "My relationship with Nazir is going OK, I think. I've been doing my best to obey him and make sure I'm following him as much as humanly possible, because I know that's what glorifies and pleases him. But I still feel distant from him for some reason. I know I'll never be perfect at being an Envoy, but I don't feel as close to him as I did at first, though I don't think I'm straying from him. I'm still confused."

Amory nodded. "These are good things to take up with Nazir—and with our trainers. How have your trainings been lately? Nazir said being trained by other Envoys was critical in our representing him. He said that this is how Envoys learn to follow him well, and that the ultimate goal is for the trainee to be able to train others, keeping the line going so that no one goes it unguided and alone."

"It's going well," said Leona. "Neisha's been giving me a ton of applicable wisdom when we've met, and our combat drills are also going well. She is a beast with those shields!"

"That's only because I've had years of practice," Neisha chuckled. "But you also have a martial arts background, so I still have a challenge."

"My training's been about the same with my parents," Edna said. "Although we haven't met at strict times, we're constantly together, and they've always guided me."

"Hey, Nazir never said we needed to meet at the same time every week or month just so long as we are consistent and keep it going," replied Amory.

"Training Bernice has been enjoyable and beneficial, I believe," added Twyla. "But it is difficult and strange because she has matured and aged more than I have. I mean no offense," she said, looking at Bernice.

"But your relationship with the Vine is far older than hers," Nels said. "You still have much to offer because of this."

"And so do you, brother," said Neisha. "Have you found someone to train yet?"

"And have you not found a trainer yet, Amory?" Edna asked. Both he and Nels shook their heads. "If neither of you have, why don't you train him, Nels?"

"We've been over this, lass," Nels answered. "I asked Nazir if that was his plan, and he said he had someone else in mind for us both, but I should at least teach Amory the basics of being an Envoy for the time being until a better trainer comes around. He said he's working everything out for everyone's ultimate good, but it requires immediate action from some and patience from others. I am teaching Amory some things that are crucial but not full-on."

Amory concluded, "I'm still talking with Nazir about this, and I suggest you all keep doing the same with all your questions and confusions. He's still the only one with the truest and wisest answers." Amory continued. "Well, I think that about wraps this up. I'm glad we get to catch up like this. Thanks again for having us over, Mr. and Mrs. Dinh!"

"It's always our pleasure!" Mr. Dinh said. "You guys have a great week."

"Oh, and don't forget our next mission starts a week from now, next Saturday morning," added Amory.

"That's right!" Leona exclaimed upon recollection. "Did Nazir give any more details for it?"

"Only to leave behind everything you think you know and to bring medicine if you tend to get seasick."

Nels slowly turned. "What?"

Slam! Dilyn shut the door as he exited the MRI results room in the hospital. He ran his hands across his face several times, unsure of how to process the news he'd just received. To avoid any awkward looks from passersby, he started walking as casually as he could to the waiting room on the same floor. He sauntered in and found his parents, chatting and waiting for him to give them the update.

"What did they say?" Reva, his mom, asked as soon as he was in sight.

Dilyn hid none of his dread as he stood in front of them. "They said it really is cancer in my liver. Stage 3."

"No, Dilyn!" Reva began to cry as she and her husband both went to hug their son. All three were silent for a long moment.

Phil, his dad, cursed. "I so hoped this wouldn't happen! Not to my son!" Another silence followed, and they eventually let go. "So what's the plan now? What do you need?"

Dilyn sighed. "The doctors said that they discovered it a little later than what's preferred, but they're going to start the chemo in two weeks. That should make it go down significantly."

"But there's no guarantee that it'll be gone completely?" Reva asked.

"I don't think there ever was that guarantee for anyone," said Dilyn.

"Does Ambrose know what's happening?" asked Phil.

"I tried calling him on my way here, but there was no answer," Dilyn replied. "I'm going to see him in a bit, but I want to head home and get a nap first. I'm exhausted."

"Get all the rest you need," said Reva. "Do you need anything else? Food maybe?"

"No thanks. I couldn't eat a thing."

Dilyn sank low in the seat of his Camaro and heaved a deep, shaky sigh. He just sat there and stared at the hospital entrance, keeping the car in park. The test results were worse than he'd expected.

What am I gonna do? He thought. *Sure, it's potentially terminal, but certainly I won't die from this! Not this early in life, anyway. I'm only eighteen, and I'm barely an adult. I've still got my whole life ahead of me. Or do I?*

He paused for a moment. Those thoughts were his, but they had an unnatural tone to them. He looked at the shotgun seat and saw a subtle shadow cast on it, but he knew that his real shadow would not be cast there from under his car lights. It was Nylid, his doppelgänger, or rather his ghost. Nylid had been haunting him for several months after Dilyn had joined the Self-Worthy. Any discouraging or distracting thought (distracting from what—he'd pretty much forgotten) Dilyn recognized as from Nylid, but now he was beginning to get used to them.

"Get away from me!" Dilyn said aloud. "I killed you. You should not be here!"

He started the car and sped out of the parking lot. He drove home, completely tuning out the traffic, wondering how on earth he was going to break the news to his brother. He got to the house gate and entered the wrong code; his hands were so trembly from fatigue and fear. He finally entered the right code and quickly pulled into one of the three garages, wasting no time to get out and crash into bed.

A couple of hours later, Dilyn woke up and called Ambrose to tell him he was coming. He then drove to Ambrose's apartment complex—a nice and secure place but not the fanciest. Ambrose himself was paying the rent, but his parents always stepped in whenever he couldn't make ends meet.

Ambrose met him at the gate and let him through, an authentic grin on his face.

Dilyn smiled meekly through the car window as he found a parking spot, rehearsing how he would tell his brother. He opened the car door and had no opportunity to say anything.

"Good to see you, bro!" Ambrose exclaimed and gave him a firm handshake and hug. "It's been a hot minute. What've you been up to all this time?"

"Not much," Dilyn said as they started toward Ambrose's apartment building. "Mostly just resting."

"Yeah, me too," Ambrose interrupted. "Ever since the Liberdane incident, everyone in the Self-Worthy's been resting. Not for long, though. It's been rumored that Maewing's resolved to try another mission."

"Really?" Dilyn's heart sank. He'd been looking forward to helping the Self-Worthy with another mission since their last one had failed, but he knew he was in no condition to trek and fight like last time.

"Yes, sir!" said Ambrose as they jogged up the building's stairs to the apartment itself, which was on the second floor. "We've gotten thousands of new recruits fully trained. Plus, our strength, arsenals, and morale have grown a lot in the past couple of years."

"When do you think we'll be ready?" asked Dilyn, hoping to have time to tell Maewing that he couldn't come.

"It's still anyone's guess at this point," Ambrose said.

They arrived at the door, but before they could enter, a blinding white and green portal burst forth with a roar right where the door was. The brothers stopped short.

"The Sword," Ambrose muttered.

They waited for whoever opened the portal to come through, for they knew that they themselves couldn't have opened it. But no one came. At last, Ambrose internally decided that it was made for him and Dilyn to enter. So he went through, and Dilyn quickly followed.

The two boys found themselves in the large, main courtyard of the Self-Worthy's castle in the high-tech world of Ourrance. It was packed tight with beings from dozens of universes. When the brothers finally got outside the crowd to get some breathing room, they realized that there were several portals open at once, surrounding the throngs entering through them. They all came from bright green, laser-like rays connected from one focal point: the Sword of *Chârâsh* itself. It was being held upright by Maewing, who stood on the stage in the center of the giant court as she often did. She was wearing a black, more formal dress made for a centaur, decked with a flowing red cape.

After a while, she saw that no one else was coming through the portals, so she slowly lowered the Sword in front of her and tilted it from a horizontal position to a vertical one. As she did this, the portals simultaneously shrank into the rays they came from, and the rays instantly were absorbed back into the Sword's blade, making a seismic boom of air when it was complete. The crowds of creatures cheered in awe and excitement at the newfound power of their leader. Ambrose and Dilyn stood in shock.

"Multiple portals at once?" Ambrose said to Dilyn. "I didn't know that was possible!"

Once the applause ceased, Maewing spoke in her booming voice. "This power to bring people from multiple worlds at once is merely a taste of the power of the Sword of *Chârâsh*!" More cheering erupted. "If our ultimate aim is accomplished, then I will be able to merge every universe into one peaceful, unified world! This is only possible if everyone in all the worlds is of one mind. What you have heard is true: we are going on a new mission at long last, and it will be a major step in making this objective a reality!"

Maewing continued. "Our target world this time is Uchu, the realm that contains mostly water and very little land. It is inhabited by shapeshifters, so always be cautious that everything you see and touch is as it seems. Thankfully we already have allies there who will help us avoid distractions or delays. The majority of Uchu is ruled and manipulated by a tyrannical wizard, who is using dark and heinous spells to keep it under his dominion. Our mission is to overthrow and kill him, thus freeing Uchu from his power. Be wary, though, for I hear his abilities are vast, and they must be if he deceives creatures whose nature is deception. Once he is dead, then we will do what we failed to do on the last mission: proclaim freedom on the peoples to be themselves without being restricted by any person or society! And this time, I will not abandon you!"

Deafening ovations were heard everywhere, even from the Brandts. Throughout the noise, though, Ambrose wondered if that last statement was a jab at herself or at him. When it got mostly quiet again, Maewing welcomed any questions. Ambrose raised his hand and sifted through the crowds to become audible to Maewing, Dilyn following.

After Maewing acknowledged him, he began, "You said you intended to merge every universe into one realm. If proclaiming individuality is our goal, why would you want to do this? Why not separate each world further and make everyone more individual instead of uniting everyone?"

"I admire your unique discernment and loyalty, Ambrose," Maewing replied. "And it is much needed. But multiversal unity is the only way to ensure that all will eternally hold the knowledge and passion of their own individuality. Otherwise, division and conflict would still occur."

Another from the crowd spoke up. "But if everyone is entitled to their own opinion, wouldn't there still be disagreements even if everyone did have that knowledge and passion? Not everyone sees eye to eye."

"If everyone did have it," said Maewing, "then they would be aware and considerate of each other's opinions and set aside their disagreements. Putting aside differences is a big step in achieving peace. Do remember that. Are there any other questions?"

As more inquiries were given about the mission itself, Ambrose looked at Dilyn with confusion and frustration. They both remembered times when their parents ignored conflict or differences between each other and that the conflicts never really dissolved until they were acknowledged and settled. The brothers also wondered if Maewing's main goal was still individuality or if it was now unity, as it had been gravitating back and forth over the past several months. They'd noticed that it had been since she'd started using the Sword of *Chârâsh* more often.

After all the questions were answered, Maewing concluded, "Since we will be using only one ship as our primary transportation, we will not be able to accommodate every soldier on this mission, so I have selected fifty troops to join me. The rest will continue to prepare for the mission I've set after this one, in which everyone will be needed. The names of those I've chosen are as follows. . . ."

Dilyn's heart jumped. He got excited for a brief moment, thinking that he would be able to sit out on the mission. His hopes were dashed when he heard Maewing call his name, along with those of Ambrose and Lisias the faun.

Yes, finally! Ambrose exclaimed to himself. He'd been waiting for a chance like this to prove his worth again.

As Maewing started to exit the stage, she said, "If you have any concerns with whom I've chosen and left out, come and talk with me. The rest of you may continue your training, knowing you will be in the next one for certain. Those whose names were called, report to my quarters to receive more specific instructions. You are all dismissed. All for one!"

"All for one!" everyone shouted.

The bustle of creatures began, and Ambrose struggled to stay with Dilyn as they made their way to Maewing's room. "Can you believe it, bro?" Ambrose said. "At last we get to go on another mission together!"

Dilyn hesitated. "Yeah, about that."

"Hey, what's up with you today?" Ambrose said. "I thought you'd be excited to go on a Self-Worthy mission as one of us officially. You don't seem enthused."

"I have liver cancer, Ambrose!" Dilyn yelled louder than he'd planned.

"What?" asked Ambrose as he stopped short, staring at his brother while the throngs passed by them.

"Stage 3," Dilyn continued. "I can't go on this mission because I'm in no condition to. Believe me, I want to, but I physically can't. That's what I've been trying to tell you this whole time."

Ambrose stood stunned, a deep surge of worry overtaking him. "You need to tell Maewing now. I'm sure she'll understand, and it won't be that hard to find another person. Dude, I'm so sorry. I don't even know what to do or say!"

"All right, I will," said Dilyn as he made his way toward her. "And you don't have to do much of anything. Just check up on me every so often and tell me how the mission goes. I'll see you around."

Dilyn politely pressed his way through the crowds and finally found Maewing at the foot of the stage, surrounded by people who were wondering why they weren't chosen. Thinking he'd gain more of an audience with her because he was chosen, he stepped in front of them all.

"Ma'am, I need a minute with you," he began.

"So does half of our forces," Maewing said, looking at everyone but him.

Dilyn wasted no time. "I can't go on this mission, ma'am. I have cancer, and I'm physically incapable of doing my part in it. I so want to go, but I seriously can't. You understand, don't you?"

"Mr. Brandt, you don't know how many battles and illnesses I have fought at the same time. Believe me when I tell you it can be done. I chose you because of your unique talents and because the armor you wear is of a rare caliber that will be needed. I will not replace you, and you are required to come along, or else I will take away some of your privileges and honors as I did to your brother. If it is weakness that concerns you, I can give you a potion from my private apothecary that could help."

Dilyn was somewhat taken aback by that last suggestion. He was too afraid to argue further, lest punishment would result. "No, thank you. If you insist, I will go, but I cannot guarantee that I will be of much use."

With that, Dilyn sauntered toward Maewing's room, downtrodden and confused. He didn't feel like his well-being was being considered at all.

2

A WORLD OF DIFFERENCE

E dna was the last to get to the Center of the multiverse—
Rôb Têbêl—where the other six Envoys and Nazir himself
were waiting. The Envoys looked much grander with their
armor and weapons—Amory with his sword and sheath,
Bernice with her spear with the Envoy flag, Leona with her
pickaxe, Nels with his crossbow/axe, Neisha with her two-
pointed shields, and Twyla with her array of knives. The Vine
and the Center never seemed to change; the spherical room
whose walls looked like windows exposing outer space was still
just as spectacular. Nazir, of course, didn't age a bit and was still
his cheerful yet solemn self.

"Right on time!" said the Vine. "How are you, daughter?"

"A little tired, honestly," Edna sighed as she held her
hammer a little higher. "I had a lot of custom résumés to tweak
last night. I'm ready to serve again, though! What do you have
for us?"

Nazir chuckled. "I have a task that's very different from
your last one yet holds the same weight. I'm sending you to the

island world of Uchu, the world of shapeshifters. The people are being terrorized by a wizard, who was empowered by Marah, our enemy. Marah then led him into that world to subdue it, and he's unjustly ruled them long enough. The time has come for his tyranny to end, so I'm sending you to find and kill him and to proclaim my freedom and salvation to those you will encounter beforehand and afterward."

"This is definitely different from our last mission," said Amory, confused, "because we weren't supposed to kill the evil ruler on our last one. Why are we supposed to now, and how does that make sense?"

"Unlike King Ever, this wizard has no right to rule," said Nazir. "I let the wizard come to power to return the people there to me, but now he's gone too far. Also, those who practice witchcraft to this extent must die because of the destruction and chaos they cause as direct servants of Marah. There have been several wizards and witches who have given up their ways and turned to me, and I've been able to do much through them. But this wizard will not repent—though, as I had with Ever, I've reached out multiple times to him. He will not listen. He has stuck to the path he's on, and his time is up."

"Does he have a name?" Edna asked.

"He did, but he forsook his identity to get where he is now. Calling him by his former name will no longer work. If you ask someone where to find him, just say 'the wizard,' and they will know who you mean."

"I've been wondering something," said Bernice. "Because of our wrongful actions in Hertengard, I've been questioning if Envoys are supposed to kill."

"Whoever put that into your head was wrong," said Nazir sternly. "Have you not imagined what would've happened if Amory and Leona hadn't killed the giant spider that you and the Brandts ran into when you first came here?"

"Good point," Bernice said. "But what about people?"

"There have been countless instances when Envoys needed to kill people in war or self-defense, whether I directly commanded them to or not. Killing is an ugly and terrible thing, but it is sometimes necessary. There will be instances when you will need to hold back and compromise to obtain peace and bring people to me, and there will be times when you need to fight and face the conflict head-on to do this. The latter is what needs to happen now." Nazir continued. "What are the gifts from me that are now in your hands? Not just tools but weapons! They have several purposes, which you will soon see, but their main purpose is to fight. What matters is who you're fighting, which is what was wrongful last time. Remember that the true enemy is Marah, and you are to show no mercy to him and his armies. People are not our enemy; their renewed and lasting relationships with me are our objective. But my condemnation remains on those who refuse this relationship, and the wizard is one of those individuals. Just know that my reasons are good and just, and my every action and command is for the ultimate benefit of everyone." Nazir looked at Bernice. "You can still trust me even when I don't give my reasons."

"Understood," said Nels. "We're ready."

Nazir continued. "All right. The portal to Uchu is to the right of the portal to *Chârâsh*. Be careful, though. The wizard draws much power from Marah and is capable of many unexpected things—which is what allured him to Marah in the first place. Additionally, this universe is filled with deception, and it's not just because of the wizard. Do not be easily swayed, or you will be lost and confused—a gullible pawn in the people's endless game. Don't worry either, for you're ready for this mission. I've equipped you with all you need to succeed. Go, and proclaim and enact my love and justice!"

"Thank you, Dad!" Amory exclaimed, and they set off into the white once again.

———

The seven Envoys entered the new universe and were instantly in awe of what they beheld. It was as stunning as Liberdane when they'd left it but in its own way. It was night now, but the constellations were in consistent rotation while remaining in one place, each made of stars of one or two or even three colors. They looked like giant, spiraling fireworks that never dissolved. There were also three orange moons that seemed to nearly meet directly overhead.

The Envoys stood on a high hill consisting of stone and dust. From where they were, they could see a shoreline to their right with magnificent waves crashing into the island they were on, which was enamored with thick trees with leaves of every color imaginable. The temperature was quite warm here, to the humans' liking and the Hertengardians' disliking (they were used to cooler weather). There were several hills like the one they were on, some with dirt pathways and some without. They discovered that they were standing on such a path and visually followed it to a torch-lit, bustling village at the bottom of the hill near the shore. Wooden docks dotted with galleons bridged the shore to the village.

"How do we proceed from here?" asked Twyla.

"We need to find out where the wizard is," Amory said, "and see if he stays in one hideout or if he roams about. Since Nazir didn't say, it might be the latter."

"I say we go to that village down there and ask to make sure," Edna added. "And if you're right, we need to see if any of them have seen him recently."

"I agree," Amory replied. "Let's go—and be careful. Be sure to stay together."

As the Envoys approached the beach town, the path became illuminated by tall torch poles. They saw that the dirt here had a purple tint to it and that the thick grass grew to the humans' height. The noise of the enormous waves became louder along with that of the villagers. Upon entering the outskirts, they found dozens of types of creatures all going about their work as if it was daytime. They saw creatures of their own kinds, as well as various animals and insects, plus beings they'd never heard of before. They all had one of two things in common: either they had a brand-like mask around their eyes, or they had several tails (or clothing made up of their tails).

As they watched the creatures operate their shops, restaurants, and markets, Bernice wondered aloud, "Why are they working so late? Do they work well into the night or during the night instead of at day?"

"Maybe they work all the time and don't know the meaning of sleep or rest," said Neisha.

"Maybe it's just always nighttime here," Leona suggested.

Amory stepped aside and caught the attention of one of the merchants, a brown minotaur with three tails. "Excuse me, do you happen to know where the wizard dwells?"

The minotaur stopped short and set down the barrel she was carrying. "Who's asking?"

"I am Amory, and these six are my friends who come from different worlds than yours. We're Envoys of the Vine, Nazir, who sent us to kill the wizard and to show you all Nazir's love for you in freeing you from the wizard's power."

The minotaur hesitated for a moment, then chuckled. "From what I hear, the wizard walks here and there, disguised as any one of us, perhaps even one of your friends. I cannot help you locate him, but I would now beware, for he probably heard you and will now hunt you down, leaping upon you when you least expect it." At that, she picked up her barrel and left, grinning.

The Envoys looked at each other with different expressions of worry.

"OK, now I have to ask: are all of you real?" Edna asked.

"Yes, but would we actually say if we were not?" asked Twyla.

"Be extra careful, and watch each other's six," said Amory.

They snuck along the streets, looking quite ridiculous (as those in fear often do), constantly looking over their shoulders and turning around on a whim. They entered what seemed to be the plaza—an empty space with a stone central street—with actors, acrobats, and other performers practicing their odd and daring routines. Even these, the Envoys watched tactfully. The actors were singing or saying lines the Envoys didn't understand.

Some daredevils were dodging deadly projectiles thrown at them by changing sizes or shapes.

Leona was studying just how these creatures were able to do this when she suddenly heard a deep, male voice float around her head.

"Your doom has come, strangers."

She stopped short and noticed that the others did too. They looked around and saw no one close enough to own the voice. "You guys heard that, right?" she asked.

The weapons being drawn and poised answered her question.

"That minotaur was right," the voice continued. "I did hear your intentions, and I will not let mere foreigners steal my power, especially some who are so few in number."

"Our strength is not in ourselves!" Neisha shouted. "It lies in Nazir, King of the multiverse and the real Ruler of this world! We are not afraid of you!"

The voice snickered. "Yes, you are. And what kind of strength must he have for you to still be fearful? Or how much do you actually depend on him?"

The Envoys simply looked at each other with concern and said nothing.

"Nevertheless, since you have threatened to kill me, you will suffer. I will personally ensure that you will each die a very slow, unique, agonizing death. Imagine it being drawn out for days, yet you feel every bit of pain, dying a little more each second inside and out, and not being able to do a thing about it. Imagine it thoroughly, for it will happen before you know it or suspect anything."

"Liar!" cried Bernice as they all darted back and forth, trying to figure out what to even do to prevent this threat from coming true.

After a minute they stood still in panic, everyone looking to Amory, wondering what to do. Amory had no idea. It was then that they heard another snicker, this one being a lot smaller and higher pitched. They followed it and found a tiny brown dragonfly on an overhead branch from a nearby tree. It had blue lines outlining its eyes, and it seemed surprised that it was seen.

Amory looked back at his friends. "Do you think that . . . no, surely not." He started to walk away, but then they heard the laughter again coming from the insect.

As quick as lightning, Twyla held the two knives in her hands in front and above the dragonfly to prevent it from flying away. "Identify yourself!" she yelled.

"All right, all right, you caught me," it said in a voice that was shriller than the one before.

"You're the one who said all those things about a slow death and all that?" Amory asked, appalled.

"Yeah, but I'm not the wizard you're looking for. I just overheard your conversation with the minotaur and thought I'd have a little fun with it."

"Well, I think it's safe to say you went a bit far," said Bernice.

"All I did was say words I didn't even mean," the dragonfly replied. "It's not like I pranked you or anything, which a lot of other people here do, especially to newcomers."

"Well I'm glad we ran into just you then," Nels said sarcastically.

"So you're really Envoys, and you're really going to kill the wizard?" asked the dragonfly.

The Envoys nodded, and Twyla pulled her knives back a tad.

"Allow me to introduce myself." At that, the dragonfly began to gradually expand, and as it did so, its color and form changed. Its head and tail grew to fit the thorax, and its whole body grew thick, brown fur. Its eyes changed from a bug's to an animal's and receded into its face (though the mask remained). Its wings and two of its legs shrank into nonexistence. It was now a dwarf-sized raccoon standing on its hind legs, with a face that was cute but hardly innocent. It appeared to have a familiar badge and long, wearable, metal claws that were fitted onto its real claws. These claws remained even when he was the dragonfly.

"My name is Masato," the creature continued. "I'm a sailor on a ship that harbored here last week."

"What exactly are you, originally?" Edna asked.

"I'm a tanuki, and this is my original form. There are two main kinds of creatures here: us tanuki and the kitsune, which are basically foxes that grow another tail every century. They are very wise and cunning, and they can also change form, but they can't do it as thoroughly as we tanuki can."

"What can you tell us about the wizard?" asked Amory. "Do you know where he is . . . really?"

Masato's smile waned as he walked around the plaza, the Envoys following.

"He arrived here millennia ago, boastfully declaring that he made himself the dictator of Uchu. He proved his power to anyone who resisted him, obliterating armies with strong elemental forces and slowly killing off our leaders one at a time through disease or other incidents. I don't know if he is omnipresent or can hear anything and everything that's said, but his might is nevertheless not to be underestimated. For the past several centuries, we've been leaderless, and the wizard has terrorized us remotely from his lair in innumerable ways, devastating families and businesses to bend the economies to his will."

"So he has a lair," said Amory. "Does he stay there all the time?"

"As far as we know," Masato replied. "Many have sailed off to his island to try and kill him or at least reason with him. He lets them see him, but then he wipes them out, leaving no survivors."

"How do you know this if there were no survivors?" asked Neisha.

"*Almost* no survivors," Masato grinned. "I was on such an expedition several decades ago. We sailed inside the cavern he lives in. Just when we caught sight of him on the rocky shore, the sea inside the cave lit on fire and burned the ship and crew into nothing. Only two of us were able to fly out without being blasted by the monster's wands; the other was a fellow crew member called Akira, who is now my captain. He's a kitsune, and he's quite brave and noble."

"Masato," said Edna, "I don't suppose you or your captain would be up for taking us to the wizard's island and helping us kill him, would you?"

The tanuki shook his head. "It'd take a lot for me to travel back there, and no amount of money could bribe me into it."

"Well, we don't have much of that anyway, and it wouldn't do much good here," said Leona.

The eight of them strolled a little further in silence.

"That badge you wear . . . ." Amory pointed at Masato's shoulder. "Is that an Envoy's badge?"

"It is, and I am indeed one of Nazir's children. Akira, our captain, became an Envoy shortly after our narrow escape, and he encouraged all of us to do the same and to listen to what Nazir told him. I came to the Center alone, and I accepted and believed, and he gave me my armor, which I left on our ship just now, and these claws, which are still made of *charisma* but are malleable for whenever I change form. Since the rest of the crew got similar armor and weapons, I assume they did the same."

The Envoys wanted very much to believe that Masato truly was an Envoy, but after his trickery and what he said about Nazir as a dragonfly, they were unsure.

"Where'd you get the Dagger to get to the Center?" asked Leona.

"I used Akira's, then I got my own," Masato said.

Another short silence followed.

"You know," said Amory, "us killing the wizard is what Nazir wants. As one of his followers, don't you think it wise to help us get to him? What else were you going to do if you weren't?"

That last part stung at Masato's heart, and he wasn't sure why. He stopped walking and looked down, thinking intently. "All right, I guess I can at least check with Akira and see what he thinks. He's much wiser about these things than I am."

"Wonderful," said Nels. "As long as we make some kind of progress."

"He'll be at our ship," said Masato. "It's right this way." He took them from the plaza into the bustle again toward the beach, where the Envoys caught glimpses of some of the docks on the shore. The Envoys looked again at the busy creatures about their work.

"Why does everyone work so late here?" Edna asked.

"Late?" Masato replied. "This isn't late. We always work when it's dark, then go to sleep when daylight comes."

"Oh. It's the opposite for us," said Edna.

"I'm not seeing a lot of meat in these markets and restaurants," Neisha added. "Do you even have meat here?"

Masato chuckled. "No, because we never know whether we're eating actual livestock or a tanuki in disguise. Don't ask me how we came to realize that."

Without warning, as soon as Masato took his next step, the paw that stepped instantly turned into thick red algae. His other hind paw also did a second later, and more of his legs melted away into it.

"What's happening?" he asked in a panicked tone.

"You're asking us?" said a shocked Amory.

"It is not the wizard, is it?" Twyla asked.

"It could be!" said Masato, who was now up to his torso in the algae that used to be his legs. "Maybe he really can hear everything, and he's trying to stop me from taking you to him! Listen closely. . . ." It was now just his arms and head. "The dock furthest to the left has our ship, *Kaze Nagare*. Akira will be there. Tell him what happened here! Nazir be with—"

Thus Masato was reduced to a red puddle with a badge and empty claws lying on it. The Envoys just stood there, stunned.

"What the heck?!" Bernice finally shouted.

"Make a run for the docks before one of us is next!" said Amory.

The seven of them bolted off, thankful that every step they took thus far was solid.

3

STRIFE REAWAKENED

T he panicked Envoys were in a mad dash to get to Akira's ship before one of them fell victim to another of the wizard's bizarre traps. They clambered along the docks, tripping over goods and crashing into flummoxed workers. No matter how fast they ran (making sure the dwarves kept up), the docks never seemed to reach their end. Edna began to wonder if this was another of the sorcerer's schemes, to keep them constantly running in a mad scramble across a line of docks that he was making endless. Finally after about ten minutes, they caught sight of the end of it, with a galleon tied to it, smaller than average.

The ship had two masts and two decks: one above and one below. It was painted white with green rims and had green sails with a yellow symbol that looked very similar to the Envoys' emblem. Out of the sides protruded a few oddly shaped and colored cannons, making the Envoys wonder if they were cannons at all. On the prow read *Kaze Nagare*. As the Envoys ran closer, they saw on deck a red, white-armored fox with six bushy tails, standing on its hind legs. The Envoys figured this was Akira the kitsune and clambered on board. The kitsune was surprised.

"My, my, what has gotten into all of you?" he asked.

"Are you Akira, captain of the *Kaze Nagare*?" Amory asked, panting.

"Yes," the pink-eyed kitsune said, who they now noticed seemed decked with as many knives as Twyla. "And who might you be, and why have you come in such a rush?"

"We're Envoys of Nazir who've come to kill the wizard who's been terrorizing you," said Bernice in heaving breaths. "We met Masato, one of your crew members, in the village, and he was leading us to you when the wizard turned him into red goo! We got here as fast as we could before the wizard targeted one of us to prevent us from coming to you."

"Is that so?" said Akira in deep thought but not seeming to have much remorse for Masato. "Yes, it is a pity what happened to dear Masato, and I will ensure he will not have died in vain. But first, tell me more about your mission."

"Nazir called us to come to your world and rid you of the oppression that's been laid upon you," Neisha replied, "and to declare to everyone we meet that Nazir cares for them enough to free them from their terror and their pride. Masato gave details about how the wizard rules this world, and he said that you were an Envoy."

"Indeed, I am, and I am proud to be one," said Akira. "Nazir has given me life, which I do not deserve. And he sent you to free us by putting the wizard to death?"

"Yes, but we need a ship and a guide," Edna answered. "Will you help us, sir?"

Akira contemplated this for several moments. "Long have I wished the sorcerer dead because he forces us to abide by certain moral standards, which in reality are not moral at all, and hypnotizes or terrorizes whoever resists. In the past, I simply lacked the wit and numbers to kill him myself. I have waited for centuries to attain a chance to, and when I did, I failed miserably. After that, I waited to grow another tail or two, for with each tail also comes more wisdom, so I would be better able to fight him next time. I have grown one more tail since then, and here you are—more Envoy troopers ready to embark on the same task. I would be a fool to refuse this new chance. Welcome aboard, my friends!"

"Thank you so much," Nels said. "We wouldn't have done this without you."

"It is my pleasure," Akira replied, taking a silver bugle from a room below that appeared to be the captain's cabin. "I'll call my crew, and we will set off at once."

The kitsune sounded the high-pitched horn, and after a few minutes about a dozen armored tanuki of varying fur colors jogged on board one at a time, all with their belongings and newly bought foods and items. The last tanuki to come was Masato in his original form.

"Oh my word!" Edna shouted, frustrated that they were all duped again. "We thought you were dead!"

"You all are so easily gullible!" Masato chuckled. "How can I not take advantage of that?"

"By using your ability for good and not trickery," Akira sighed. "You did not fool me, but these newcomers don't deserve to be frightened this way, especially if the wizard really can do all of the things I assume you elaborately described."

"I'm a tanuki. It's in my nature to prank and deceive. Surely Nazir could use that."

"Not in that way," Akira replied. "What have you accomplished by tricking these Envoys who have so graciously obeyed the Vine in helping to free us?"

"I got them here, didn't I? One way or another?"

Akira frowned more. "But you didn't want to go, did you? You thought I'd say no, and you avoided coming yourself."

Masato paused for a second. "No, I don't want to go because of what happened last time. But I think it's my duty as an Envoy to go, which is why I came back. Forgive me for not being as willing as you would like, but I am at least physically prepared to go there again."

"You're forgiven," said Akira. "Now, to your post. We shove off immediately."

Masato then changed to a brown-haired, clothed human (still with the mask over his eyes) and began to help hoist up the anchor. Akira himself turned into an elf with six arms to help guide the ship from the wheel. The Envoys watched everyone prepare the ship, then heard Akira call out as the ship began to move: "To the wizard and to freedom!"

The tanuki all cheered, according to whatever form they were taking, as did the Envoys.

Akira turned to the seven visitors. "It's an eight-hour trip to the island. Get below deck and get some sleep. I'll awaken you when it's getting close. The women can have my cabin, and I'll tell Masato to leave all of you alone while you rest."

The Envoys grinned and went below.

Akira never had to awaken most of the Envoys, as they were up by the time the three suns were rising to replace the trio of waning moons. The only exception was Nels, who discovered the hard way that he got seasick quite easily. If he wasn't moaning in his hammock below deck, he was leaning over the side rail above deck releasing anything he'd eaten in the past week. His sister and the humans tried every kind of medicine they'd brought to try and help it subside, but his stomach accepted nothing.

"How long have we been afloat like this?" he asked his sister who stood by the hammock he laid in.

"About three hours," Neisha replied.

"Have we been in a tempest all this time? I feel like we're in one of those deadly storms back in Hertengard."

"No," said Neisha. "We've actually had fair weather the entire time."

"Then tell Akira to slow down! I've never been at sea in my life until now, but I'm sure boats shouldn't rock this much!"

Neisha told this to Amory and Akira later.

"Quite honestly, I do not think this ship has ever swayed less than it is now," Akira chuckled. "This weather is remarkable."

"I think he'll be fine in a few hours," said Amory. "I took Bernice on a ferry ride earlier this year, and she was the same way at first, but she got better. Continue to keep an eye on him, though."

"I hope you're right," Neisha said.

A while later, Amory stood on the edge of the starboard deck, soaking in the sights and sounds of this strange world. It was so similar to Earth, but the differences were bizarre. The ocean was a cold blue like Earth, but with three moons there were also three intersecting currents which created abnormal wave clashes in places where the currents collided. The three suns varied in color—one was yellow like Earth's, one was dark red, and the other was blueish white (indicating that they were of various ages), which made this world on the hotter side but not as hot as Amory thought it should be.

Amory then turned to watch the crew eat their dinner (and the visitors, the breakfasts they'd packed) in random spots on the deck. The plants the tanuki ate seemed to all have the same hint of purple as the soil from which they grew, although their sizes and shapes were very different. Like on Earth, though, the creatures ate the leaves of some plants, the stems of others, and the roots of still others.

Amory then noticed Leona chatting with Masato over their meal and stepped in a tad closer to overhear.

"Akira also said the wizard has a certain set of standards that he forces people to live by and that it's immoral and hurts people more," Leona said.

"Akira said that?" asked Masato. "It's true, but that's strange coming from him. Akira also gave us a code of conduct to live by."

"What?" asked Leona.

"Ever since he became an Envoy. In addition to our armor and weapons, he gave us Nazir's rules to abide by, and he said that keeping them will ensure that our status as Nazir's children remains."

"Wait, he said that you could lose that status?" Leona asked.

"And he gave you your weapons?" Amory cut in, stepping closer. "I thought you said you went to Nazir yourself and got yours."

"Well I did, yes, but for the rest of the crew, Akira simply gave them theirs after they repeated a few phrases and vows after him, and he said he got their equipment for them so they wouldn't have to. I think they still went to Nazir like I did, though."

"I see," said Amory indifferently. He knew that Nazir would've given the tanuki their weapons immediately after redeeming them, not through someone else later.

"What kind of vows did they make?" Leona asked.

"Just things about committing to Nazir and no one else, striving to act exactly as he would, staying pure, and fighting as if the universe or even the multiverse depended on it."

"Those aren't bad vows to make, except that no one could keep them perfectly," said Leona.

"Don't pay too much attention to him, Leona," Amory said. "He's just jealous of Akira because Akira can actually go a day without tricking anyone. I don't know about you, but I don't feel like being fooled again."

Masato grinned slyly, and Amory walked off, quite proud of himself for wising up to Masato's lies.

———

Dilyn lay in his bed alone on the bottommost deck in the Self-Worthy's massive, steam-powered ship, en route to the wizard's island. The white, hot, wooden room was full of beds and went as far as the eye could see. Dozens of hammocks and lamps dangled from the ceiling. Ambrose had helped Dilyn in his struggle against the other troops to claim a bed instead of a hammock so he could easily get the rest he needed to fight in and survive this mission. He'd laid there since the beginning of the voyage, deep in thought.

I'm this much closer to dying because I just had *to go on this mission. I'm in no state to fight! Even if I don't die in battle from exhausting myself and making myself an easy target, the battle will hurry the cancer along, and I'll be worse off than before! Why am I even on this boat instead of at home? What am I doing this for?*

It's certainly not for me, even if that's what the Self-Worthy's about. There's no escaping now, though. I'm in the middle of the freaking ocean, in an ocean world! I'm going to die soon, if not today, and there's no way out of it!

Dilyn stopped and recognized the toxicity of his thoughts. He looked around at every light and shade above and beside him. "Nylid, get out!" he shouted. He had to say it twice before he caught a glimpse of a shadow that moved in the opposite direction of the other shadows—and at a quicker pace. Dilyn's eyes finally settled on one of his own shadows (for there were several lights), except this one moved on its own, not parallel with the swaying lamps. "You're not supposed to be here!" Dilyn said.

But I am, said Nylid in Dilyn's head. *Because you let me back in. Now you're mine and under my influence.*

"I don't think so. I'm your killer."

And for that I don't intend to let you go.

"Then I'll just have to kill you again!" Dilyn hurriedly snatched from under his bed his bow and an arrow from his quiver. He found Nylid darting along the walls toward the entrance from upstairs. Before Dilyn realized there was someone coming down the stairs, he fired straight at his doppelgänger, and the arrow lodged into the wall about two inches from Ambrose's head.

"Bro!" Ambrose yelled. "What are you doing?!"

Dilyn froze in horror. He looked at the arrow; Nylid had disappeared, though Dilyn was certain he wasn't gone forever. He finally dropped his bow.

"I'm so sorry," Dilyn said in an alarmed, gasping voice. "I think I saw a ghost or something, and I was trying to kill it. I think it tried to get me to kill you instead, but I'm thankful I didn't. I seriously didn't see you coming, and I'm positive I wasn't trying to kill you!"

Ambrose calmed his temper a bit. "It wouldn't be the most outlandish thing I've heard of lately. This world is absolutely nuts. The creatures here are so unpredictable. And the captain of this ship is so weird. He leads like two dozen crew members, but he seems like a pushover for whatever Maewing says. I guess that's what loyalty is."

"I've heard some strange things too, even before we left Ourrance," said Dilyn. "Did you know that Maewing has a private apothecary?"

Ambrose's eyebrows furrowed. "No, actually I didn't know that. What's so strange about making medicine?"

"She never said medicine; she said potions. When I told her about my cancer, she offered to give me a potion that could help. I refused, assuming she meant some sort of witchcraft."

"*Potion* can also be another word for *medicine*, you know," said Ambrose. "Why didn't you take it if it could help? Don't you want to be healed from this? You're jumping to conclusions that don't add up, and it's costing you."

"But what if it does add up?" said Dilyn thoughtfully. "Could that be the reason she's been around so long and yet looks so young? Is that the reason she healed from her injuries from the Hertengard tornado so quickly?"

"I don't know," said Ambrose, more frustrated. "I do know, however, that there are dozens of worlds out there, and maybe one of them has the remedy for quick recovery or even cancer. Over the centuries, Maewing's been to several universes using a Dagger that a former Envoy gave her. Surely she's found something!"

"Even if that were so, I don't know if I feel comfortable following someone who practices something so evil. If it were true, what separates her from the wizard we're going to kill?"

Ambrose became even more defensive. "The wizard is a terrorist seeking only power. Maewing is an advocate seeking to free people from tyrants like him!"

Dilyn still feared his brother's disapproval, especially now that Ambrose seemed to care for him. But he still had to say, "By what means, and at what cost?"

Before Ambrose could lash back, Lisias bolted down the stairs. "Hurry upstairs, both of you! All hands on deck!"

"Are we there already?" Dilyn asked.

"No, but we're close. There's been another ship sighted portside, and Maewing's ordered that we bring it down."

"What kind of ship?" Ambrose asked. "Who's on it?"

Lisias looked concerned. "It's an Envoy ship."

———

Amory stood with Bernice by the wheel, chatting with Akira as he skillfully piloted his vessel.

"So can you guys turn into pretty much anything?" Bernice asked.

"Well, it has to be a living thing and in accord with each creature's gender," Akira said.

"Then how did Masato turn into goop?" Amory asked.

"He turned into algae," Akira chuckled, "which I am sure you know is alive. If we turned into a non-living thing, we would become dead ourselves and unable to return to a live form."

"So what do you think about Masato?" asked Amory more quietly, making sure the trickster wasn't around. "I have mixed feelings about him as you have probably guessed, but I haven't known him as long as you."

Akira grinned. "He is a skilled sailor and a noble warrior. His craftiness is what saved our skins when we escaped the wizard the first time. His wit can be used for good; I just wish he would use it for good more often than for fun. It makes me question his relationship with the Vine, sadly. I am intrigued and concerned to know how many commands he's held compared to how many he's disobeyed."

Before the conversation could go further, they heard Twyla shout from the crow's nest, "There is an island straight ahead!"

Everyone who wasn't currently working sprinted to the prow and beheld a thin, green island with a towering, grassy butte in the middle.

"That is the place," Akira said somberly. "The cave where the wizard resides is at the center of the isle underneath the butte. The only entrance by boat is straight ahead. We should arrive in less than an hour."

Just then, Twyla called out again, "There is a large vessel on our right!" She didn't yet know the difference between starboard and portside.

Akira and Amory both grabbed telescopes as the other Envoys and the crew members who were able went to the starboard side to see. It was a massive, white ship that seemed to be powered by steam. Amory looked through the telescope and saw a familiar black flag on the funnels.

"Oh no," Amory mumbled.

"What is it?" Bernice asked.

"It's the Self-Worthy."

Bernice and the others were silent as Amory tried to look through the troops on deck who seemed to be increasing rapidly as they came up from below deck. They all looked prepared to fight but were also confused.

"Are Ambrose and Dilyn there?" Leona asked.

Amory sifted through the people he saw and finally caught a glimpse of both of them nudging their way to the portside rail.

"Yes, they are," Amory said in a despondent tone. "And they look worried."

"Are any of them doing anything?" asked Neisha.

"Some of the soldiers are going back below," Akira said. "This is not a good sign. They might be preparing to fire upon us."

"Dang it, I thought as much," Amory sighed. "We've had run-ins with them before. Although they had an army last time, and now I don't think they can have nearly as many on just one ship."

"You fought an entire Self-Worthy army?" Masato asked.

"Well, we weren't their primary target," said Edna. "And my guess is that we aren't this time either. They're probably headed for the wizard the same as we are."

"But this is our mission—from Nazir himself," said Amory, putting down his telescope.

"I'm sure the Self-Worthy believe this is their mission too," Edna replied, "which might be a good reason to attack us to ensure no hiccups occur like last time."

"Now calm down," said Bernice, talking to herself as well. "We don't know that they're going to do anything yet."

"Look out!" Akira said.

Out of nowhere, a large object flew into the crow's nest, knocking Twyla off. Luckily some tanuki were there to catch her. The Envoys watched as the object, obviously alive, started to fly back in their direction. It looked like a female centaur but with wings. She had a sword in each hand, one of which looked a little familiar. No one on that ship knew who she was. The creature made no noise or diction as she dove for Amory, Bernice, and Edna. They ducked and blocked with their weapons as she tried stabbing and kicking them from the air mid-swoop before ascending again. Edna was knocked over the side, but Amory and Akira caught her before she plunged into the warm depths. Bernice stood amazed, staring at her flag. She was certain that one of the creature's swords had pierced through it and would therefore pierce her, but when she looked, there wasn't a scratch on the flag.

Can nothing tear this cloth? Bernice thought. *Could I actually use this as a shield?*

Her thoughts were interrupted by Akira, who'd just pulled Edna back on deck and was bolting for the steering wheel.

"Get that fiend off of us before it kills us all!" he said.

Before all the words were out of his mouth, their attacker dove at Neisha, but she was able to bash her away with her shields. The creature then flew up and landed stiffly on the crow's nest. Her weight made it top-heavy and threatened to tip it over.

"You have interfered with our plans one too many times, Envoys," the being shouted.

"Who are you?" Leona asked.

"I am Maewing, the leader of the Self-Worthy. Are you familiar with this comradery?"

"Yes, we are," said Bernice. "We ran into your forces in Liberdane." She regretted saying this.

Maewing's eyes flared. "You're the ones?! You're the Envoys who stole the kingdom of Liberdane and the people's freedom?"

"Liberdane is better than it has been in centuries," Neisha said. "And the people, I can personally attest, are freer than they ever thought possible."

"But they are not independent," Maewing replied, still teetering on the mast. "Now many of them lean on Nazir for strength and sustenance, rather than tapping into themselves and seeing their own potential."

"Nazir is the only one who can bring out our potential!" Twyla shouted.

"Deceitful liars!" Maewing cried. "I will not let you spread your illusions on any more worlds! Turn back now, and we will inflict no further harm on you."

Amory looked ahead of them. They were almost to the island, and he could see the ominous cave and could almost peer inside it. They were so close. He looked back at Maewing.

"Nazir himself has tasked us with killing the wizard, and we will not stop until he's dead."

Maewing breathed in deeply and raised her arm, which held the Sword of *Chârâsh,* and alighted from the crow's nest with a shove of her hooves. The mast didn't break, but the whole ship swayed unnervingly. Suddenly the Envoys and the crew heard distant explosions from the other ship and a second later were bombarded with cannonballs. Everyone barely had time to think or take cover. One crew member was killed, and there were several holes in the hull. The *Kaze Nagare* began to slow down.

"We're taking on water!" Akira cried. "Patch up those holes and fire our own cannons!"

All of the crew went below deck as Nels trudged up in full armor after having spent several minutes mustering the strength to get out of bed. Leona and Neisha went downstairs to help with the repairs and passed him.

"What's going on?" he moaned.

"We're under attack from the Self-Worthy," Leona replied. "And their leader is here trying to stop us from going any further because they're on the same mission, apparently."

Nels made it on deck just as the ship was hit with another onslaught. He swore in dwarfish as Maewing swooped right above him and attacked Akira. The kitsune was ready and used four of his arms to counter and strike Maewing with his knives at an impressively rapid pace. Maewing blocked almost every slash he made with her swords, but they each managed to cut the other's arms once or twice. They went at it for a solid minute before Maewing saw Amory and Edna charging toward them and Nels drawing his crossbow. She darted away behind her right before Nels fired, and she kicked Akira into the rail in the process. Akira limped back to the wheel as the two vessels gradually shortened the distance between themselves while drawing less than half a mile from the cave entrance. The tanuki crew finally started firing upon the Self-Worthy's ship with well-aimed shots that looked like colorful fireworks.

Maewing saw this and started to fly down to try and take out the cannons. Before she got there, a winged horse with dark gray armor and metal claws on its hooves assaulted her and pushed her away. It took the Envoys a moment to realize the horse was Masato. Maewing stared at him for a second.

"Don't lay a hand or hoof on them again," Masato said through his horse teeth.

"Fine," said Maewing. "I'll lay them on you . . . then on them once you're dead."

At that, they sped toward each other and clashed hooves. Masato tried to claw at Maewing's horse body while she tried to gash his head. Both were good enough at weaving to evade these attempts. They flew to and fro, trying to find an opportune time to shoot in, but seldom did. Nels and Twyla tried shooting their weapons at Maewing but to no avail. The others got distracted while watching them and barely dodged another set of projectiles. They saw that the Self-Worthy's ship was taking on almost as much damage. The ships continued to tear each other apart as they approached the arch of the island entrance.

The Self-Worthy got sidetracked too as they watched their leader and Masato, who were crossing blade and claw closely still. Masato decided to try and headbutt her but was too slow.

Maewing wrapped her arm around his neck and dragged him to the cliffside above the archway. With a great heave, she flung him into the rocky wall. He recovered and resumed flying but was obviously much weaker. She swiftly grabbed him and hurled him into the cliff again. He fell further but still managed to take flight before hitting the water. Maewing grabbed and threw him a third time, and this time he landed on a short edge protruding from the rock and remained still.

"Masato!" cried Akira. He called a time or two more with no response back. He bowed his head in remorse. "Nazir, have mercy on him."

The ships were almost inside the cave when Maewing threw Masato the third time, so she flew to her own ship and attacked the Envoys no longer. As they finally entered the cavern, darkness and a heavy sensation overtook them all. Nothing could be heard except for the stirring of each crew, the water lapping at each fractured hull, and the flickering of the torches on each ship, which were the only sources of light other than the dusk sky through the diminishing entrance. Even with the torches, they could hardly see anything, save whatever was just in front of them and the black water.

"Everyone, be prepared for anything," Amory said. "This is it."

Everyone was quiet and somber for the next few minutes. Absolutely nothing happened, and each crew almost forgot the other was there.

Bernice couldn't stand the silence any longer and approached her boyfriend. "Amory, I found something strange about my flag. When Maewing swooped at us, I felt one of her swords hit it, and I thought it ripped. But it's still in one piece, even though it shouldn't be."

"That's interesting," said Amory, who was paying more attention to the darkness in front of them.

"Do you think that's what Azarias meant when he said our weapons have several purposes? Do you think all of our weapons might be like Edna's and Nels's, having multiple functions and abilities?"

"Possibly," Amory replied.

Nels interrupted. "Hey, where's Akira?"

Everyone looked and saw that he had indeed disappeared.

"Maybe he went to see if Masato's OK," said Amory as he ran to the wheel.

Before he got there, he heard Edna shout, "Amory, we're headed for the cave wall!"

Amory lunged for the wheel and steered it hard to starboard, luckily evading the collision. They ran parallel to the wall as Leona panted up from below deck.

"Where's Amory?" she urged.

Bernice brought her to him.

"The holes are mended, and the ship is intact for now, but I found something else." Leona held out her hand, which dripped something slightly thicker than what should've been water. "The water's not black because of the dark. It's oil."

It didn't take Amory long to figure out what would soon happen. A look of sheer panic overtook his face. "Get the crew on deck now!" Leona and Bernice trotted down the stairs. "Now!" Amory cried.

Every Envoy scurried below and summoned the tanuki. Everyone was startled and baffled.

"Get every grapple and harpoon we have and throw them portside into the cave wall!" Amory shouted. "This ship will soon be destroyed!"

Everyone complied and rushed around to find anything on a rope that could hook onto rock. Amory steered a little closer to the wall to get in range of catching the rock. As he got in position and the Envoys tossed the hooks two or three at a time, Amory looked ahead. He thought he could see a faint light about a quarter of a mile away. His foot nudged the telescope he'd dropped during the attack from the Self-Worthy, and he quickly nabbed it. Through it, he saw a cloaked figure standing on a rocky shore with a large, thick stone column behind him, possibly the exact center of the island and the butte. The figure held two long wands that were the size of drumsticks, its tips on fire. He ominously skulked to the shore and knelt down, the wands getting unnervingly close to the oil. That was enough for Amory. He dropped the scope and sprinted to the others. Twelve ropes were now attached to both the cave wall and the ship.

"OK, someone weigh anchor, and the rest of you start climbing," Amory panted. "We only have seconds before we die!"

The tanuki, who could grow wings if needed, let the Envoys go first, except for Amory, who would go last. Twyla's elven agility brought her to the top of the rope quickly, and the humans followed shortly afterward. Nels and Neisha had the hardest time climbing, and all the tanuki eventually scampered up every rope other than theirs to avoid getting stuck underneath them. Soon, everyone was hanging onto the ropes waiting for Amory, who had just grabbed his.

Before he pulled himself off the deck, Amory heard a deafening roar. He looked and saw a giant, tumultuous fire on the pond of oil advancing swiftly toward him from the cave's center. He felt the heat greatly intensify as he instantly leapt from the ship, just as the fire consumed it. Within seconds, the *Kaze Nagare* was reduced to smoke. The ropes burned free from the ship, and the Envoys dangled on the cave wall. They looked behind them and saw the entire cavern illuminated by the blazing pond.

The Self-Worthy ship was shockingly still in one piece, sailing toward the shore. A bright green bubble could be seen encompassing and protecting the whole vessel, whose source was the Sword held by Maewing on their crow's nest. The Envoys then saw pink blasts bombarding the bubble, coming from the wizard's two wands. The wizard was trying to break the otherworldly shield but without success.

"We have to get to him before they do!" said Nels, recovering well from his ailment.

"Get off these ropes now!" Amory yelled, just realizing the bottoms of the ropes were on fire from the ship. "Start climbing toward the center of the cave. I can see where this wall leads there. And please be careful!"

Suddenly, a knife appeared very close to one of the crew's faces. They all looked behind them and saw Akira in fox form, flying on two wings transformed from his tails. His eyes glowed pink, and his other four tails turned into arms to throw his knives. He grabbed two more.

"Akira, what are you doing?!" Bernice cried.

The kitsune threw one knife at her, and she jumped from the rope to evade it. She managed to catch herself on a tiny ledge before falling into the fire, though she struggled to hang on. One tanuki got stabbed in the hind paw, and the rope onto which Leona and two other tanuki held was cut through. All three managed to grab hold of some stony divots when they dropped. The crew wanted to change form and fly toward either the land or their crazed captain, but assaults of knives prevented them.

"His mind must be controlled by the wizard," said Edna, using all of her strength to climb while carrying her hammer on her back. "His eyes are the same color as the wizard's wands." She was the next to receive and dodge a blade.

Amory watched all of this happen, paralyzed with dread. *Please, Nazir,* he thought, *give us a way out.*

Without warning, Akira was struck by another flying creature, a winged horse with claws.

"Masato!" Leona shouted.

Akira took a pair of larger knives and came at Masato, who, tired and hurt though he was, blocked every slash.

"Akira, what's gotten into you?" Masato asked between clashes. "Don't you remember me? Don't you remember the crew? What would Nazir think of this?"

Akira said nothing and continued to dart here and there, attempting to kill Masato or those stranded on the wall.

"Break free, my friend!" said Masato. "The wizard has you bound by your greatest strength: your mind! Break free from his rule, Akira. You're cunning enough! Don't you want to taste freedom again, like you've told me for decades?"

Masato waited to see a change in his friend's expression or behavior. He waited in vain. The kitsune was still bent on death.

"It's not going to work," Amory called out. "My guess is the wizard's had a hold on him since the last time you both were here and just decided to turn up the throttle now. We have to get to the wizard, Masato, and you know what we have to do to get us there."

"But he's an Envoy!" Masato cried. "I can't kill him anymore than I could kill a brother!"

"I'm beginning to doubt that," said Amory, dodging another blade. "An Envoy would never do this, and I think he's deceived you into thinking he was an Envoy just so you could trust him more and follow him to your death. Nazir is not in him."

Masato flew still for a moment, his horse head hung low. He watched as more knives were tossed at his new and old comrades. Finally, being careful to dodge the projectiles, he soared to Amory.

"Jump on, but you'll have to be the one to do it. I can't bear the thought of doing it myself," Masato said begrudgingly from underneath him. Amory hesitated for only a second and let go of the wall while the others kept trying to climb.

"Hey!" Masato yelped as Amory landed. "Watch where you hold your sword!"

Confused, Amory looked at his sword which he'd deliberately held above his shoulder to avoid cutting Masato. He knew for a fact that it didn't touch him. Then he realized it was his sheath that was cutting him. Amory had always thought that his sheath seemed a bit too sharp, and he now saw that it scraped Masato's hide enough to draw blood. Only then did he notice the detachable buttons on its straps and the flat bottom that was less wide than the rest of it—but still wide enough to fit the sword through.

Does this sheath double as an extra sword? Amory thought. He decided to find out.

As Masato weaved over the fire as they were chased by Akira, Amory, holding on tightly with his legs, carefully unbuttoned his sheath from the belt. Holding it by the apparent handle at the end where it was thinner felt uncomfortable yet somehow natural. Amory sat poised to strike now, then gasped as Masato dove for the fire and swooshed around to catch Akira behind them. Claw and knife met again. Akira used two arms to fend off Masato and two to fight Amory. Akira then realized he was using the only four knives he had left, and his fury increased. Amory was able to use this anger against him. As Masato kept him distracted with his own jabs, Amory took an angrily and clumsily thrown arm with his swords and knocked the knife out of it. Now with one knife against two swords, there was little Akira could do. Amory blocked the hand holding the knife with his sheath and stabbed Akira in his chest with his primary sword. Akira reeled back in silence as he plunged into the fiery pond.

Masato proceeded to take Amory to the place where the inside island met the wall the Envoys were climbing. Everyone else was there, as the other tanuki were free to fly the others to safety once Amory and Masato had distracted their now dead captain.

"Is everyone OK?" Masato asked as Amory dismounted him.

Everyone nodded, though they were obviously shaken.

"We're so close to finishing the mission, you guys," Amory said. "Let's try and sneak behind the wizard and kill him before the Self-Worthy get here. But let them continue as a diversion to him. Think of this world being freed and its people not living in terror anymore. It's this close to becoming a reality."

The eighteen crew who were left trotted quietly around the large column on the island while Masato hung back a little to recover from his injuries. Bernice grinned as she saw Amory holding both his sword and sheath. The wizard stood in front of the column, awaiting the Self-Worthy's arrival after giving up trying to burst their shield.

As the Envoys came around to the back side of the column, they saw the Self-Worthy's ship turned to its side at the fiery shore. A door in its hull opened downward onto the rocks, and dozens of soldiers sped out, charging at the sorcerer.

"It's now or never," Amory whispered. "For Nazir, and for Uchu!"

The Envoys sprinted toward the wizard from behind, advancing closer to him than the Self-Worthy were. Then they noticed that his figure seemed to fade. Before they realized it, he had teleported behind the Envoys, leaving them between him and the Self-Worthy. Everyone hesitated for a moment, then they heard Maewing's voice.

"Don't let these dogs get in our way again!" she said. "The wizard is escaping! Keep moving!"

The Self-Worthy consequently continued to charge at the Envoys. The Envoys were able to hold themselves steady against them after their weapons clashed once again. The troops who weren't presently fighting ran around the scuffle toward the wizard, and Maewing flew over the battle toward him. The wizard produced illusions of himself, which could still do harm, to keep the troops at bay and took on Maewing in person.

Amory saw this and deflected his way out of the battle. "Keep these guys busy," he told Leona quietly while he left. He darted past the soldiers and illusions before he could be seen and leapt at the wizard from behind again with both swords. The wizard blocked his blow and one from Maewing at the same time with each wand. Maewing still had a free arm and took a jab at Amory, who managed to pull his sheath away to block it. Now all three of them were at a circular stalemate, each blocking with a sword or wand in both hands. They stared at each other in determination and rage. The sorcerer's wands started to glow brighter, and Maewing realized her double-sided sword was beginning to melt where the wand was. Amory also noticed that his sword wasn't melting, and the wand did nothing to it. Before Maewing's blade melted completely, she spun it around to the blade on the other side of the hilt and almost cut the wizard's arm.

From that point on, the trio struck and blocked and parried at each other at a furious pace, each wanting the other two dead. Amory at first felt a bit out of his league. Maewing was the largest and most aggressive of the three, and she often flew about to juke or escape her opponents.

The wizard drew on unnatural powers to remain unscathed. Then Amory remembered that Nazir's own power was pumping through his veins, and he knew he could survive and accomplish the task at hand if only because the Vine enabled him. With newfound passion, he swung at Maewing and then the wizard several times, becoming more on the offensive. The wizard stayed on the defensive, and Maewing began to parry and counter Amory's strikes and even tried batting him away with her wings, which tested his temper. His focus and strikes slowly gravitated toward Maewing, and both of them swung at the wizard less frequently. Soon, the wizard realized that he wasn't getting attacked at all anymore, and he sneaked away while the other two persisted to take each other out of the way of their missions, which they momentarily forgot about.

The Envoy team was doing exceptionally well at keeping the troops in front of them and not letting them get past, but they began to get worn out. Each blow and block took its toll, and it became harder to survive. The tanuki had changed to various beasts, which helped, but even they felt fatigued. Bernice and Leona fought side by side, with a bear beside Leona and a leopard beside Bernice. Bernice waved her spear in every direction, with newfound confidence in her flag. She blocked two opponents with one upward strike and managed to slit both of their throats bringing the spear back. She thrust it between their falling bodies and caught a glimpse of a familiar cutlass blocking it.

From the crowd emerged Ambrose, who was just as surprised to see Bernice as she was to see him. It had been two years since they'd met last.

"It's you!" Ambrose exclaimed as they both stood staring at each other. "You guys were the ones on the other ship?"

"Yes, and we have the same objective as you," said Bernice. "You can't let Maewing win, Ambrose. It will only lead to more ruin and confusion for this universe. You can stop this."

Ambrose paused for a moment, not letting his guard down. Then he heard the voice of Esorbma, his otherworldly doppelgänger who followed him on every mission, from within the fray.

"You don't have to follow Maewing, but you don't have to listen to this deceiver either! Look, the wizard's alone. Take him yourself!"

Ambrose and Bernice both looked and saw the wizard sneaking to the other side of the column, trying to get away. Confused, Bernice glanced at Amory, who was only dueling Maewing. She looked back at Ambrose, who started walking toward her in the wizard's direction. She instinctively held out her spear to bar his path. He stopped short, taken aback.

"Let me through," he said. "I can finish this, you just said so."

"I said you could stop the Self-Worthy from causing more harm," Bernice replied. "Nazir tasked us Envoys with this, and I intend to see that that happens. I can't let you through."

Ambrose stuck his sword underneath her spear to try to sweep it away. "You do know that Nazir can use non-Envoys too, right?" he asked.

Bernice held her spear steady. "Of course, but not when he gave us specific orders. I'm not compromising on this."

Ambrose stood still and sighed briefly. "Fine." At that, he thrust his sword directly at her, though she was able to slide out of the way and parry it. Knowing she wasn't going to argue her way out, Bernice brought her spear around and smacked him on his armored shoulder. Ambrose grinned and began to deal faster strikes.

"Ambrose, is that you?" the Envoys heard someone call. It was Dilyn, squeezing to the front to catch up with his brother.

Dilyn, wearing his bow on his back and holding a staff in his hand, wormed his way behind Ambrose and unexpectedly locked eyes with Leona, who was fighting nearby and had just killed a Self-Worthy dwarf. They sauntered closer.

"What are you doing here?" Dilyn asked.

"I'll give you one guess," said Leona. "You got a new weapon, I see."

Dilyn glanced at his staff. "Oh yeah. I was told it's better for close combat. I still use my bow a lot, though." Dilyn expected her to say something about using more of his Envoy tools or doing more Envoy things, but instead he saw her eyebrows furrow as she looked him over again.

"Are you feeling all right?" she asked. "You look pale . . . and tired."

"Yeah, I'm fine," said Dilyn. "It must be the weird light from the fire. How are you?"

They heard Esorbma again, calling to Ambrose. "Do you want Maewing to ever respect you again or not? The wizard's getting away, and you have a chance of finishing this task yourself! Forget about past sentiments and push through!"

Dilyn and Leona watched as Ambrose grabbed Bernice's spear with his free hand and punched her in the head twice with his sword's guard. Bernice fell to the ground, unconscious and exposed to enemies, while Ambrose sprinted free of the Envoys' barricade and to the sorcerer. Leona jumped over to her to protect her, and Dilyn followed.

"They're going to try to kill you too if they see you helping us," Leona said.

"I'm not about to let one of my friends die—on either side," said Dilyn.

"Let's stage a fight just to blend in," Leona replied. "But stay over her so no one touches her. Just block every swing I throw. I promise I won't hurt you."

Leona dealt blows that were slow yet convincing, and Dilyn did well to deflect them. Edna caught a glimpse of all of this, and she too saw Amory still trying to kill Maewing. To free herself up for a moment, Edna knocked one opponent silly and stabbed another with the cat's-paw of her hammer.

"Amory! Maewing's not our target!" Edna yelled angrily. "Where's the wizard?"

Amory and Maewing both heard this and paused for a split second to find the wizard. They found him climbing the other side of the column, almost out of their view. Ambrose was darting after him. Out of the corner of his eye, Amory saw Maewing trying to fly off, which failed, and he saw that a snake—small enough to be fast and long enough to not be ignored—had curled its way around her hind legs and wing coverts. It was Masato, who'd recovered enough to creep around to the battle and take Maewing by surprise.

"Go get him, quick!" Masato shouted.

Ambrose started to climb the column in hot pursuit of the tyrant, but he wasn't sure how he'd make it. The rocky pillar wasn't man-made, but it was still rather smooth. He managed to find a crevice or knot here and there, and they were close enough to reach to and from. The higher he got, the more convinced he was that the wizard had never even climbed and was just using his powers to hover or something. When he got about halfway, he looked up and saw that he was indeed using one wand to remain in the air at the ceiling of the cave near the top of the pillar. The other wand he held close to the pillar itself. Unsure what the fiend would do next, Ambrose kept climbing and failed to see the wizard draw his wand back from the wall, ready to thump it.

Suddenly an arrow appeared above the wizard's head, which was fired by Nels who'd also broken free from the battle. As Nels got his next arrow, the sorcerer smacked the pillar, and a small rockslide occurred just above Ambrose. Ambrose instantly let go and slid down the column, tripping and crashing onto the stone floor, a pile of rocks building up behind him. To avoid any more arrows, the wizard himself slid down after the rockslide, though he did this much more gracefully. Upon reaching the bottom, the wizard leapt to Ambrose, who was still on the ground recovering from his fall. Ambrose's heart stopped as he suddenly beheld the sorcerer about to smite him. Then a sword pierced the wizard's wilted heart from behind, and a second sword relieved him of his head.

The body fell, revealing Amory behind it. In an instant, the fire dissipated, the cloned illusions faded, the flaming oil turned back to pure water, and that dark feeling left every soul. Amory slid his blood-stained sword into his blood-stained sheath and reached a hand out to Ambrose. When Ambrose took it, Amory heaved him up, patted him on the back, and whispered, "Now we're even."

4
A REALM DIVIDED

U pon seeing the wizard's corpse, with much toil Maewing shook off Masato's serpentine form. She immediately took flight and boarded the Self-Worthy ship, which was surprisingly still seaworthy. Without looking back, she called out to her crew.

"Back to the ship with haste! We must spread the word that the wizard is no more and that the people are now free!"

Ambrose started to tear after the ship, though he managed to look back at Amory for a brief moment. Amory took it as a thank you. The rest of the Envoys watched as the Self-Worthy forsook the waning fight and scurried onto the ship. Bernice began to regain consciousness as Dilyn slowly backed away to follow the others, fearing he'd be left behind. He took one last concerned look at Leona, who decisively said nothing. She'd tried almost everything to bring him back to their team in the years past, but nothing prevailed. He was in Nazir's hands (or leaves) now, and it hurt her deeply to let him go without saying a word.

Dilyn was the last one aboard the ship before it turned around and sailed off. The Envoys reassembled as they watched it head for the cave entrance, which revealed a finalized sunset.

Bernice cleaned her bloody brow, and Twyla and several tanuki were limping.

"So, how exactly are we getting out of here?" Neisha asked.

Dilyn saw his old friends stranded on the cave island. He turned and looked the other way but then realized they had no way of getting out. That was their problem, though, not his. Besides, what could he do when everyone around him would stop him? But those Envoys were his friends, old though they were, and he knew he couldn't just leave them there. He quickly looked around, mostly for ideas but also to see if anyone was looking. Then it came to him. It was something that everyone would notice, but he had to do it. He grabbed his bow from his back plus one wide arrow. Before anyone could stop him, he shot the arrow through the ropes holding one of the lifeboats over the side of the deck. The sliding of the ropes and the splash that followed was louder than Dilyn wanted. He looked back to see who else had seen him. Everyone had. Ambrose and Lisias came over to him.

"Why did you do that, son?" Lisias shouted. "We had the advantage, and we could've pronounced freedom to the peoples with a guarantee that the peoples wouldn't also hear lies about the Vine!"

"That's funny coming from you," said Dilyn. "But I couldn't just leave them stuck on this island without any way out. They're individuals too, you know."

"I thought they had their Daggers," said Ambrose. "And if they're powerful enough to kill sorcerers then surely they'd be able to get off the island. If not them, then that Plant would."

"His name is Nazir," Dilyn said sharply. "Shouldn't you be a little more grateful that they saved your life? Their interference has saved our skins before."

"Our interference saved theirs! Amory said so himself just a bit ago," Ambrose replied. "I thought you'd forsaken Nazir. Why get so defensive about him now?"

"Enough," Maewing's voice came behind them. Ambrose, Lisias, and the others stepped aside while she faced Dilyn directly. Dilyn had seen her give this cold stare to his brother, but he never felt its impact for himself until now.

"If I but catch a glimpse of those Envoys near us again while we are in this world, I will not be able to trust you to join us on any subsequent missions for a very long while," Maewing said coolly in front of everyone.

Great, Dilyn thought. *Precisely what I wanted* before *we got here.*

Maewing turned aside. "Full steam ahead to the nearest civilized isle, captain. We must waste no time. Everyone not operating the ship, get below and get some rest. Let's get what recovery we can before we reach out to these freed souls."

Everyone either slept or took care of their wounds, but they didn't have long to do so. It was only a couple of hours to the next island, and they were called up without expecting it so soon. Maewing gave Lisias a silver bugle, and as they approached the shore, he blew it with all the might he had left, emitting a low-pitched, almost high-tech-sounding boom.

By the time they arrived on shore on some precariously creaky docks, dozens of villagers in various forms had gathered nearby. Curious and puzzled, they saw Maewing burst into flight from the ship, perform a few loops and twirls, and then alight before them as her comrades strolled out of the ship behind her.

"Hark, the wizard is finally dead!" Maewing began in her well-known, loud public speaking voice. "We have come to proclaim to you that that tyrannous terrorist is no more, and it is because of us that you now possess more freedom than you could ever imagine!"

"Who are you?" one intrigued kitsune asked.

Maewing grinned. "We are the Self-Worthy, and our sole purpose is to reveal to every being their individuality. You don't need superior forces or ideas to tell you who you are. You are each your own person with your own unique personality, talents, skills, and stories. Authorities like the late wizard often suppress your personalities and strengths for their own benefit, but this no longer applies to you! There is no one to impress their agenda on you anymore, and you are finally free to be yourselves!"

Dilyn almost cracked up laughing but managed to hold it in. The gathering crowd, however, seemed interested. A few of them stepped forward.

"We've noticed that the wizard has died," a female tanuki said. "The night is all of a sudden clearer, and the heavy, oppressive sensation in our bones is gone. It's been so long since we've been free of his rule that many of us have forgotten how to live on our own. Are you saying you'll teach us how?"

Maewing beamed. "That is exactly what I'm saying, and we would be delighted to show you and to invite you to join our ranks! That way we will walk alongside you and show you what freedom and being yourself is really like. In addition, we will equip you to fight battles so that you can help us go to other worlds to free more beings—so that everyone in the entire multiverse will be able to unlock their true potential!"

"So you are an exclusive military?" asked another kitsune. "I assume, then, that it was you who killed the wizard?"

Before Maewing could answer, everyone heard a deafening squawk. Behind the Self-Worthy ship came the lifeboat Dilyn had released, and it was the Envoys who rode it. One of the crew turned into a shark and pulled the boat using a rope tied to the prow and its dorsal fin. Another tanuki changed into a phoenix, which was giving the long shrieks everyone was hearing. The Envoys nearly crashed into the docks as they struggled to disembark.

They all clambered up the shore to the crowds, Amory all the while shouting, "Wait! Wait! These people are lying to you! They offer vain hope, and it will not satisfy. We've come to show you the only true hope in the multiverse!"

Maewing, frowning intensely, glanced at Dilyn while the Envoys stopped beside them and gasped heavily, their weapons all drawn.

"What are these maniacs doing here?" Maewing asked.

"Indeed," said the first kitsune. "Who are you?"

"We are Envoys of the Vine, Nazir, King of the multiverse," panted Amory. "We've come to tell you about him and his love and power."

"Don't listen to this deception," Maewing said.

"A plant for a king?" a tanuki asked. "You speak as if this Vine was a person. Is he a shapeshifter like us?"

"No, I don't think so," said Edna. "But he is real. I've spoken to him on many occasions, and he's spoken to me even more often."

"How?" shouted another creature. "Where is he?"

"In the Center of the whole multiverse. We can take you if you wish," said Twyla.

"Enough of this!" Maewing cried. "Comrades, get these intruders off this island—no, out of this world and back to the Center and the Vine they claim. Use force if you must!"

The Self-Worthy started toward the Envoys, who stood their ground and determined within themselves not to budge.

"Now hold on," another creature bellowed, approaching the gap between the two groups. "There is no need to cause any further bloodshed. I am quite interested in what both of your groups have to offer. Leader of the Self-Worthy, if you truly value our individuality, you will let us be the judges of who is lying and who is not, and if there are any liars among you at all. You have already stated your case. Now we want to hear these Envoys. Tell us, Envoys, of this Vine's love and power."

"We can't thank you enough, sir," Amory replied. "The Vine, Nazir, through us, brings you bad news as well as good news. The bad news is that everyone once had a good relationship with him, but we broke it by disobeying him, since he is King of everything. We have fallen short of the perfect standard that he has established—a relationship that allows us all to be with him forever in a paradise world called *Paradeisos*. Those who die without this relationship spend eternity in torment without him in a world called *Pur*." Amory continued, "The fact is that every single being in existence has fallen short of that standard and is destined for and deserving of *Pur*. But the good news is that Nazir loves us so much that he wasn't OK with that. He gave up everything and experienced everything we mortals do, and he took our punishment so that we wouldn't have to. The only way to escape *Pur* and have your relationship with the King redeemed is to accept and believe that he can and will redeem you and that he can take over your life and make it into something beautiful and glorious and clean and whole, just like him—even using our past mistakes. That is what every one of us Envoys has done, and we can each attest that we were totally different people before him. Would you like to meet him now?"

Dilyn and Lisias looked at their hesitant audience, Lisias with contempt and Dilyn with contemplation. About a score stepped forward.

"You have stated your view, and you made it very clear," said one of them, "but how do we know this is true?"

The Envoys started pulling out their Daggers and were about to say that they could meet Nazir in person and talk with him, but Maewing interrupted.

"That is truly a breathtaking story, but yes, how do we know if it's true? To clarify, I myself believe in Nazir's existence because I've seen him too. You can go with these Envoys if you want, and you'll probably meet the Vine. He'll say something to make your emotions tender, and he'll embrace you and perhaps even give you weapons and armor, but how will you know if anything has truly changed inside? Nothing will change, but he'll tell you what to do and how to live the rest of your life because you got soft and made a commitment that you'll be guilt-tripped into keeping. No one has the right to control anyone else's life."

"How do *you* know all this?" Amory replied. "How can you make these claims? Have you experienced this and gone to him yourself?"

"No, but I have close friends who did, and they forsook him because of all of the regulations and standards they had to live by."

"They were taught wrong, then," Neisha said. "Nazir gives us more freedom than even you could offer, and we as his Envoys are called to act as he does. He is perfect, so there are clear things we should and shouldn't do, but there is only so much mortals can do. He is inside every Envoy, guiding and equipping those who'll listen and obey."

"See, it's that word *obey* that makes me cringe," said Maewing. "Who has the right to assume authority over anyone? Yes, there are rulers in each world, but they simply try to make life easier and less complicated for their subjects."

"Using what? Suggestions for the subjects to follow?" Amory retorted. "For any society to thrive, there must be clear and assertive laws put in place to help the people not go astray and ruin not only their own lives but countless others' lives."

"Who said going astray was bad or even existent?" Maewing asked, now more focused on Amory than the crowd. "*Astray* is a relative term. What's bad for you might not be bad for me, as we have different personalities and backgrounds. There are no such things as absolutes."

"Is that an absolute statement?" Amory replied, almost grinning. "If our definitions of evil are different, then why are both our groups constantly on the same battlefields with the same targets? Why were we both trying to kill this wizard for almost the same reasons?" Then he turned to the crowd. "By the way, did she tell you who actually killed the wizard?"

"Not directly," a tanuki answered. "We just assumed she did it."

"I thought not," Amory said. He then lifted high his bloody sword and sheath. Many in the mass gasped. "I'm the one who killed him. His blood is on my blades. Nazir sent us Envoys to kill him so that you'd be better able to turn to him without the sorcerer interfering. You will notice that Maewing's swords have no blood on them."

"That's because I'm responsible enough to clean mine," said Maewing, knowing she was losing ground. "It seems these Envoys are careless slobs who like to go around spreading their mess across the multiverse."

Now Amory was losing his temper and focus. "No, actually I figured it'd come down to this, arguing about who actually freed the world. So I thought I'd bring the evidence."

Nels leaned over to Bernice. "Wait," he whispered, "who actually freed Uchu, Amory or Nazir?"

"You said that was the wizard's blood!" Maewing exclaimed. "Dare you deny to these people that you also fought against us?"

"You fought against each other?" asked a tanuki.

"Isn't that obvious by now?" snorted another.

"Why didn't you just join forces and team up against the wizard?" the first one asked.

"We tried that once in another world," Amory answered. "It didn't work. We don't have the exact same goals in mind, and we have different beliefs that conflict with each other. Both of our beliefs can't be true; one of us has to be wrong. And I'll let the wizard's blood stand as proof of who's right and who's wrong."

Maewing's passion was becoming unignorable. "Our ideals do clash, yes, but how does that automatically mean that someone is wrong? Even if our beliefs are perpendicular instead of parallel, is it possible that there are several 'right' paths instead of merely one?"

"Not according to you," Amory chuckled. "Earlier you called us liars and deceivers, implying that we were wrong and you were right. You're contradicting yourself, and it's discrediting you. Seriously, Maewing, decide on a statement and stick to it! You're simply proving the fact that absolute truth not only exists but is the only way anything makes any sense!"

Maewing was now fuming but refused to give in. "Your stubbornness and narrowmindedness will be your downfall. It will bring you many enemies."

"That's to be expected in the life of an Envoy," said Amory. "Questioning every statement and fact has already become your downfall. It will bring you many admirers until they become disillusioned with the truth."

"What is truth?" Maewing asked. "And again, how are you so sure that Nazir holds it? Because he told you? What proof is that? That's the same as me saying I'm right. But where does that get us? Right back to where we started. Why can't we just ignore our differences and go our separate ways?"

"People have tried that for millennia," said Amory. "The conflict always comes back around at the next clash, now fiercer than before. Addressing and resolving conflict is the only way to attain peace."

"That's ridiculous. That just leads to more conflict. The true way to peace is to live and let live—to follow one's own path and let everyone else follow theirs."

"Even if those paths lead straight to *Pur*?" Amory asked. "Sorry, we Envoys can't do that."

"That's another thing," Maewing exclaimed. "How do you know *Pur* and *Paradeisos* are real? Have you been to either of them?"

"Actually, we do know someone who Nazir resurrected and rescued from *Pur*."

"How do you know he wasn't making it up?"

Amory grinned. "You should've seen the look on the elf's face when he came back to life. *Pur* is as real as death and pain and is in fact the epitome of both."

"That's not what I've heard," Maewing shrugged. "I've heard rumors that *Pur* is where all the free-spirited people go who resisted societies and cultural norms and rebelled against Nazir and ticked him off. It's where all the fun and vivacious people go. That honestly makes that place more appealing to me than the other one."

"Bull crap," said Amory. "That is where rebels against Nazir belong, yes, but it's full of unending torture and devastation. On the other hand, maybe you would be better suited there!"

Ambrose nudged Dilyn and whispered, "Looks like Maewing's not the only one discrediting herself."

Dilyn had to agree.

Bernice and the others watched all of this with growing worry. The argument was getting hotter and hotter, and no progress was being made. None of the locals were convinced one way or another; they just watched as both Amory and Maewing made fools out of themselves.

"This is getting nowhere fast," Bernice said aloud to herself.

You're right, said a voice in her head. She recognized it as Nazir's.

"What?" Bernice said under her breath.

No more progress will be made while you're here. Return to me; your mission is over.

Bernice looked at her teammates and found they were all looking at each other with the same expression. Everyone heard the same voice and the same message. It was time to pull out. They looked at Amory in front of them. He was still arguing. It seemed he wasn't given the same message, or at least he didn't heed it. Bernice stepped up beside Amory who had just given another dastardly insult to Maewing.

"Time to go," she said aloud. Amory apparently didn't hear her. She repeated it as Maewing dished out a comeback.

"What?" Amory turned to Bernice, perplexed and angry. "We still have work to do, souls to win!"

"No, we don't. Nazir does," Bernice replied. "He'll take it from here. He said it's time to go back."

"Cowards," Maewing grinned. "Leaving just when things become intense."

"If that were the case, we'd have left when we first saw you," said Amory. "Who was it who left Hertengard after one dicey storm, so I heard?" He turned again to his girlfriend. "Our mission was to kill the wizard *and* tell others about Nazir's redemption."

"We've done that," Bernice said. "The mission is complete."

"We can't leave these people to be deceived by these liars!" Amory shouted.

"Do you not trust that Nazir can take care of that?" Bernice asked, maintaining her original tone. "What makes you think we're the only Envoys in Uchu and that our presence is critical to the world's survival? We're not Nazir's only tools, Amory."

Bernice looked back at the others and nodded. Twyla took her Dagger and produced a green portal. Leona beckoned Masato and the crew to join them since they had helped with the mission, and they complied with hesitance. Bernice walked back in their direction and glanced back at Amory.

"We're leaving," she said. "Are you coming with us?"

As the Envoys stepped through the portal one by one, Amory took one last glare at Maewing before following them. "You're wrong, and these people will find out sooner or later."

Maewing waited until Amory was almost through the portal to reply. "That's their choice, and you won't be around to influence them."

Amory was clenching his swords tightly as he entered the Center. Everyone else frowned in concern or frustration as they stood before the Vine. The entire crew had changed into their original tanuki forms and seemed to be in shock. Nazir himself did and said nothing.

Amory sauntered presumptuously to his King. "Why did you pull us out? There's still more to be done!"

"Indeed there is, my son," Nazir said calmly. "But there is nothing more I could've done through you. Lingering there would only have caused more division among the peoples, and that is just what I'm working to prevent and undo. What's important is that the world is now free and seeds for my Kingdom are now planted. Getting caught up in disputes interfered with your focus and impact, but I will use it regardless."

"Then who will you get to cultivate those seeds?" Amory said, his anger subsiding but still present.

"That's a good question, which I will address now," said Nazir, turning to the crew. They all stared at him.

"Us?" one crew member asked.

"I see you all are doubtful," Nazir replied.

Every one of them—Masato included—knelt before him.

"We've never seen you in person before. At least I haven't," said a second tanuki.

Masato glanced at him in surprise.

The second tanuki continued. "I don't know if I'm worthy of being in your presence because I don't know my standing with you." The rest of the crew nodded in agreement.

"Your standing with me?" Nazir asked, not surprised but prying for more honesty.

It was Masato who spoke up now. "Akira was the one who taught us about you and helped us become Envoys. One of the things he taught us was that we could lose our redeemed Envoy status if we misrepresented you enough or strayed far enough from you."

Nazir sighed deeply. "Akira was never my child to begin with, and the wizard planted thoughts of deception and ruin in his head upon your first disastrous visit, Masato. The wizard sought to deceive more souls through Akira, since he was of such good repute. Akira thought he could use my teachings and ideals to better himself and others, but he purposefully neglected the most critical part of the Envoy role: his or her relationship with me. It's not obeying a moral code that will restore your status and relationship with me but rather accepting and believing that I am your King and your only hope of life. I do give commands to follow, but that's not what will redeem you, as no one can follow me perfectly. The point is that I alone can redeem you."

"We know this," said the crew. "We know we don't have the power to attain peace in ourselves."

"Then how do you think you have the power to lose it once you've received it?" Nazir asked. "You will fail me at times, but my mercy covers that, and my grace equips you to get up stronger and more resilient against temptation than before. No matter how much you mess up, if you're my child, you will always remain so. Once an Envoy, always an Envoy."

"My Lord," another tanuki asked, "are we truly Envoys? I mean, we do believe in you as King of the multiverse."

"Marah himself and his armies believe in me, so much so that they quake upon hearing my name. Belief is not enough. Have you truly turned to me—not just my ideals—from your pride, and have you come to me to give up your wrongdoings and your whole lives? Did you simply repeat words that Akira had recited to you, or did you authentically mean them?"

Every one of the crew's heads dropped in guilt and introspection—all except Masato. He remained kneeling and staring at the one he knew to be his multiversal Father. As Amory's team looked closer, they finally realized that their badges, along with the flags and sails of the *Kaze Nagare*, had portrayed symbols that didn't exactly match the true Envoy emblem. They then saw that Masato's badge did match their own. The crew members finally spoke up.

"I must admit that I was only following Akira, not you, my Liege," the others said at the same time.

"Are you OK with that?" Nazir asked.

"No, we're not!" they answered. "We need to make this right—now. If today has taught us anything, it's that we might not get another day or another chance."

"Indeed, you're right," Nazir grinned.

"We want to turn to you as King and redeemer of our lives right now, Nazir. We want to throw all our pasts away."

"Your pasts will always come back to haunt you," said Nazir. "Throw them to me, so I can properly dispose of the bad and use the rest for my Kingdom."

"All right, it's all yours," the crew said. Then they said in unison, "We accept and believe in you as our redeemer."

Nazir chuckled, and no one save Amory could help but smile. Nazir embraced them all at the same time with his branches and vaporized their old blood as he had with everyone else present. After letting them go, he held out some leaves in front of them and unfolded them, revealing Daggers and metal molds.

"These are for your *real* Envoy equipment!" Nazir laughed. "Now go to the portal behind me to *Chârûsh*, and the forger there will construct your new armor and weapons. Take your old equipment off and use it to fuel the forge's fire."

The now excited tanuki trotted through the portal, all the while thanking Nazir. Masato and Amory's team remained.

"Masato," Nazir said, "you were the only one who was dissatisfied with someone's teachings about me, even though it was your closest friend. You wanted to see me for yourself, and I restored you as a result. Since you've had the longest relationship with me out of the whole crew, I'm appointing you as the crew's new captain. Your new task is to return to Uchu, train up your crew in my ways—knowing your Envoy status is permanent—and show them what it looks like to reflect me. As you do this, travel across the islands and declare that the wizard is dead and my Kingdom is coming. Prevent the Self-Worthy's deception from gaining anymore ground."

"Thank you, my Lord!" Masato exclaimed as he bowed again. "I would love that! I do have questions, though. First off, how are we to go throughout the islands? Our ship was destroyed. You're not suggesting that we change to aquatic creatures and swim to each civilization, are you? We'd get tired too quickly."

"I will provide a new ship for you," Nazir answered. "You must trust my timing on it, though."

"Yes, my King, thank you! Also, are you sure you want me to show the crew how to follow you? I don't feel like I've done the best job at obeying you myself."

"Oh?" Nazir responded.

Masato glanced at the other Envoys. "I feel like I've had more fun than was productive. I've enjoyed using my abilities to prank people, but Akira's constantly told me that I shouldn't do that. Now that I know his real motives, I don't know which of his teachings are true or not. And I might tell the crew something about you that's untrue."

"Those are very good concerns to have," Nazir replied. "First of all, Akira did tell the truth in some areas, but not in others, which made him more believable. Marah is a master at that. If you're unsure of which is which, come to me, and I will tell you. Always come back to me. And in this case, Akira was right to an extent. You were taking advantage of people by tricking them. Your talents were given to honor me, not to exploit others. Fun and sarcasm are good things and are one method I designed to help start and strengthen relationships. But like every other good thing, they can be taken too far, and you did that."

"I'm sorry," Masato said, bowing lower.

"I forgive you," Nazir replied.

"So do we," Leona chimed in.

Masato looked at his new friends and sighed deeply.

"Remember, fun and humor are good," Nazir continued, "and I invented them. I can accomplish much through those who possess these traits but only if I am their King."

"You are," said Masato. "Everything I have and am is yours to use."

"That is exactly what I want," Nazir smiled.

By that time, the crew began to come back to the Center, one by one. They all beamed as they wore their new armor and badges and bore their new, unique weapons. Once they all arrived, Nazir resumed.

"Most impressive! I like this new look on you all!"

"We do too," said one of the crew members. "We feel so much freer and eager to serve you!"

"Good!" Nazir said. "Now, I just made Masato your new captain. He's going to show you what it's like to follow the real me. I am sending you back to Uchu to proclaim my freedom and restoration to every island. As you declare this more, word will spread, and more Envoys will be raised up to help you advance my Kingdom until it penetrates the whole universe. Don't worry about how this will happen; simply trust and hold fast to me and watch with wonder as I provide. Now go; use your gifts not for deception but for the advancement of the truth!"

Masato and his crew elatedly turned back toward the portal to their home world, passionate to start telling others of the hope they'd found.

Nazir chuckled as he turned to Amory's group. "Well done for not backing down when you were attacked and for persevering until the mission was accomplished. Now that it is done, I can use this crew and many other creatures in Uchu to build my Kingdom there. Once enough progress is made, I will have Masato join your team."

"That will be awesome!" Bernice said. "But why didn't you tell him that earlier?"

"One step at a time, my daughter," answered Nazir. "Speaking of which, now is the time to tell you all your next step. You got heavily distracted by the Self-Worthy's interference, and I see that some of you are still distracted by it. Therefore,

I'm sending you back to Earth to rest and refocus on what truly matters—on the real mission and the real enemy. I want you to come to me often during this time and continue training each other. I will finally give you to another trainee, Nels. And I will provide a new trainer to you, Amory. Be watchful but not presumptuous."

"By rest, you do mean that there will be another mission for us, correct?" Twyla asked.

"Yes," said Nazir. "You didn't fail me today, and even if you did, I would still pick you back up and use you. You succeeded in this mission, though not perfectly. But many things must happen before your next assignment. Do you all understand?"

Yes was the general, more dejected reply. They all turned to the portal going to Earth.

"Always remember that I love you," Nazir called. "I am making you more beautiful through both the trials and the times of rest and waiting. *Waiting* is not a passive term. Continue to follow and serve me while you're at home."

Amory was the last to walk through. He said nothing to his Father as he plunged through the white, deep in thought and frustration.

PART II

THE FIRE IS COVERED

5

WEIGHTS LIFTED

It was a Thursday afternoon. Dilyn sat in the blue bean bag chair in his room, deeply troubled. He could've been working to catch up on an English assignment, but he felt no desire to do so. He just got back from another check-up at the hospital. They had started the chemo treatment over two months ago, and every test result showed no improvement. In fact, things seemed to have gotten worse. His skin was getting yellower, he constantly felt weak, and when eating, he got full faster, even though he was losing weight. And now, his hair was getting lighter and thinner. What's worse, no one outside his family seemed to care. Even Ambrose appeared to have lost a bit of interest in Dilyn's welfare. Ambrose was promoted again to lieutenant for his actions in Uchu and became busy with his new, eagerly received role.

Ambrose was right when I first joined the Self-Worthy, Dilyn thought. *Maewing is as wishy-washy as they come. Man, those were some good times, those first several months with them. But now those days are clearly over. Nobody there cares about me, my health, my future, or my personality. They've got an agenda to keep, and I'm not a priority anymore. One thing's for sure: I am done with the Self-Worthy. I'm not going back. So now the question is, where do I go from here? Back to Nazir? Back to Amory's team?*

Dilyn then thought back on his reunion with his Envoy friends—how valiantly they fought against the wizard and against the Self-Worthy. He remembered Amory's heated public debate with Maewing and how offtrack he got. Amory lost focus big time, that much was obvious. Everything he said made sense, and might even be true, but he totally lost his temper and did not portray Nazir well at all. *Is this how they've been for the past couple of years?* Dilyn thought. *Have they been this angry and unreasonable in every world they've gone to since I left? If that's the case, then I don't want to be on their team anymore. Maybe I could come back to Nazir without rejoining them. But what if every Envoy is like that? What if Nazir lied to me?*

Dilyn felt something was off about those thoughts he had, but he overlooked it.

Assuming that everything Amory said was true, is that how Nazir taught them to teach it? Through intense debates that actually get nothing accomplished? Did Nazir task them with killing the wizard and either destroying or discrediting the Self-Worthy? That sounds a little exclusive to me. But then again, how do I know everything Amory said was true? What if some things Maewing said were right, like about how Nazir might make it seem like we're redeemed but really nothing inside us has changed?

Dilyn's thoughts continued. *I know that's not true. I felt a weight lifted off my shoulders when Nazir cleansed me, and I felt a sense of peace that I hadn't felt at all before then. But why haven't I felt that peace since then? Did I lose my redemption by joining the Self-Worthy? Do I need to be cleansed again?*

Dilyn pondered this for a long while but came to no conclusion.

I don't know. If I do need to be cleansed again, I want to fix that as soon as possible. If I don't need it, I'd like to know for sure. But I don't know for sure! I need to ask somebody. I could ask Nazir himself, but I kind of want it to be a human. Besides, I'm not quite ready to meet him again. It's been a long time, and he knows that. But who else could I ask? It needs to be an Envoy, but none of the Envoys I know care about me. No one from Amory's team has asked how I'm doing in over a year! But wait . . . Leona did, in Uchu and a few times way before that. I don't think she knows about the cancer, but she saw something wasn't right. Aw heck, I'll call her. She would know the answer.

Dilyn pulled out his phone and sifted through his contacts to find her, which took a minute. He paused to look at several contacts he should delete, especially now. None of them were his true friends, and they weren't about to be now. He got over the distraction and kept scrolling.

But does she really care, though? Other than Uchu, she hasn't asked me how I'm doing in a while. Plus, it's been a couple of months since then. Why hasn't she come back to me now?

Dilyn recognized Nylid in those thoughts and kept going.

Something's holding her back from checking up on me. I've noticed at school that she constantly glances over at me but does nothing. It could be Nazir, or it could be fear. I do know that Leona's not the timid kind. She might be waiting for me to come to her.

He finally found Leona's number and pressed the call button. She answered before the second ring. He told her everything about the cancer and the Self-Worthy's behavior. Leona sounded devastated to hear about it all.

After Dilyn had finished catching her up, there was a brief silence before Leona said anything.

"So has the Self-Worthy done anything at all to help you? Have they given you any kind of emotional or physical or financial support?"

"No one but Ambrose, who gave all of the above. But now he doesn't as much because he just got promoted again."

"That is sad—and frustrating at the same time," Leona said. "So what will you do now if you're not going back?"

"I don't know," Dilyn answered. "I'll have you know, I am considering coming back to Nazir, but I'm hesitant. That peace and joy that I had when he first redeemed me is gone, it seems, which leaves me to wonder about my relationship with him. It can't be on good terms. I haven't seen him in forever. Do I need to get adopted again?"

Leona could've answered that herself but intentionally chose not to. "Why don't you ask him?"

Dilyn paused and sighed. "Will he even welcome me back?"

"Of course!" Leona replied. "I've seen his mercy and forgiveness in action before, even firsthand."

"You mention forgiveness as if he has something to forgive me of. Are you saying my leaving him and you was wrong?"

Leona paused. "Let me put it this way: You can't be loyal to two opposing forces. Nazir and the Self-Worthy don't clash on everything, but they do in some things. Nazir demands all of our loyalty and lives, and if you believe him to be the loving King of the multiverse, you know he deserves it all. If you fall short on this, that's disobedience to his demand. So yes, it was wrong."

"So I do need to be cleansed again?" Dilyn asked.

"That's something to discuss with him," said Leona. "I can come with you if you want. I'm getting my Dagger out now."

"Now?" Dilyn asked.

"Right now," said Leona.

"OK. I'll meet you there," Dilyn replied.

Dilyn hung up and sat there a moment longer, wondering what he just got himself into. He got up and entered his closet to get his Dagger. He had to stop and remember where he'd put it because it had been so long since he'd used it last. He recalled that he'd placed it in a small box he kept for old, sentimental things. He opened the box and found his Dagger buried underneath some family photos and some love notes from an ex-girlfriend.

Wait, said Nylid. *Don't go through with it. It won't be what you expect.*

"I hope not," said Dilyn aloud. "I'm expecting the worst." At that, he made a portal (after having to remember how) and plunged through.

Dilyn entered the Center of *Rôb Têbêl* and stopped to soak it all in. It had been well over a year since he'd come here, yet everything looked the same, including the Vine he'd dreaded meeting.

Nazir was delighted to see him. "My son! Welcome! It's good to have you back here."

Dilyn was shocked and overwhelmed. "What are you doing? Why are you being so welcoming to me? I left you!"

"You're my child," Nazir replied. "Since the day you left, I've never stopped calling you back to me."

Dilyn recalled a voice he'd heard when he first joined the Self-Worthy, urging him to return. "I don't remember hearing you recently."

"That's because you crowded out my voice with many others: Ambrose, your parents, your friends, Maewing. All of them were feeding the primary voice in your head—Nylid."

Dilyn looked behind him and saw his doppelgänger's flat, shadowy form on the ground cowering behind him. Nylid jumped when he saw Leona and the whole team—the humans, dwarves, and Twyla—come in to join them. Dilyn was happy and scared and confused to see them all, but they each seemed overjoyed to behold him—even Amory, who Dilyn hadn't seen smile in quite a long time. He also noticed that Amory and Bernice were holding hands. He turned to face them.

"I guess we all have a lot to catch up on," Dilyn began. "This seems like a good time to tell you guys something, though Leona and Nazir probably already know. About two months ago, I got diagnosed with liver cancer, stage 3." He gave no pause to allow for empty pity. "I started chemo a while back, and nothing's changed. I'm still hoping for a breakthrough, but nothing's come yet." Then, after thinking for a moment, he turned to the Vine. "Nazir, you unnaturally healed me of stings from a giant spider, and Leona told me several months ago that you brought that one elf back to life. If you can do those things, I know you can take this cancer away. Will you? Please?"

Nazir gave a glad and understanding sigh. "Not at this moment, my son. You must understand that I allow people— especially Envoys—to endure terrible trials, but if they press on by keeping close to me and my love and strength, it leads to many coming to me. Remember the storm you went through when you first came to Hertengard? I could've taken the storm away, but I didn't. What was the result? You ran into Eoin and Fynballa, who you know you wouldn't have met otherwise. Because you met them and showed me to them, they came to me for redemption, and I gave them the entire kingdom of Liberdane, which has flourished ever since."

Nazir continued. "Yes, I do heal some people, but not others yet. These I leave unhealed because I see they can be faithful in reflecting me in spite of their physical or mental imperfections. Either way, I heal or don't heal according to what will most glorify me. Ultimately, though, I do heal every Envoy, even if it happens after death. Dilyn, do you trust me and my goodness and love, even in the painful waiting to be healed?"

Dilyn stared at the ground for several moments before sighing deeply and saying, "Yes, I do." Then he looked up. "But speaking of redemption, I've been doubting mine lately. I know I left you, but still that peace and joy you talked about isn't in me, and I was wondering if that's a sign that I lost my relationship with you. I thought I meant it when I accepted and believed you the first time."

"I know you did," Nazir said, his voice undeniably clear. "You've been my child since that day. Nothing has changed that. No guilt, no fault, no misunderstanding, no mindset, no lie, and no falling away. Once an Envoy, always an Envoy. As far as the peace and joy go, I do happily and freely give these to you, but you can't pursue other things in search of them. I am the only source of this, and depending on me completely is the only way you'll experience this. Now, your falling away is something we need to address and take care of."

Leona stepped forward. "Dilyn, what persuaded you to join the Self-Worthy in the first place?"

Dilyn nodded. "I thought they offered more comfort, security, and welcomeness than you did, Nazir. But I was wrong. They did at first, but once I discovered the cancer, all of that vanished, along with every friend I thought I had there. I know now that no one was as welcoming to me as you were and, surprisingly, still are."

Nazir replied, "There will be toils in the life of an Envoy, and there will—or at least should—be times when you lack comfort and safety. Marah ensures this, and not only that, but I will personally put you in hard places on occasion to test you and to turn heads to your resilience, thereby turning heads toward me. No matter what, I will always be with you to strengthen you, and I will never leave. All you have to do is keep stepping forward and not give up, knowing I won't give up on you."

"I understand," said Dilyn, who began to kneel. "I'm sorry for leaving you, Father. I now know you to be the only true source of peace and fulfillment. Please forgive me."

"I forgive you," Nazir smiled. "As long as you forgive those who wronged you, including Maewing and your brother."

Dilyn thought only for a second. "They're forgiven. They don't owe me a thing, not even an apology."

Nylid, who'd been quiet this whole time, lunged up from the ground at Dilyn's knees, screaming for attention. He got it. Nazir used a nearby leaf to whap and pin his flat figure to the ground by his head, and Dilyn flung his Dagger into the shadow's chest.

"No!" Nylid shrieked as he dissipated, never to be seen or heard again.

Dilyn took back his Dagger and stood again. "Thank you, Nazir. I've been fed up with him for a while now. I think I'm ready to join this team again and work through some things."

The others quietly celebrated his return, and each gave him an affirming hug or handshake.

Amory said, "I mean this. If you need anything, especially with the cancer, let us know without hesitating. I want to be better at leading you."

Dilyn grinned. "I appreciate that. Actually, I'd like some catching up on what you guys have been doing and learning while I was gone."

Nels wrapped his arm around his new trainee's waist, nodding at Nazir. "I believe I can help with that."

It was eleven o'clock at night. Leona lay in bed after a long day of teaching and grading, plus parent-teacher conferences. It had been over a week since Dilyn's return, and that spiritual high was long since over. Busyness and stress overpowered her joy to have him back, and she knew it. She laid there, replaying the whole day in her head, recalling all the moments when she said or did or thought things that might have helped or hurt Nazir. Certain scenes concerning the latter stuck out to her, and she couldn't get them out of her head. She tossed and turned for almost half an hour, trying to go to sleep. The thoughts never left her, and she was still as awake as when she'd first laid down, overcome by worry. Shaking her head, she finally got up, put on her robe over her pajamas, and took her Dagger.

At the Center, Nazir turned to Leona, his voice filled with loving concern but not surprise. "My child, what are you doing up at this hour?"

"I can ask you the same thing," Leona answered, rather amazed. "Don't you ever sleep?"

"No. As a being with infinite power, do you really think I need sleep?"

"No," said Leona, "but I thought I heard stories where you rested and then made that a tradition for us to follow."

"Yes, I did," Nazir replied, "but that was rest, not sleep. The difference obviously is that one is conscious while the other is not. The similarity is that both are intentional breaks from work to recharge either the body or the soul. I made that tradition because mortals need it constantly. And yes, when I was mortal for a time, I too rested because I needed it. If even *I* needed rest, don't you think you should make the effort to rest too?"

Leona chuckled to herself. "Wow, that's not even the reason I came, but you already told me what I needed to hear!"

"What's the real reason you came?" Nazir asked.

Leona sighed. "I've just had something nagging on my mind. I think I've been doing better with obeying your commands—please correct me if I'm wrong—but I feel more distant from you than before. I've been coming to you and trying to apply everything you tell me, but somehow I don't think I've been getting any closer to you relationally. What am I doing wrong?"

"Why are you trying so hard to obey me? Which, mind you, is a good thing."

Leona had to think for a second. "Because you told me to, and because I want to do my best to please you so that you'll be proud of me. I don't have a human dad with me, and I have no chance of making him proud of me. But you're the Dad who really matters, and if I can't please you then I've lost." Tears began to form in her eyes.

"Leona," Nazir said, "I am already pleased with you, and you can't change that any more than you can change your status as my beloved daughter. Similarly, it's not because of anything you did or can do but because I love you and because my blood is inside your veins. The distant feeling you have is because you don't love me as you did at first. You're not obeying out of love but out of obligation. Envoys who make a constant habit out of this wander far from me."

"But I do love you!" Leona replied.

"Yes, but there's something missing in that love. You revere me, but you don't adore me. Both are critical. You must both fear my authority and anger and cherish my mercy and faithfulness. Remind yourself of who I am: your eternal Father who gave my life to have you as my treasured child. I am your just and powerful King who does mighty and unimaginable things so that everyone will come to know me and know me more—relationally. I am always fighting for and forgiving you, even when you don't see or acknowledge it."

Leona lunged to hug the Vine. "Thank you, Dad! Thank you for always wanting to make things right in me and not giving up on me! I have never known a father like this, and I know I never will! Thank you for everything you do just to help us know you. I can't believe I'm your daughter!"

"You'd better believe it," Nazir laughed, "because you are mine forever. Go and get some sleep . . . *and* some rest."

Bernice and Twyla sat at an outdoor table at a street corner café to catch up over lunch since the last mission. It was a quiet Saturday afternoon, and there was hardly anyone walking or sitting nearby.

"How are you?" Twyla asked before biting into her cherry Danish. "How is your scar?"

"The scar's healing up fine," said Bernice, feeling for the gradually fading scab on her temple. "I'm doing OK. I've just been frustrated with all the waiting."

"Have you still made no progress on landing any occupation in human resources?" Twyla asked.

"Nope." Bernice shrugged flippantly while sipping on her mocha. "Honestly I don't know if I ever will at this point. Almost every door is shut tight, figuratively speaking, and any that have opened got slammed in my face as I tried to walk through. On top of all of that, I've been waiting for Amory to make any move that would take our relationship further, but he hasn't seemed very interested in *us* lately."

"By 'take your relationship further,' do you mean marriage?" asked Twyla.

"Yeah," Bernice grinned. "I think we've dated long enough to commit to something deeper, and I've wanted to spend my life with him since before you even met us. I think we're both ready for it, but I don't know if he agrees or if he's even thought about it."

"I am sure he has much on his mind at the moment, and from the glances he gives you, I am positive that you are one of those things on his mind."

"Thanks," Bernice said apathetically. "Honestly, I'm just ticked because life isn't going how I thought it'd turn out. Two things I'd dreamed of, an HR career and a lasting relationship with Amory, are in the doldrums, and I have no way of making any progress on them, no matter how much I try. I keep asking Nazir why this is, but he hasn't directly told me. I'm getting tired of him withholding his plans from me."

Twyla looked intently into Bernice's eyes. "Marah is attempting to distract you from Nazir and every good thing he has already done for you. You have been faithful to him, Bernice, and Marah is trying to undo that. Let me ask you: do you believe Nazir loves and cares for you?"

"Yes," Bernice answered. "I just wish he had my best interests in mind."

"He does," Twyla replied. "They simply might not be what we expect or initially desire. I was almost fifteen years old—or seven, in human terms—when my parents died. Before that happened, I wanted to be an athlete. I believed I had good coordination, and I loved any sport involving a target for which to aim. My talent and competitive nature allowed me to beat everyone I challenged. That was my dream, and even at such an early age, I was certain that would be my destiny, and I was excited. However, the loss of my parents and the oppression of King Ever utterly dashed that dream. I was brought to Ida's orphanage shortly afterward, and she can attest that I was ashamedly upset. I was so sure of my destiny, but I was wrong. Then, I was led to and redeemed by Nazir, and he rewrote my fate. This would not have happened if my dream had not been crushed first. Because of him, I am still doing the things I enjoy, such as throwing knives, but I am no longer doing them for sport or a wreath but for the greatest kingdom in all the worlds! I say all of that to tell you that Nazir has unimaginably amazing plans for every Envoy, but those plans might not be what we think."

"Wow," Bernice said. "I had no idea what your past was like, other than that you were orphaned."

"That's simply one trial Nazir faithfully led me through," Twyla replied. "Let me ask you something else: what makes you certain that human resources is the ideal job for you?"

Bernice replied immediately. "I'm good with people, authentic, thorough, and efficient, to name a few things."

Twyla nodded. "Those are all wonderful things to be, and Nazir will use those traits one way or another, especially since that is how he made you. Remember, he gave you those traits, and he will use them for his Kingdom if you let him. Just make sure you are prioritizing his Kingdom over your own. I have one more question: why do you think that Nazir calls people to one specific career or need?"

"Because that's what I've been taught most of my life, by Envoys and non-Envoys alike," Bernice said. "Even our gathering talks about that."

"In all honesty, they have made no sense to me when they talk of 'callings,'" replied Twyla. "I am not entirely sure that lines up with what Nazir actually does."

"He called several people to follow him, if you remember the stories we've been told and have even told ourselves," said Bernice.

"He called them to himself," Twyla interjected. "Our relationship with him is the priority in our lives. He will iron out the rest if we lean on him. To my knowledge, Nazir has said nothing about specific callings to certain things—only to individuals with a certain task right in front of them, and when that task was completed, he gave a new one. He commands us to do certain things and equips us to accomplish them, yes. But to me, waiting for a big moment where he tells us our *life* purpose seems like a distraction from what is actually our *daily* purpose—that is, to be faithful with what is right in front of us and to glorify him in simply being the Bernice Banner he made you to be, in the seemingly big and small ways."

"But what is the Bernice Banner I'm supposed to be?" Bernice asked.

"The friendly, authentic, thorough, efficient, flag-bearing daughter of the king," Twyla answered. "The amazing part is that you can be these things no matter what you do on a daily basis, whether you are working in human resources, as an actress, as a multiversal Envoy, or as a stay-at-home mother."

"Hmm." Bernice thought for a second. "Thank you. I'll have to work on that."

"I have had to work on the same things, in addition to other struggles," said Twyla, looking around. "Nothing could have prepared me for this world, this culture, and the advancements and hinderances within. Dwarves are difficult enough to live with, but western humans are an entirely different ordeal. While you—speaking generally, not specifically—are outwardly or even genuinely kind and considerate, each of you deep down is pursuing something for yourself. You are always seeking or making something new or current, and none of you ever stops to breathe. I still do not understand this."

"This is just our culture," replied Bernice. "None of what you mentioned, except for maybe the last part, is inherently wrong unless it's taken too far. The same is true of your Liberdanian culture. One example of taking things too far is when I first found Nazir. Amory, Leona, Ambrose, Dilyn, and I were exploring some woods near Amory's house when we discovered this underground cavern. Being the constant seekers we humans are, we decided to go inside and see what we could find. After a long time, we came across some Daggers. We had never seen anything that powerful before, and we were afraid to use them. Ambrose was the only one of us who wasn't scared, and he convinced us to go through a portal he'd unintentionally made. When we went through, we met Nazir, and he told us about himself and his love. That's when Amory and Leona accepted and believed, but the rest of us were hesitant. We still sought more, and that's where we went wrong. The Brandts and I decided to explore another world, where we were attacked by a giant spider that would've killed us all if not for Amory and Leona coming back for us. Dilyn and I accepted and believed in Nazir after that, but it took a misadventure to persuade us to slow down and think about what we really needed versus what we wanted."

"That is an amazing story," Twyla said. "Thank you for telling me. That does help me understand a little bit. I will have to think about it more, though."

"Oh, so will I!" laughed Bernice, getting up. "Are you ready to practice fighting again?"

"I am," answered Twyla. "To the park we go."

Bernice started to walk to her car. "Hey, next time I'll pay!"

"We shall see," Twyla grinned.

That same day, Amory sat inside a coffee shop in uptown Philadelphia, deep in thought. Forgetting about his rapidly cooling tea, he mentally replayed everything that went on in Uchu and what he could've done better.

Things were going along just fine until the Self-Worthy showed up, he thought. *Then, even with their intrusion, I still managed to kill the wizard. That was when everything started turning sour. They got to the people first and probably got a head start in converting them. I wonder how much ground they've gained versus how much ground Masato and his crew have gained? I have no way of knowing, nor do I have any control over it, though I wish I did. All I have control over is my own actions, and I know I could've done better when we were there. Was there anything I said to Maewing that was untrue, though? I mean, saying she should go to Pur was probably a bit much, but besides that, I think I was pretty on point, honestly. Perhaps I could've worded it all better. But how else would they have listened?*

Amory's expression hid no amount of frustration and bitterness. He figured no one who saw him would care. He was wrong.

"Excuse me, are you Amory Walters?"

Amory looked up to see a man in his late forties holding a latte, wearing a blue polo and khakis. "Um, yes, I am."

The man extended his hand. "Theodore Thompson. How are you, sir?"

"I'm good. How are you?" Amory said instantly, forgetting to stand up as he shook Theodore's hand.

Theodore grinned as he observed this. "I'm doing well, thank you. May I have a seat?" Amory nodded hesitantly. "I bet you're wondering how I know you."

"No, I know how," Amory replied. "I recognize you from the weekly Envoy gathering I'm a part of. I just never met you until today."

"Yes, it is quite a large gathering," Theodore said.

"So tell me a little more about yourself," said Amory, looking intently at his uninvited companion. "I recognize you, but I don't really know who you are."

"I've been an Envoy since I was seven," said Theodore. "Though I'm not the kind that travels throughout the multiverse. Nazir's called me to stay on Earth and spread his kingdom here. I'm a retail warehouse manager, and I have a wife and three sons. Nothing extraordinary, but it's what Nazir's called me to and it's what he's equipped me to be faithful to him in, and it's been very fulfilling."

"That sounds like a great life to me," Amory said. "So what brings you here? It's pretty obvious that you meant to find me and talk to me. What about?"

Theodore leaned closer with a thoughtful expression. "I've been keeping an eye on you and your team during our gatherings, ever since you came and gave a report on your mission in Hertengard. Everyone on your team has a certain rawness and authenticity, which is unfortunately rare to see in an Envoy, and I've been intrigued by that. That sort of thing draws attention, and I want you to know that people see it, even if it goes unacknowledged. I watched you from a distance, seeing how you lived and interacted with others—only at the gathering, so don't be creeped out. I must say, the Vine's work was quite evident in your life . . . until three months ago, when you came back from Uchu. I then noticed that you seemed a little out of sorts. I sensed some bitterness and regret in you. I wanted to come talk to you about it, but Nazir kept telling me it wasn't a good time yet. Then lo and behold, I happen upon you here. As I was ordering my drink, Nazir told me it was time to talk to you. All of that to say, how are you—really?"

Amory raised his eyebrow and nodded. "Hmm. I'm thankful I at least used to bear the Vine's image well. How obvious has my recent attitude been?"

"Let's just say you don't have a poker face," Theodore smiled.

"Well, I guess there's no escaping now," Amory began and proceeded to tell him in detail about the mission, the Self-Worthy's interference, his argument with Maewing, and the division that resulted. "I just wish the Self-Worthy would come to realize that they're living a lie and stop trying to convince other people to join in with them. It's hurting our effect on each universe we clash in, and fewer people are coming to Nazir than the amount that could be."

Theodore pondered this for a second then replied, "You don't know that. Until Nazir decides to get the Sword of *Chârâsh* back, the Self-Worthy can come and go as they please, and there's nothing you can do to stop them."

"How did you know the sword Maewing had was that Sword?" Amory interrupted.

"That weapon has a lot of multiversal power and influence," Theodore answered. "News of its theft spread far and wide. With that said, I know Nazir would never let it be taken unless he had a good reason. People have stolen it before, and Nazir has always gotten it back before any serious harm could be done, drastically expanding his kingdom in the process. I suspect something similar could come of this time. In the meantime, you need to trust his judgment and not let the Self-Worthy be your main enemy. Marah will use groups and agendas like them to hide behind them, trying to fool Envoys into thinking the group is the target. But it's a false target. If there's to be an objective at all, it must be to bring them to Nazir, the ultimate source of truth. As far as the arguing goes, you can't let your temper control your actions and words or you'll misrepresent Nazir. Additionally, stop trying to do what only the Vine can do: persuade people to change their hearts."

"Wait, I thought it was our job to persuade people to come to Nazir," Amory said.

"Many Envoys do believe this, but they were taught wrong. It is our job to simply tell them the truth in a loving way that sees where they're going and desires to show them a better way—the only way. You can't convince them to change their beliefs and lifestyles any more than you could convince me that tea is better than coffee—no offense."

Amory chuckled, looking down at his Earl Grey. "None taken."

Theodore sat back a tad after thinking for a few moments. "Do you have an Envoy trainer yet, Amory?"

Amory looked up in surprise. "No."

"Would you like it if I became your trainer?"

Amory thanked Nazir in his head. "I think I would, sir. I think it's apparent to both of us that I need one. Are you sure you want to, though? We barely know each other."

"We have to start somewhere," Theodore shrugged.

"All right, though I must warn you that I'm a slow learner."

"I've got three sons," Theodore smiled. "I think it'll be fine."

"Thank you," said Amory. "Oh, while we're at it, do you mind if I ask your advice about something else?"

"Not at all," Theodore answered. "I've got all afternoon."

6

NEW STEPS

It was a beautiful Sunday afternoon, uncharacteristically warm for January. Bernice and Amory had decided to go on a walk through Amory's wooded acreage after their Envoy gathering that morning. For a while, they said nothing as they soaked everything in and processed what they wanted to discuss. A gentle breeze brought them a pleasant pine scent, and the towering trees gave plenty of shade from what heat there was. The occasional columbine and mountain laurel added some life-giving color.

"It's not nearly as thorny as I remember," Bernice finally remarked as Amory led her by the hand among the trees.

"I've been gradually clearing out a path to the old cavern," Amory replied, holding a branch over them both. "Just in case I ever wanted to go back, which I have once."

"You mean you went back in that cavern?" Bernice exclaimed. "You're nuts! We never would've gotten out without the Daggers the first time!"

"No, certainly not," Amory laughed. "I still think there are traps down there. I just meant visiting it from the outside."

"Dude, if I ever get a call from you and you say you're stuck down there, you will never hear the end of it," Bernice snickered.

"Rightfully so!" said Amory.

"Is that where we're heading now?" Bernice asked.

"Yes, unless you'd rather not."

"No, I'm good with that. I'd kind of like to see it again. I haven't since we first found it."

There was a pause before Amory spoke again. "Man, that was a memory I won't forget: the time we first went exploring together with Leona and the Brandts. So much happened that day, and so much has changed since then."

"I know," Bernice replied. "The woods themselves have changed quite a bit from how I remember them. You cleared out a lot of the thorns, the trees and bushes have grown so much, and I'm seeing so much more fruit and flowers, even though there was a bunch last time. The forest just seems more alive."

"I agree, and I can only take credit for the thorns," grinned Amory. "Ever since I was little, I've been amazed at how this forest has flourished, and I wondered how it could do so without help from someone, even if it was someone behind the scenes of nature. I knew it was impossible for something as complex and beautiful as this to exist—and remain—without it being orchestrated by some form of intelligence. Intelligence with good taste, I might add. I always wondered what or who it was, but nothing from what I was told by others made any sense after a lot of thought. But then we came across those Daggers together and found Nazir. After several conversations following our first one, I knew he was the one behind it all, holding the universes together, and I don't foresee or want anyone else taking his place."

"Neither do I," replied Bernice. "It's not just the forest that's changed. You and I are not the same people we were before him, and our lives have dramatically changed course."

"I know!" said Amory. "Our friendship has grown a ton since then. For several years, you were so kind and welcoming to me when no one else was, and I often took wrongful advantage of that. Remember that time I had you and your friends over, and I made you all stay up all night and watch every season of that one show?"

Bernice chuckled. "I'm still trying to catch up on sleep from that, even if it was eight years ago. Remember when you convinced me to follow you and jump over an ash heap on your property from a fire you'd made the day before? I've still got that scar on my foot."

"Hey now, it wasn't my fault you didn't jump far enough, or that your boot had a hole in it," Amory said. "And let's not forget the time you told me it'd be a good idea to smuggle candy and jerky into the movie theater."

"How did I know they'd catch you, let alone be serious enough to make you leave it behind?" Bernice shrugged. "You still owe me for the candy I ended up buying for you! Just kidding."

They both trekked on amongst the trees in a silence frequently broken by laughter as they recalled more memories in their heads.

"Hey, I know I haven't asked this in a while, but any luck with an HR spot?" Amory asked.

Bernice frowned. "None. I must have applied for dozens of jobs and tweaked my résumé nearly to perfection. I felt confident in the few interviews I made it to. I don't know why I keep getting rejection after rejection."

"I completely understand that," said Amory. "I really wish you could get a job in this. I don't get why you haven't either. How's the receptionist gig right now?"

"It's still not the best, but at least my boss treats me fairly," Bernice answered. "Other than the rude callers, it's not a terrible job. It's just not the career I want, the one I think I'm more skilled in."

"I agree that you have all the qualities for human resources and perhaps not for reception. If the moment comes that Nazir allows you to get in, pursue it wholeheartedly and leave this job in the dust! But in the meantime, we both have to be faithful to him wherever we are, including but not limited to our occupations. Remember those Envoys of old we've read and heard about at our gathering? They were famous for one certain trade or task that they did, but who's to say they weren't faithful to Nazir before they caught people's attention? It makes sense to think that Nazir would give more responsibility to those who were faithful to him no matter what they were doing, while remaining unseen. They spent time with and grew from the Vine and were focused on what was right in front of them and how they could please Nazir with it. If it worked for them, it should work for you and me."

"That's what Twyla told me," Bernice replied. "Are you even sure this career is what Nazir wants me to do?"

"I have no way of knowing that," said Amory. "Do you?"

"Not for certain," Bernice sighed.

They walked on in awkward silence, beginning to ignore the beauty around them as well as the vines that were starting to gather. However, they managed to continue holding hands.

"So I heard you finally found a trainer," said Bernice after trying for several minutes to find something to talk about.

"I did! Or more like he found me. His name's Theodore, and he's apparently been an Envoy for quite a while."

"So you're saying he's super old?" Bernice grinned.

Amory laughed. "No, just in his forties. I don't know him that well, but I like him so far. I only met him a couple of weeks ago, and he's already shared so much practical wisdom with me, things I needed to hear."

"That's great!" replied Bernice. "I'm guessing that's what trainers are for, in a sense."

Amory continued. "We've talked about Uchu a lot in the few times we've chatted, and one thing he brought to my attention was that I need to apologize to you for what I did there. I've been bitter about it too long, and I'm sure it hurt you to wait this long for me to come around. I could've been much humbler and more reasonable after the wizard was killed, and I regret not noticing or caring when you were knocked out and when you were telling me about your flag. I got so sidetracked with Maewing, and it got you hurt and made many other people confused. I'm so sorry, and I'm working on being more attentive to my attitude and what's going on around me."

Bernice smiled. "You're forgiven, Amory. I should've forgiven you the day it happened, whether you apologized or not. But we're all good now, and thank you for turning back and trying to make right. Honestly, you weren't the only one at fault. Maewing and the Self-Worthy have caused a lot of problems for a lot of universes, and they too have confused thousands, if not millions of people."

"I guess it hit home for me once I realized they were following a half-truth," Amory said, "and that they'd deceived some of our friends into chasing it too. I'm very grateful Dilyn came back, but I wonder how long it'll take Ambrose and even those he hangs around with to be disillusioned?"

"How about a good whack on the head?" chuckled Bernice.

"Hey now, remember what it took for you to turn to Nazir," Amory replied.

"I know, I know. But you have to admit he's a lot more stubborn than I am."

"Which could be useful or detrimental," Amory said.

At last, the couple arrived where they had hoped: the overground top of the cavern they'd entered on their first multiversal adventure. Careful not to trip over the vines that blanketed the ground, they paused their conversation to reexplore this place that held so many nostalgic and frightful memories. They stared at the flat stone roof below them that was gradually deteriorating as it gave way to life. Under the thick trees shading them from the sun, they found the hole Dilyn had made in the roof when he'd stepped through it. The duo even knelt down and peered inside. It was just as dark and dreary as before. None of the fire basins within were lit, and it seemed colder and emptier than ever.

"Wow. This was a great idea!" Bernice exclaimed and soon got up. She didn't notice that Amory was still kneeling.

"Bernice," Amory said faintly.

Bernice turned around. Her eyebrows soon furrowed. "Are you OK?"

Amory gave a light laugh. "Yeah, I am. I just need to breathe for a second." After a few deep breaths, he continued, still on his knees. "Bernice, I want you to know that I love you, and I have for quite a while now, as hopefully you have seen. Initially your looks caught my eye, but later your firm character caught my heart. Ever since then, I've chosen to date you of all people every day, and you have been infinitely worth it! Today I do the same to a further extent."

Amory proceeded to pull out a small blue box, which revealed an ornate diamond ring. Bernice gasped deeply through her nose, which was covered by her hands.

"Bernice Banner, will you marry me?"

With tearful eyes and a gleaming smile, Bernice took Amory's hands, which still held the box, and guided him to his feet. Then she flung herself on him and embraced him tightly.

"What took you so long?" she cried. "Of course I will!" She felt the tensity in his body cease in a joyful chuckle. She looked back at him. "What, did you think I was going to say no?"

"With how I'd been acting lately, I wasn't sure how you'd react," Amory smiled. "I don't deserve your *yes*."

"Newsflash, I don't deserve yours either," Bernice said.

Now that the decision was settled, Bernice allowed Amory to place the ring on her finger, and she took the time to look at it more closely. It was a pure gold ring with an emerald-cut diamond, which was surrounded by vine-like threads of gold around the band.

"I love it!" Bernice beamed. "So, do you have a date in mind?"

"I was thinking maybe April, so three months from now," replied Amory. "That should give us enough time to plan, don't you think?"

"Not for most couples, but for us, I think so," Bernice grinned. "How does the fifteenth sound?"

"Perfect!" said Amory, leaning in for a kiss.

Suddenly, both of their phones dinged. Bernice's ding came from her pocket, but Amory's came from behind some nearby bushes. Perplexed, Bernice grinned as she watched Amory walk away and reveal from the shrubbery a tripod where his phone was sitting.

"It's just the two of us here. I had to capture the moment somehow," Amory shrugged.

Bernice laughed as they both checked what the message was. Twyla had texted on their group chat saying that she had just come from the Center. She said Nazir wanted the whole team there immediately.

"Won't they all be surprised!" Bernice exclaimed as they unsheathed their Daggers.

―――――

The fiancés were the last of their crew to arrive at the Center. Masato in his normal form was there as well, who was recently told he was to join this team. Everyone was welcoming him in when the couple arrived.

"So are you excited about all of this?" Edna asked.

"*Excited* is a strong term," Masato chuckled. "*Ready* is what I am. I've been training up my crew, and while I'm gone I've put them under the charge of Taka, who's grown the most out of them all. I'm prepared for the unexpected, but that's also what I'm dreading."

"I thought you were used to unexpected things," said Neisha.

"I like keeping things unexpected for other people, like with the pranks I used to pull. But those were things I could control—mostly—as opposed to when I'm the one who's kept on my paws, which is what I hate because it's out of my control. But I'm working on that."

"Everyone," Nazir called, and instantly he had everyone's attention. "I've called you here to embark on a new mission. But first, Amory and Bernice have some news they'd like to share." His voice echoed his delight.

Amory and Bernice beamed at each other. Bernice held up her hand with the ring as Amory proclaimed, "We're engaged!"

Everyone lit up with excitement for them, and the couple was bombarded with hugs and the word *finally*.

"Did all of you really see this coming?" Amory said, surprised.

"Well, we sure hoped so at this point!" laughed Leona.

"I thought you were already married when I first met you guys," exclaimed Dilyn. "After I found out you weren't, I knew it was just a matter of time until you were."

"Man, even I saw it coming!" Masato said. "Didn't you notice when you were in Uchu that she never left your side unless you left hers first?"

Amory paused to ponder this, and his heart sank a little when he realized it was true. "Well, shoot. That'll be something I can work on."

"Hey, it's not like we'll be able to be literally side by side at every moment," Bernice replied.

After all the congratulations were bestowed, everyone turned back to the Vine.

"What mission do you have for us now, Dad?" Bernice asked.

"I'm sending you to the olden world of Binosia, which is peopled by half-human creatures, such as centaurs and fauns," said Nazir. "Your objective is to find new recruits for your team. Your every mission following this one will require more people. You need only to tell these newcomers what I've done for them and testify about my love and power. Do not try to persuade them to join you; that's still my job."

"How many recruits are we talking about here?" asked Dilyn. "Do you mean a few hundred or thousand?"

"Do you not remember our prophecy?" Twyla said. "Our team will consist of only a score of people. Are we going to get the rest of them?"

"No, you will only need three more for now. I have prepared the hearts of these certain people for the specific work you'll be doing. Again, the weaker you are, the more strength I can display to those around you. But before you ask what the point of this is if we want my power shown more, these three individuals will prove essential to your team. Additionally, like Edna and the non-humans when they joined you, there will be those who are already Envoys for whom it's time to become Envoys throughout *Rôb Tĕbêl*. When you find them all, bring them to me."

"OK," Amory replied. "Who are they? Who are we looking for?"

"You'll know when you find them," Nazir answered.

"OK, but how will we know?" Edna asked. "Aren't you going to give us any clues or hints? At least the last times we were supposed to find someone, you said it'd be the first people we met, or they'd look exactly like us, or it'd be an evil wizard."

"I will guide you as you go," answered the Vine. "Since when have I followed a certain pattern in everything I do? My love is constant and unchanging, and my wrath will inevitably spill out on those outside my Kingdom. But there are several times when I will do one thing in one situation that calls for it, and then I'll do something different in a situation that calls for something else. Everything I do will always be in line with my character and Word, but if I did the same things for every similar situation, I would become predictable, and people would be able to control and manipulate me by foreseeing what I'd do next. It'd be quite unnerving to think that the King of the multiverse who controls everything could be controlled by others, don't you think?"

"Yes, it would be," Nels affirmed.

"Do you all understand this mission before you head out?" Nazir asked. Everyone nodded, some slower than others. "All right. Go through the middle portal to your left, and go expand your team!"

———

As the nine entered Binosia, they breathed in the full yet stale air. Immediately they could tell that this world had been around for a while. The solitary sun in this world was bright red, soon to die, and gave off little heat. The air around them was clean but thick and did not have that fresh feeling when one inhales it. Beyond that, Binosia seemed to still be teeming with life. There was flat stone everywhere, but grass and trees enveloped every slope and structure in sight. The plants here were quite similar to that of Earth and Hertengard, the only difference being that these here were much drier. They seemed to thrive regardless.

The Envoys now seemed to notice just how much stone there was. There were gray, brown, or red mountains left and right, and it took them a moment to realize that there was no dirt between the rocky ground and the grass above it. Soil did not exist here and did not seem to be a necessity for this vegetation. The Envoys also marveled at all the stone buildings they found. They saw villages in the valleys between mountains as well as towns in open fields protected by high walls. Then they turned around and beheld a city carved inside a light brown mountain range, consisting of multiple levels held by intricately carved columns and statues. From the outside looking in, it seemed to be bustling and thriving.

"I say we check in that city first," said Amory. "We'll cover more ground sooner that way."

Everyone agreed, and they began making the trek to the cliffside of the nearest mountain. The city grew larger and larger with every step they took, and they soon realized it had to be at least fifty miles long. They discovered that this task was going to require more time and effort than they thought.

After about two hours of walking, they stopped and sat down for dinner, which was mostly fruit and snacks. They wished very much that they had a blanket or pillows or something to provide cushion for the hard ground. Dilyn was the first to finish since he'd only had an apple.

"Are you feeling all right?" Leona asked him.

"Yeah, it's just that I don't have that much of an appetite anymore," Dilyn replied as he tossed the apple core aside. "I'll be fine. I wouldn't be going with you guys if I was unsure."

"OK," said Amory. "Let us know if we need to walk slower or help you out with anything."

"Will do," answered Dilyn.

Soon they had all eaten their fill and were on their way again. They were only a couple of miles away now.

Twyla approached the new fiancés. "Have you decided when you will be wed yet?"

"April fifteenth," Bernice said with a broad smile. "Assuming we can find a good venue for that date. And yes, you're all invited, including your crew, Masato."

"Well, I was going to give you a good piece of my mind if we weren't!" Nels laughed.

"Have you thought about where you want your honeymoon to be?" asked Edna.

"No, not really," Amory answered. "We haven't had the chance to talk about much of anything yet. I had just proposed when Nazir called us all."

"Ah, OK," said Leona. "That decision might prove difficult seeing that you have several places in several worlds to choose from."

"Oh, that's true. That never occurred to me," said Bernice. "Hertengard and Uchu were certainly pretty . . . and possibly this place too once we get to know it a little better. I don't know though, there's something special about Earth."

"Yeah," Amory said. "As fantastic as those places are, I think home would be the best place to spend that time."

"I agree," said Bernice.

The nine now approached the nearest city gate at the foot of one of the mountains. Much of the cliffside remained uncarved here on the first level, acting as a natural city wall. Four burly minotaurs in gray armor standing outside the portcullis caught the Envoys' gaze as they approached them. The guards tightly grasped their axes and stood poised to strike at a moment's notice.

"Desist!" one of them said. "Who are you, and what is your supposed business in Glatinth?"

Don't say you're Envoys, came a thought in Amory's head. He knew it was Nazir's voice, but he was confused. They were almost always open about that before, but why not now? Amory just decided to comply.

"We are travelers from other worlds," he answered. "We seek to visit and sightsee your truly magnificent city."

"Why come you armed?" the guard demanded.

"Merely for protection," Leona said truthfully. Amory deduced that she'd heard the same voice. His deduction was confirmed when he saw Bernice subtly roll up the flag on her spear.

"We've been to several worlds that were wilder and more hostile," Leona continued, "and this equipment's proved helpful."

"You will not need it upon entering these walls," the minotaur said. "We are a part of the Binosia Legions, which has long since been the most powerful and prominent military in this world. The Legions protect the city of Glatinth faithfully, and I assure you no harm will come to you on our watch unless you initiate it."

"That is very kind, and I fully take you at your word," Amory replied. "But if it pleases you, I request that we keep our armor and weapons as we explore this city. We mean no harm to anyone and only desire peace. I know peace will be kept since no one would attack us if we remained armed."

"I cannot trust you in this," the guard said unwaveringly. "You must prove to us that you have no ill intent and will not use your weapons at all."

Amory had to think for a moment or two. "Provide us with an escort to watch us. If we meant harm, it would have to happen in your plain sight. If we didn't, that means extra protection."

All four minotaurs looked at each other and discussed this. Some from the team looked frustrated at Amory, who just shrugged.

"I know we won't be able to search as freely," Armory whispered, "but we can't compromise on what Nazir clearly said."

"All right," the first guard declared. "You may enter the city of Glatinth fully armed. Your escort is waiting for you on the other side of the gate."

The Envoys thanked the guards as the gigantic portcullis was raised. Some creatures exited as the newcomers came in. Five more minotaur soldiers stood on the other side, one of them the escort.

"Greetings, travelers!" said the escort, who seemed much friendlier and more professional in his tone than the first guard. "My name is Zeno, and I will be watching over you during your stay in Glatinth. Thank you for your cooperation."

"Of course," Amory replied. "Thank you for your protection."

"Now, where would you like to begin?" Zeno asked. "Are you hungry, or would you like to have your currency exchanged?"

"Actually, an exchange would be helpful," Edna said. "Could you take us to the nearest and most honest place?"

"I can," answered Zeno. "It is strategically placed nearby for trekkers such as yourselves. Follow me."

As they started walking, Bernice whispered to Amory, "This guy seems nice. Do you think he's one of the three?"

"I don't know," Amory said. "Time will tell."

Now the Envoys began to take in all the sights and action surrounding them. There were holes and doors and windows carved into the mountain inside, and each business and home they saw had either a unique shape, engraving, or both, to keep it recognizable. Various centaurs, minotaurs, and fauns strolled in and out of these places with seemingly much liberty. Many of them were customers or friends, but others carried goods with methods according to their species. The minotaurs carried everything over their shoulders, the fauns held things with their hands in front of them, and the centaurs carried things in their arms and on their horse backs.

As the group went deeper into the mountain, torches and lamps attached to the structures lit the streets. Huge, detailed statues of various creatures held the second level above them. Every carving and every form of craftsmanship—even down to Zeno's armor and axe—were intricately and carefully made.

"This place is massive!" Masato exclaimed. "None of the islands back home ever compared to this, and I've been to several!"

"Glatinth does boast Binosia's size, fortitude, and beauty well," Zeno said. "Frankly, one drawback is the sheer population here. It is difficult to discern the rebels from the loyalists."

"What do you mean by that?" asked Leona.

"All of Binosia, or most of it, is ruled by Emperor Dion, the purest of all creatures and the commander in chief of the Binosia Legions. Dion's dynasty has governed here for the past millennium, and they have ushered in great peace. They have been attempting to rule the entire universe here and are quite close to it, thus engulfing this whole realm in its peace. But I am straying from your question. There are rebels who appear every once in a while to try and persuade people to not be 'oppressed' by the emperor. The greatest of these uprisings was led by a winged ponytaur called Maewing, who herself was part of the Binosia Legions. But she is long since gone."

The Envoys glanced at each other with either concern or intrigue as Zeno continued.

"Some of her followers remain here and there, but they are not the biggest concern for us at present. Mostly it is cultists, namely the Envoys of the Vine, who claim freedom even from Emperor Dion. Their lies have penetrated deeply into several hearts, and it has been extremely taxing and lengthy in time to silence them. But I am worrying you too much. I assure you, you are completely safe. Anything less than loyalty to his highness is strictly illegal and therefore uncommon."

Now the Envoys knew why Nazir told them to keep their identities hidden and that Zeno was not one of the three they were looking for. They knew they had to somehow lose him, but they had to figure out a way to do it civilly and legally.

They soon approached the currency exchange center, a wide building made to accommodate multiple species and even worlds. It sat in between a bar and an open grill serving meat and produce on sticks and in bowls. They went inside the exchange center and were immediately overwhelmed by all the stations, crowds, and overhead signs. If not for Zeno who pointed out how much of a hassle it was for the nation to come under one currency, which they were still working on, they surely would've gotten lost. He led them to a booth that shockingly took US dollars, as well as pesos, yen, and several other forms of Earth money. They then found a place where Masato could exchange his Uchu money, which looked to be like pearls. Once everything was finished, they sifted their way back outside.

"Thank you for guiding us through, Zeno," Amory said.

"It is my duty and pleasure. Where would you like to go now?"

"I'm not sure," said Amory as he began to saunter along down the street, trying to think of their next move. Everyone else followed him. They found themselves right in front of the bar, when suddenly a fat, more elderly centaur stumbled out, obviously drunk, almost trampling Neisha and Nels on his way out the door. Both the dwarves let out a swear word or two as the centaur struggled to step around them. They managed to get out of the way, and the centaur took a minute to get his bearings, landing and keeping his gaze on Zeno. The centaur simply groaned and hobbled away, yelling and murmuring.

"Are you all right?" asked Twyla as she and the others helped the siblings up.

"Who the heck was that?" Neisha shouted.

"That would be Chadmight, the city's notorious drunkard," Zeno said with frustration. "He has been that way for a few centuries. He has earned a reputation of being a troublemaker and disturber, but when he is sober, he is mostly harmless. When he does get into the occasional skirmish, he fights incredibly hard and does not give up easily, if at all. We have been trying to keep him under control and keep his disturbances to a minimum. I apologize for letting this happen."

"It's quite all right," said Nels, brushing himself off.

Zeno briefly went to some nearby soldiers to discuss being more watchful of Chadmight. As he did, Amory stared at the centaur as he drifted further away, trying to discern his thoughts. The others took notice of this.

"What are you thinking?" Bernice asked quietly.

"I don't know," Amory said, not taking his gaze away. "But I've got a funny feeling about that guy."

"So do I," said Edna. The others concurred.

"He seems like he needs some hope, and we've got that," Leona added. "No one gets that drunk on accident. He's trying to numb or forget something."

"Let's follow him and learn more about him," Dilyn suggested. "Maybe he's one of the people we're looking for. Even if not, it might be good to chat with him. Once he gets to his house tonight, or wherever he lives, and once he sobers up, maybe we can talk with him then."

"Yes, but we must lose our guard," Twyla said. "If we constantly follow him, Zeno will become suspicious, and he certainly cannot be there when we attempt to talk to Chadmight."

Amory looked back at Zeno, who had returned from talking with the troops. "We've decided to just stroll around and look at everything. No particular destination right now, just browsing," Amory said.

"Lead on!" Zeno said cheerfully. "If you have any ideas or would like any recommendations, please simply say the word."

The group started walking further into the mountain, trying to pick back up on Chadmight's trail. They heard his murmurs a ways off and finally caught sight of him. They kept a distance from him to avoid suspicion.

Amory leaned over to his fiancée. "If we get into a crowd, split up and keep following Chadmight from a different route. Maybe we can lose Zeno that way and avoid getting caught afterwards. Make the rendezvous point wherever Chadmight stops. Help me tell the others."

They eventually spread the word through whispers to the whole team. The group soon came to a busy marketplace where the street was blocked by customers. Chadmight roared and shoved his way through, much to the Envoys' delight.

"I wonder what kinds of food are sold here?" Neisha said nonchalantly.

"Oh, this certain market boasts a wide variety of products . . ." Zeno began to explain as they entered the throng. At that point, the Envoys subtly stole away and found different paths amongst the people. Some of them went behind some of the vendor stands and others found alleys in between the stands to escape through. Even though they weren't running, Zeno suddenly realized he wasn't keeping up.

"Slow down!" Zeno called in a suddenly urgent tone. "Come back!"

It was too late. He had soon lost sight of everyone under his watch. He cursed under his breath and went to find more troops.

Many of the Envoys used routes that made them lose sight of Chadmight, but thankfully they each figured out how to find him again. They each stayed separate from each other—other than times when some of their routes inevitably joined together, then they would separate again when they could. They followed the brown-skinned and gray-haired drunkard to a wide staircase that led to the next floor up. After ascending to the second floor, Chadmight stumbled further inside the mountain until they got to the city's border, which was a long, uncarved cave wall. The Envoys realized he had led them to a small, abandoned stable next to the cave wall. The area surrounding it seemed to be long since unattended. The torches sat unlit, and the road was covered with trash and manure.

The Envoys tiptoed to the stable's entrance where Chadmight had sauntered. No animal had lived here for years, it seemed, but the place still smelled like a stable, likely due to its sole occupant. They saw that Chadmight had lain down and immediately fallen asleep on the old and only hay bed in the building.

"He should be mostly sober when he wakes up," Nels said.

"We can talk to him then," said Amory. "In the meantime, let's wait and stay out of sight, but still nearby. The sun's setting. The night cover should help."

Everyone agreed and split up individually or in pairs to different hiding places in the stable's general vicinity, whether behind corners or in other nearby abandoned buildings. Amory gradually found and kept track of each one of them. The sun had long since set and a cool blue moon arose, although the Envoys wouldn't see it until later when it could be seen from the front of the city. Time went on, and Chadmight was still dozing soundly, and one by one his visitors did the same. Only Amory and Masato, who was accustomed to nighttime but had fought to stay awake during the day, remained awake and separately kept an eye on their friends and the streets nearby. It must have been two in the morning—assuming Binosia had the same system for time as Earth—when they finally heard stirring in the stable. Amory and Masato tiptoed to the entrance and saw Chadmight sitting up on the hay, sniffing and groaning, likely from a new headache.

"It's time," Amory whispered to Masato as they backed away. "Let's get the team up."

In a few minutes everyone was awake, some more so than others. Twyla and Leona were alert within seconds, but everyone else was still drowsy. They assembled and entered the shed. It was not a quiet entrance, as several of them coughed and gagged from the smell. Chadmight slowly looked up and, upon seeing his armored visitors, struggled to stand.

"Who are you? What have you come here for?" he groaned.

The Envoys approached slowly with their hands empty and raised.

"We mean no harm to you," Amory said, stifling a yawn.

Chadmight jumped at them, kicking and punching. Some of the Envoys drew their blades and arrows.

"We don't intend to hurt you, but we will fight if you attack us first," Nels said firmly, now less drowsy. "Remember, you're unarmed."

The centaur stood still for a minute, then sat back down on his bed of hay as the Envoys put back their weapons. "Well, I can see you're not a part of the Legions, so I suppose I wouldn't have any quarrel with you," he said, having forgotten that he'd already had a run-in with them. "What do you want?"

"We can see you're hurting and that you're in need of hope," Bernice said. "We've come to help with that."

Chadmight grinned. "I am fully aware of my condition and how gluttonous I am. It's obvious, and I know it. You're not the first group of idealists and nonprofit *helpers* to come to me in an attempt to fix me. Every one of them eventually gave up, and I accepted that I am a lost cause, and you soon will too. However, you're the first ones to come armed with no intent of arresting me. So again, who are you?"

Amory looked at the others, who nodded. He then knelt beside the centaur as the others followed suit. "We're Envoys of the Vine Nazir, and we've come to tell you more about him."

Chadmight snickered. "You know, now I do recognize you as Envoys. You have the badges and the armor for it, and you can't shut up about that Vine to save your lives. Perhaps the Legions were right to illegalize you, although it's impossible to take all of you away."

"So you've met Envoys before?" Neisha asked patiently, using her arm to bar Leona from losing her temper. "What was your experience with them, and what makes you say that?"

"I haven't met any in person, just from a distance," replied Chadmight. "With the exception of one, they've all preached to the masses about either the Vine's love and tolerance or his intolerance and anger toward our mistakes. There've been two very different opposing forces claiming to represent one being, and it just didn't add up. Additionally, I know how some of them lived, and I've been in some of the same places where they've secretly been. Their behavior doesn't match their message."

"Hmm," Leona said. "There have been a lot of Envoys like that in our world too. I know this changes nothing, but I'm sorry that's been your experience."

"You said there was one exception," Dilyn said. "What was he or she like?"

"His name was Panos," Chadmight answered. "He said that there was a balance between the Vine's love and his wrath. He taught that the Vine sees and punishes the evil in us but also loves us enough to make us not evil. His words made the most sense . . . but still not completely. Also, he lived more consistently with his words. He wore his badge and armor everywhere, and if he ever made a mistake, he would acknowledge it instead of hiding it."

"It sounds like this Panos told more of the truth," Amory said. "What he taught is what we wanted to tell you. We also want to tell you that each of us was without hope before we met him. We have each done things that angered Nazir, and we all equally deserve his punishment. He hates all the selfish and hurtful things we do—even to ourselves—and we all deserve to spend eternity in torment after we die, which is all of our fates."

"But Nazir didn't want that to be our fate," Masato added, "even though it was just, as he is just. His original plan and desire, which we messed up, was that we would spend eternity with him, and no matter what we did, he was going to stick to that plan. By giving up his own life and coming back from the dead, he enabled those who turn back to him to be free of the debt of death we owe and to live with him after death and even now in a relationship with him. Throughout that relationship, he shapes us to be like him in our attitudes and actions."

The centaur pondered this for a while. "Did he really do that? How would I be able to know?"

"Each of us can attest to how much better we act and think and feel after coming to him," said Edna. "We can take you to see him yourself, and he'll tell you."

Chadmight nodded. "What about the armor and weapons? How does that play into all of this?"

"Nazir gives us these things to enable us to go throughout our own worlds and others and tell people about him," Nels said. "They also equip us to fight battles to establish peace and freedom for those who otherwise won't see him."

"I see," Chadmight said. "And you came all this way to find me?"

"Nazir sent us to find three people from your world to bring to him, to add to our team," Dilyn answered. "Yes, in a way he did lead us to you first. He loves you and wants the very best for you, which is proven to be himself. I can personally vouch for that."

The centaur got up slowly. "All right, I'll accompany you until you return to him. At any rate, I'd like to see how you act and how you find the other two people."

The Envoys smiled as they hugged him, while holding their breath. Chadmight couldn't remember the last time he was hugged.

Twyla said, "I am sure Nazir cannot wait to see you!"

"I hope so," said Chadmight. "Actually, should I tidy myself up before we see him, and should I stop eating and drinking excessively? That's going to be a hard habit to break, and I'm not sure I'm willing to wait that long."

"Neither is he," Bernice said. "Just come as you are right now. He won't mind as long as you're turning from it to him. After he makes you an Envoy, he'll put it on your heart to stop doing hurtful things, and he'll equip you to stop. It's so much more worth it after meeting him than before."

"All right," the centaur replied. "Where to now? Who's the second person to find?"

"I'm not sure, but I have an idea," Amory said, looking to the others. "Do you know where Panos is now?"

The other eight nodded, affirming Amory's notion.

Chadmight frowned. "Panos is in prison."

7

UNLIKELY RECRUITS

W hat do you mean Panos is in prison?" Dilyn asked, dejected along with the others.

"He was arrested about a month ago after continuing to talk about the Vine even after it became illegal," Chadmight answered. "He was stealthier about it, but they eventually caught him. They will catch you too if they recognize your badges."

The whole team was disheartened, but they all still felt a peace about finding him. Amory looked intently at the centaur. "Do you know where the prison is?"

"You're not seriously considering going there, are you?" Chadmight asked.

"Hey, we've broken people out of prison before!" exclaimed Neisha.

"But you don't understand," replied Chadmight. "The Binosia Legions are the best military development I've ever heard of, and they take guarding their prisoners seriously. If even one person escapes them, everyone working and serving at that prison is immediately killed and replaced. That alone is enough motivation for the guards to always remain alert. I haven't heard of a single breakout in Glatinth in over a century."

"He's got us there," Edna said.

Amory thought for a moment. "All I know is that I'm pretty sure Nazir wants us to find Panos. I have no reason to doubt this. If he wants us to do this, he'll make it happen."

"But last time we broke people out, it was because people from the outside helped us and even distracted the guards," Edna said.

"Remember what Nazir told us before we left?" Amory replied. "He doesn't always do things the same way. He'll make it happen the way he wants to."

"Are you positive that the Vine wants this?" asked Chadmight. "All of this risk over a feeling?"

"You'll soon learn it's more than a feeling," Amory said. "It's a voice."

"Agreed," said Leona, and the others eventually did too.

"Do you feel up to getting us there?" Bernice asked the centaur.

"I gave my word that I'd accompany you for the rest of your stay in this world," Chadmight said. "If you don't know the way, then I suppose I'll be your guide too. Besides, what have I got to lose if we all get caught? Follow me."

"Also, is there a way you could get us there by backroads or alleys?" Twyla asked. "We had to escape the watch of an escort from the Legions to get to you, and I fear he might have acquired help in attempting to recover us."

Chadmight grinned. "I thought as much, which is why I intended to take hidden routes anyway. Beware of bandits, though. No universe is exempt from them."

At that, the group of now ten started off into the night. The centaur led them down several quiet alleys that lacked torches, and they all strained to see two feet in front of them. They often bumped into or almost tripped over each other and sometimes could not avoid the occasional clashing of armor. If this happened, they'd stop and check their surroundings to ensure nobody heard them, and then they would continue. They journeyed up to the fourth and top floor of the city and proceeded to sneak further inside the peaks. All the while, no thieves ever showed themselves to them. If there were any, they likely strayed from the trekkers partly because of the Envoys' weapons and partly because of the size of their guide.

"I suppose you're wondering how I ended up in this state," Chadmight said abruptly after a while of silence.

"We were, but we weren't going to press the question on you," Bernice answered.

"You might as well know anyway," The centaur began. "Ever since I was a foal-lad, I've longed to join the Binosia Legions. It gave me such a deep sense of purpose to think that I could contribute to the welfare and protection of the country and the emperor. I would train myself vigorously every day as I grew up, and I wanted there to be little to no doubt that I would succeed and be sworn in. When I was still a child, there came along an elite warrior from the Legions' ranks who started appealing to the masses. I will never forget the words she spoke. She reminded her listeners that we are each individuals with specific purposes, and nothing should confine us or keep us from reaching our own potential. This inspired me deeply, as no one had ever told me that before, and it made so much sense. So I trained harder than ever, so certain this was my potential and destiny."

Chadmight continued. "I applied to the Legions as soon as I was of eligible age, and to my surprise and dismay, I was rejected. I was not distraught for long, and later I applied again. And again. And again. I must have been rejected a dozen times before I was finally told I was never going to get in because I 'wasn't enough.' That stung me to the core, and I couldn't bear the pain of the disillusionment. That's when I tried to use alcohol and the pleasure of food to lessen the pain. It only worked temporarily, so I kept trying more and more until I got to the point in the habits where I'd almost lost interest in the reason I was in this state. That is the point where I was when you found me."

"Do you happen to know the name of that warrior and speaker?" Amory prodded.

"I won't forget it; it was Maewing," Chadmight grinned. "Her words are potent and convincing. I will give her that."

"Indeed," Bernice said, glancing sharply at Amory. "Although not all of her teachings are true, what you said that she taught matches what Nazir says too. She just took it too far."

"The half-lies I believed were powerful," said Chadmight. "Falling for them can cause so many changes in one life."

"Those days of misery, though, are about to be over," Dilyn said. "You won't have to live that way anymore."

"Part of that is exciting and relieving," Chadmight replied, "and the other part is still difficult. I want to be free of this, but I'm also getting quite hungry and quaky. The withdrawal is setting in again."

"Don't worry, I'm sure we'll be able to eat soon," Nels said.

"It might be later than you think," said Chadmight. "We're here."

The blue moon shone coolly through the city now, as it was a couple of hours until daybreak. They saw that the outside of this prison was also an ominous, uncarved wall, with only two windows in the iron doors in the middle. Only a few strategically placed lanterns exposed it to light. The ten stole away in a nearby alley and beheld with dismay the dozens of soldiers of varying species patrolling the entrance.

"Have you had any bright ideas on our way here?" Chadmight asked.

"Not any good ones," Amory sighed. "Anyone else?"

"I have a few," said Masato who was more experienced in the arena of stealth.

"Wait, look there!" Twyla interrupted.

The Envoys saw that every guard's attention was stolen by something out of the Envoys' sight. The guards marched in that direction, away from the Envoys and the prison entrance, within seconds.

"I smell a chance to get in," Dilyn said.

"Let's take it because I don't know how long we have," Amory said.

They all snuck to and fro throughout the buildings and alleys toward the cave wall. Along the way, they found that it was Zeno who'd caught the guards' attention and had called them over to give them an order. He shouted it all, so the Envoys heard every word.

"There are nine fully armed individuals roaming this city who have escaped my watch. I have tarried all night in vain to find them, so now every soldier in Glatinth will receive the order to arrest them immediately upon seeing any of them. They will be hard to miss as they are all wearing armor of varying colors, and they are not creatures from this universe. If they do not look like one of us, it is them."

"Extra caution must be made now," Twyla whispered as they neared the wall. Once there, they tiptoed along its edge until they got to the steel doors. Thankfully Zeno was still talking, elaborating on what each Envoy looked like.

"His memory serves him well, dang it," Dilyn muttered.

"Wait here," Masato said to the rest of the team. He slowly morphed into a faun that looked like one of the troops listening to Zeno. With his back turned to the door, after glancing to see if someone was on the other side, he said to the gatekeeper, "You might want to hear what he is saying out there. It sounds urgent. I will keep watch until you get back."

The gatekeeper took the bait. He opened the door, and Masato grabbed it. Keeping his head low to hide his eye mask, he nodded at the keeper as he left his post. Masato beckoned for his friends to enter.

"Hurry!" Chadmight said. "It likely won't be long before they realize what just happened."

There were two lanterns on each side of the now shut door and a few in the first room they stood in, which seemed to be an empty hexagonal meeting room for the guards, but beyond that there was no source of light to be found inside. It seemed all prisoners here sat in complete darkness. If they were ever fed, they would not know what they were eating.

"This is awful," Neisha said looking into the darkness.

"Do you know where Panos would be kept?" Amory asked the centaur.

"I don't have the slightest idea," Chadmight answered. "I've heard though that each category of criminals is kept in the same area. All thieves are kept together, and all murderers are together, and so on. I suppose we can look around until we find where the Envoys are kept."

They started roaming into the dark, Chadmight carrying one of the lanterns as he was by far the tallest in the group. Careful to be quiet so as not to awaken the prisoners, they sauntered down a long, downward-sloping hallway, with iron doors on either side. Above these entrances hung wooden signs with glyphs known only to the centaur, which stated what kind of convicts were kept in the rooms they hung over. They continued to journey deeper into the mountain where it became undeniably cold.

"Wait a minute," Edna said suddenly. "If there's a whole room devoted to keeping Envoys, shouldn't we free them all?"

"That's a good point," Dilyn replied. "As far as I understand, they're here on unjust grounds. They've done nothing wrong; they've been put here because they're telling the truth."

"I never thought of that," said Amory. "We can see when we get there."

Several minutes passed until Chadmight finally stopped in front of them, reading a sign above a room on their right.

"This is it," he said. "This is interesting. This is the second deepest room in the whole prison, second only to those sentenced to death. I suppose they seriously don't want these people to have any hope of escape."

The Envoys entered the room surprised that the door was unlocked. This room held about twenty large cells, all packed with creatures slumbering in unavoidable clusters. The visitors were appalled by the sight. Keeping the door open behind them, they snuck into the middle of the room.

"OK, what are we looking for?" Amory asked. "What does Panos look like?"

"He's a minotaur with black fur," Chadmight said. "He's hard to mistake. He's rather small and scrawny for his kind."

They all split up among each of the cells, straining to see into them with the light coming from Chadmight's lantern. They could barely make out silhouettes of the piles of creatures.

Nels, who was searching with Masato, whispered, "We should have brought more lights."

Suddenly, they heard the centaur's booming voice, loud enough to awaken anyone. "Panos!"

Some of the prisoners jumped as the others stirred. The visitors themselves were quite startled as they looked back at Chadmight, who was staring into one of the middle cages.

"Dude!" Edna shushed. "We don't need the whole prison to hear us!"

Chadmight shrugged in apology, then turned back to the cell. The convicts within arose one by one, emerging from among them a minotaur with wide, full-grown horns, only an inch or two taller than Dilyn—the tallest human present.

"Chadmight?" the minotaur said in a high, rumbly voice. Murmurs were heard that the drunkard was here. "What are you doing here? Where are the guards?"

"Soon to return from their meeting, which is why we must hurry," replied Chadmight as his Envoy friends came closer. "Panos, I've come with these Envoys from other worlds who've convinced me to join them on their mission and to come to the Vine."

"Yes!" Panos shouted aloud, concerning the visitors further. "I have been hoping this would happen! That is wonderful, my friend! Now, what is this mission?"

Amory spoke up. "Nazir sent us to find three people from Binosia to add to our team for future missions. He led us to Chadmight first, and next he's led us to you."

Panos was silent for a second, pondering it all. "The Vine's timing is unmistakable. You have just awakened me from a dream where Nazir told me directly that he had a new assignment for me and that I needed to trust him with what follows."

"I can concur," chuckled a faun in the same cell. "Every prisoner in this room knows you talk in your sleep."

"It is plain to me that Nazir wants me to go," Panos said. "But what of the others here?"

"As far as we're able, I think we could free you all," Nels answered. "It'd be tough to get past the guards outside, though."

"No, we will stay," came a voice from a distant cell. "The Vine's will is for Panos to be free, but his will for now is for the rest of us to stay here."

"But how could that be?" said Neisha. "Don't you all want to be free?"

"Yes, very much," said another prisoner. "But there's also a certain inexplicable fellowship and glory in this suffering, as we have discovered. Nazir will be made known in this somehow, and we're willing and honored to be used to make that happen even if we don't understand."

"But I wish to partake in that fellowship and joy too," Panos replied. "I have grown much in the Vine because of this."

"But it is clear that he doesn't want you here anymore," said another Envoy's voice. "You will grow no further here in disobedience to what he has clearly commanded you. This is likely your only chance. Trust Nazir and take it!"

Panos sighed deeply, struggling to come to a conclusion. "All right, I will join you if this is what Nazir wants."

"Wonderful!" Leona exclaimed.

Twyla took one of her smallest knives, shorter than one's finger, and started to pick the lock. As she worked, Dilyn and Masato peered out the door to see if any soldiers had returned.

"I hear nothing," Dilyn whispered. "Either they're asleep or still outside."

At last, Twyla got the door open. It creaked terribly as Panos tiptoed out, sighing again. With great reluctance, Edna and Twyla shut and locked the cell door again, having freed only one Envoy.

"Let's go," Amory whispered. "It was a miracle that we even got in here, so let's hope for another miracle to get us out."

As they left the room, they heard the Envoy prisoners say, "May Nazir generously equip you for the work he has for you, and may his love and truth be obvious in you all!"

Panos turned around and replied, "May the Vine's peace and joy and strength overflow from within you, brothers and sisters!" At that, the eleven exited the room and begrudgingly locked the door behind them.

"It hurt to do that," Edna said. "It felt like I just caged my own family in there after giving them a tiny hope of escape."

"I assure you they had no intent of leaving unless Nazir himself or one of the troops told them to leave," Panos replied. "They will be all right. Their resilience and endurance has inspired me greatly. Now, we must hasten to find my equipment, then we can go!"

The Envoys trotted stealthily back up the long hallway, peering to and fro for any unseen guards. They found none. They soon beheld the light from the entry room and also heard a noise from within. The Envoys stopped for a moment to figure out what the noise was. It didn't take them long to make it out as snoring.

"Remarkable!" Chadmight breathed. "I didn't know it was possible for the Legions to sleep!"

"Usually it does not seem so," Panos said.

The minotaur quietly led his liberators into the main room, finding six returned guards out cold in their respective corners. Panos snuck to one of the side doors and opened it ever so gently. The Envoys found inside a long room of shelves and hooks filled with plunder.

"The Envoy armor will be at the very end," Panos whispered. "The Legions know an Envoy cannot live life without our armor and Daggers, so they keep them well secured."

They crept along the walls of this thin chamber until they came to the back wall. They then beheld dozens of sets of armor with unique colors and patterns, accompanied by chests filled to the brim with Daggers, badges, and innovative weapons. Chadmight, who was at the back of the line, gazed in wonder at it all.

"You're sure I will get armor like this as an Envoy?" the centaur gasped.

"Well, if you're going to be with us, you're guaranteed to need it," Edna grinned.

"There is no use coveting it, my friend," Panos said candidly. "It is a gift Nazir freely gives and freely takes back. Although your Dagger and badge will be yours to keep."

Panos finally found his own equipment—rich, brown armor with golden borders and decorations. His weapon was a wide, gold-and-chrome fork, similar to a trident. He hastily and silently put it all on.

"I am ready," he said, sliding his Dagger into his newly strapped sheath.

"All right. Let's hope those guards are still asleep," Amory replied. "I should also warn you that the Legions have a warrant to arrest us too. They don't know we're Envoys, but they let us inside the city with our armor and an escort, whom we evaded."

"I had figured you wouldn't be in good standing with the Legions," Panos smiled. "That does not sway me one bit, but thank you for letting me know."

They crept out of the treasure room with difficulty because it was too thin for Chadmight to turn around, and it is almost impossible for centaurs to walk backwards. The soldiers were still snoring when they finally got out. They tiptoed to the main entrance, peeking through the door windows to see how many guards stood outside. There were still dozens out there, but their attention was now fixed on something else. Some citizens in nearby houses were yelling at Zeno through their windows for waking them up so early in the dawn with his orders. He and some of the troops went to appease them, and it seemed as though both sides were starting to use force. The guards who weren't there watched this intently, ready to reinforce Zeno if need be.

"This is as good of a chance as any," Leona whispered.

"Be more careful and quieter than you've ever been before," Amory breathed.

They silently opened one of the main doors, surprised that it didn't creak. They only had it open by a couple of feet, as four fauns stood right in front of it, ready to run to Zeno's aid at a moment's notice. Twyla was the first to exit, holding her breath as she slipped behind the guards to one of the neighboring buildings. Then came Panos, Dilyn, Masato, and Neisha. As Bernice came next, the end of her spear accidently clanged against one of the soldiers' sheaths. The guard instantly looked down at it. Bernice just as quickly pulled her spear close and froze, trying not to breathe on the curious guard a foot in front of her. The Envoys still inside the prison hurriedly shut themselves back in.

The faun looked up at the soldier beside him. "Back away," he said. "Your sheath keeps touching mine."

The four fauns shuffled further away from each other and from the door. Bernice slowly let out the breath she held and proceeded to join the other escapees. Edna opened the door again and snuck out, followed by Leona and Nels. Now only Chadmight and Amory remained. Amory saw that the centaur was sweating and shaking profusely.

"What's wrong?" Amory whispered.

"I've never been a quiet walker," Chadmight answered. "My withdrawal is getting worse. They're going to catch us! There's barely enough room for me to get through without touching the guards!"

"Hey, listen to me," Amory said soothingly. "We're going to get out of here. Nazir will get you out just the same as he did everyone else. Now go; it's your turn."

Chadmight fearfully opened the door, only to realize that the fauns weren't there anymore. Zeno had apparently needed them, as the citizens were only getting angrier. Chadmight gave a huge sigh of relief as he sidestepped his way to the others, unnoticed. Amory, ensuring he was the last of the group, stepped outside and quietly closed the door behind him. Thanking Nazir in his head, he sauntered along the prison wall until he found the others.

Before anyone could say anything, he walked right past them and said, "Run now, talk later. Let's put some distance between us and the prison before we plan any further."

Everyone followed him as they went back through the alleys, all the way down to the third floor of the city. They stopped at an empty, quiet street, making sure no one else was around.

"Well, that was certainly an adventure!" Nels said, still in a whisper.

"Yeah, I vote that we don't do that again," Bernice replied.

"Even so, we succeeded, and I am extremely grateful for you all," Panos added. "Now, you said that you were sent to acquire three individuals?"

"Yeah, we've still got one to go," Amory answered. "Any suggestions? You know the people here far better than we do."

"That did not stop you from finding Chadmight and me!" Panos chuckled. "As a matter of fact, I do have someone in mind. There's a certain faun named Agabio, whom I had been reaching out to frequently, and he seemed very close to wanting to come to the Vine by the time I was arrested. I would like to visit him one last time."

"Lead on," said Amory. "Let's hurry before the Legions realize they don't have you anymore. Do you think he'll mind if we drop in at this hour?"

"We shall find out," the minotaur replied.

They began to trek into the night once again. They stayed on the third story but traveled further to the outside border of the mountain. The shops and neighborhoods were now brightly illuminated by the giant moon, which faced Glatinth's opening head-on now. Once they arrived at the balcony on the city's edge, they turned toward a neighborhood filled with small yet pleasant wooden homes. They made several turns within the neighborhood before Panos stopped and turned to one of the houses, which seemed to be one of the more mundane ones. The Envoys gathered around the front door as Panos knocked.

"Agabio lives with his parents, who are also Envoys, so there's no need to hide your identity here," said the minotaur. "They too have been telling Agabio about Nazir, though his heart has been hardened toward him until recently."

Panos must have knocked five separate times before a sleepy, gray-haired faun opened the door. His drowsiness vanished upon seeing Panos free.

"Panos?" he gasped. "Is that you, or are my tired eyes deceiving me?"

The minotaur laughed aloud and engulfed the faun in a burly hug. "It's me, my friend! It's good to see you again, Lysander!"

"It's good to see you too," Lysander replied. "Who are your companions, and what brings you here at this hour?"

"Nazir sent these Envoys here to recruit three new members for their multiversal team," Panos answered. "He led them to Chadmight here and also to me. We have just broken out of the Glatinth prison and are currently on the run."

"Well come in, all of you!" said Lysander. "This is a safe place for Envoys, I can assure you. Panos, my friend, you must be starving. Allow me to feed you all."

"Thank you, friend, but we are all right," Panos said. "I only ask you this one thing. We still need to find one more recruit, and I believe Nazir is leading us to your son. May we see him, please?"

Lysander's smile faded a tad. "You may, if I am able to awaken him. You know how hard he sleeps. You must know that not much has changed in him since you were arrested. He still isn't an Envoy yet."

"Neither is Chadmight here, technically," replied Amory. "It doesn't matter to Nazir their standing with him right now. We've just been told to bring them to him, and he'll do the rest. I think he's guiding us to your son."

Lysander nodded and beckoned his guests to sit on a plush mat on the floor as he went into a nearby room to retrieve his son. The eleven—all except Chadmight, who thought it best to remain standing—took a seat, listening and watching for Lysander and Agabio to emerge. Panos leaned close to the rest of the team.

"There is something else you should know about Agabio. While his body is fully mature, his brain is not as physically developed as most. He might act as if he was younger than he truly is. Additionally, his condition has made him mute. His parents do not know if he will ever be able to speak."

"That's all right with us," Neisha whispered back. "Nels and I have helped and nurtured children with various disabilities in the orphanage we used to work at."

Panos grinned and nodded, then stood up upon seeing Lysander and Agabio—still rubbing his eyes. Agabio had curly red hair on his head, face, and legs. Like his father, he was dressed in a simple orange night robe and was as tall as Twyla and the humans. His face lit up when he saw Panos. With silence and a smile, Agabio rushed to the minotaur and gave him a tight, affectionate hug.

"It's good to see you too, my friend!" Panos laughed. "How are you?"

Agabio signed with his hands in reply, *I'm doing well, especially now that you are here. Father said you were in jail, and I thought I would not see you again.*

"I was worried about that too," Panos replied aloud. "But these other Envoys helped me escape because Nazir led them to me as well as to you."

It was then that Agabio noticed the other Envoys. He stepped back as he looked around at them, an apprehensive look on his face.

"We mean you no harm, friend," Neisha said as she got up, which startled him more. "No, it's all right!"

"You will have to forgive him," Panos said. "He's never seen a dwarf before. He is used to fauns being the shortest intelligent being here, and your stature surprises him."

"Oh," said Neisha, only a tiny bit insulted.

"I'm sorry, should I morph into a faun or a centaur or something to make him feel more comfortable?" Masato asked.

"Please, no," Panos laughed. "I do not think he's seen anyone change form before either. I'm sorry, Agabio. I should have said earlier that these Envoys are from different universes. Remember the stories I've told you about people going on missions in other worlds? These people hail from some of these worlds. They've come to tell you more about Nazir. Would you like to sit down and listen?"

Agabio paused for a second, then sat down comfortably between Panos and Edna.

"What should we tell him?" asked Amory. "What've you already told him about the Vine?"

"Quite a lot, actually," answered the minotaur. "Just tell him about your adventure here, and we can go from there."

By this time, Lysander's wife, Eulalia, had awakened, and she and her husband began to prepare some dry meat dumplings for their guests, despite the visitors' pleading. The dumplings were ready within minutes, and every Envoy there ate amply, realizing now how hungry they were. Chadmight was given an entire plate and downed it all before anyone else had even finished. However, he was courteous enough to thank his hosts and refrained from requesting any more.

After the Envoys finished telling their story, Agabio processed it all, then signed, *So you think I'm the third person you are meant to find?*

The visitors stood still for a moment. "I'm sorry, we don't know what he's saying," Leona said. "There are sign languages in our worlds, but we aren't familiar with his."

"That is all right. I can translate," Panos said, then orally repeated the question.

"Nazir was very clear in what he said to us and how he led us," Bernice answered. "He didn't outright tell us to come to you or Panos or Chadmight, but he gave us signs and peace inside us that we were going in the right direction."

Agabio shook his head fervently. *Nazir must have made a mistake. He doesn't know me. He hasn't seen me. Look at me. Do you think I can fight and go on adventures like you? It cannot be me you are looking for.*

"But he does know you, and he does see you, even now," Twyla replied.

How? Agabio motioned. *He is a Vine. Surely he doesn't have a face. That would be very creepy. Even if he did, how could he see me? He is not here. He is in the Center.*

Masato shrugged. "I honestly couldn't tell you exactly how he sees you, but he does. He is everywhere and every moment happens at the same time for him. You can't always see him, but when you talk to him he proves that he even knows your thoughts and motives and knows how prideful we are and how much we need him and don't even know it."

But why are you so sure he wants me? signed Agabio. *I have thought a lot about being an Envoy, and it sounds like I should. But I would not be of very much use as an Envoy. What is the point?*

"Agabio, listen to me," Panos said, almost placing a hand on his shoulder but remembering that he didn't like any physical contact that he himself didn't initiate. "None of us are much good to the Vine on our own. The strengths, gifts, and abilities we do have come from him. He gives us what we need when we need it, and he also gives us special abilities when he redeems us. Think of the skills you already have now! You are able to observe and acknowledge things that the rest of us couldn't. You boldly and instinctively disregard unnecessary cultural rules that the rest of us still need to break through. And the sign language you use is something only a few of us know, but they could reach so many people who would otherwise be unreachable! I have told you this before, and I will tell you again: you have unique talents, Agabio. Talents Nazir gave you and wants to use in the best way if you let him."

I do, don't I? Agabio motioned. *Thank you, Panos. But why is his way the best way?*

"Because he loves you," Dilyn answered after Panos translated. "Seeing everything, he knows what's best for everyone, and he loves us enough to bring that about. But he gives us a choice to follow him on that plan or not. Since he knows what's coming, he'll do what he plans one way or another, but we still have to choose it. He goes based on our choices and his sovereignty. We aren't puppets where he controls everything. We're like actors in the show, and he's the director. What he says is final, but we can choose whether or not to obey him. When we don't, it always ends in chaos and pain."

Agabio pondered further, shaking his head slowly and fidgeting with his hair. *Are you sure he would love me? My parents and my siblings love me, and Panos loves me, but strangers don't love me. If Nazir is perfect, then I would not be that loveable to him.*

"I'm positive he does," Leona smiled. "He already sees and knows you, and he loves you enough to want to save you from all the wrong you've done."

Agabio slowly shook his head with more fervor, processing it all. It was a long, awkward moment before he made up his mind. *OK. I will go with you to see Nazir. I still think I am right, but I want to see for myself.*

The Envoys were thrilled at this decision, none more than his parents. They trapped him in a short, twofold embrace.

"We are so excited for you to see him!" Eulalia exclaimed. "I know you are going to love him."

Thank you, Mother. Wait a minute. . . . Agabio motioned, turning suddenly to the visitors. *Will I ever see my parents again? I don't want this to be the last time. I want to still see them.*

The Envoys thought about this for a minute. They weren't entirely sure.

"Nazir would've wanted us to tell you to pack your things if you were leaving home for a long time," Amory finally replied. "But he didn't. He just wants us to bring you three to him. He'll work out the other details later. I'm sure you'll be able to return home soon."

"I hesitate in hoping for that," Panos interjected, "not because it does not make sense but because we might all be Envoys when we return, which means if we are found out, we will continue to be on the run here."

"Let's hope Nazir has it figured out one way or another," Masato said. "Shall we go?"

"We've found our three," answered Amory. "There's no reason to tarry further. Let's go. Ready, Agabio?"

The faun gave a simple shrug in return and bade farewell to his parents. Everyone stood up and gathered their weapons.

"Stop!" Chadmight instantly whispered as he neared the door. "Nobody move!"

Once everyone was quiet enough, they heard the stomps of soldiers rushing to and fro, in a frantic search for the escapees.

"We have to leave, now!" Nels whispered, hurriedly pulling out his Dagger.

"Wait, put that back for a moment!" Lysander cried. "If the troopers see that green glow, we will all be doomed, and you will not be going anywhere save prison. We have a secret basement underneath the kitchen. That is how our family and companions have gone so long without ever being caught. Get inside and make a portal from there. Agabio, show them where it is. Your mother and I will keep an eye out."

A very stressed Agabio rushed into the kitchen, walking back and forth, trying to make sure he wasn't forgetting anything. He finally got his bearings and took his new friends to the back corner of the kitchen, where he revealed a trapdoor that looked identical to the rest of the brown stone floor. It was pitch black inside the basement. Agabio jumped in first, confirming that there was space enough for everyone. One by one, the visitors hopped in, and Twyla quickly made a portal.

As the centaur figured out a way inside, Lysander and Eulalia said, "Make haste, and may Nazir give your team all the strength and victories needed to glorify him!"

Amory thoroughly thanked them as he jumped in last and rushed through the portal.

Amory took in his surroundings as he arrived at the Center again. The original nine from the team stood in front of the Vine but behind the three newcomers. Chadmight and Agabio stood side by side, just staring at Nazir and trying to swallow the fact that he was indeed real. Panos stood in front of everyone, bowing low toward his King.

"Welcome, all of you, and well done, my children!" Nazir said jubilantly. "You brought the specific three individuals I wanted. Well done for listening to my voice."

"Thank you," said the team as a whole.

"Greetings, Chadmight, Panos, and Agabio," Nazir continued. "I am very happy to see you."

"The same to you, my Liege," Panos replied, bowing again. "I did not know if I would be able to see you in person again before death."

"One way or another, my plans might not be what you expect," the Vine smiled. "Welcome back, my son. You have fought well and have shed many tears for my sake thus far. But your journey is not yet over, and I have more in store for you."

"It gives me joy to know I can still be used by my King," replied Panos.

"Good," said the Vine. "Go and join Amory's team. Go wherever they go. Fight wherever they fight. Speak whenever they speak. They will need your zeal, and you will need their discretion."

"It would be my pleasure!" Panos grinned as he got up and walked back to the others, leaving Agabio and Chadmight at the forefront before the Vine. Both of them became scared stiff.

"I-is what they told us true?" Chadmight stuttered, searching for words. "Did you truly die and come back for us? Do you truly seek to fix us?"

"I did, and I do," Nazir said solemnly but with a smiling tone. "I love you both, and you mean everything to me. I have waited a long time for you to come to me."

But why do you love us? Agabio signed. *It is obvious that we are not perfect, and it seems so far that Panos was telling the truth when he said you are perfect. How could someone perfect love someone who is not perfect?*

Agabio waited for Panos to tell Nazir what he'd signed, but to his astonishment, Nazir immediately replied, "Because all of your species were once perfect, and I want to restore that. In the beginning, I created the whole multiverse to be perfect. Everything in every world was perfect, but all creatures I made with free will. They were free to either choose me or their own ways. One by one, each species eventually chose themselves over me, and since I'm perfect and they went apart from me, the things they did made them flawed. But I want to bring them back to perfection—back to me."

The centaur and the faun chewed on this for a little bit.

Wait, Agabio began, *if you want to take away my flaws, does that mean you will heal me and make me like everyone else?*

"Eventually, yes, but not in the way you are thinking," the Vine answered. "I will not heal you now, because like Panos told you earlier, your ailment has given you abilities that the others have to work harder to attain. But if you come to me and let me redeem you, then death will not stop you from living, and you will be healed more than you know after you die."

Agabio looked disheartened but seemed to understand and accept what he was told. He was also amazed that Nazir knew about conversations he and the Envoys had had earlier. *You really do see everything!* he motioned.

"What about me?" Chadmight asked.

"You, I do intend to heal before death, Chadmight," replied Nazir. "While Agabio's condition is not a result of any wrong done by him or his parents, yours is a result of your overindulgence, which I want to correct. I want you to crave the right things, things that will glorify me and benefit you instead of destroying you all for a little pleasure. However, like Agabio's healing, yours will not be immediate either. It will be a long and difficult process, and you must lean on my love and strength and peace to get through it."

"I understand," replied the centaur. "I've seen enough of these Envoys in action to believe that what they say and what you say is true. I want to be redeemed by you and become one of your children and warriors . . . and to be free from myself."

I do too, Agabio added. *If you really want me, then I want you too. I believe in you, and I want to be yours.*

"I've been waiting centuries for you two to say that!" Nazir exclaimed. "Come, my new sons, and be cleaned!"

"Yes!" Panos bellowed as the pair inched closer to their new Father. The others also cheered.

Nazir hugged them tightly with his branches—both of them reciprocating—and he drained and replaced their old blood just as he had done thousands upon thousands of times before. Agabio and Chadmight finally felt whole and at peace for the first time in their lives.

Now I know what you and my parents were talking about! Agabio motioned to Panos.

"I told you!" Panos beamed.

"Here," Nazir said again, revealing from his leaves Daggers, medals, and instructions.

"Are we truly to become warriors for you, my new King?" Chadmight said excitedly.

"Yes," Nazir grinned. "You will need to be. Go through this portal behind me, and the forger there will construct your equipment."

"Please tell me there's some sort of food there," Chadmight muttered as he and the faun entered *Chârâsh*. Everyone else chuckled.

"He'll live," said the Vine.

"Hey, I just remembered something," Bernice said abruptly. "Chadmight told us that if even one person escapes the prison in Glatinth, then everyone working there gets killed. Is that what will happen to the guards once they find out that Panos isn't there?"

"That is a fair point, and I'm grateful you brought it up," Nazir answered. "I too considered this, and I softened the heart of the emperor and Glatinth's mayor to pardon every worker and soldier at that prison. They were still on duty; they were simply distracted by the order given. Such a thing was unheard of until now, and I will use it to bring those guards to myself."

"OK, good," Twyla sighed. "I would hate to be the cause of any more unnecessary deaths."

"Now," Nazir continued, "once Chadmight and Agabio get back, you need to help them kill their doppelgängers and then take them back home to gather their things; they will be moving in with some of you. Train them and teach them how to obey and love me. This is your new assignment. There is also something else that must take place as this goes on . . . ."

8
ORIGINS

Chadmight and Agabio eagerly stepped into the forge of *Chârâsh* carrying their Daggers, badges, and molds. The large room they entered was dimly lit with a handful of ceiling chandeliers and a giant oven, illuminating the several tools, shelves, weapons, and armor-filled stands throughout the forge. It was a lot to take in, and Chadmight was thrilled like a kid in a candy store. He was certain no armory of the Binosia Legions compared to this. Agabio, on the other hand, was a tad startled and overwhelmed with it all, though he was still excited to see what his equipment would look like.

At the central anvil stood a very tall creature, even taller than the obese centaur. It had brown skin and long, black hair and sideburns. It possessed four wings, two of which were silver, larger, and thinner, and were used for flying. The other two were dark silver, smaller, and thicker, and were used as clothing and armor. The being was banging away at a thin piece of glowing metal that would soon be a knife. It stopped once it beheld its visitors.

"Welcome to *Chârâsh*, the forge world of Nazir and his Envoys!" uttered the creature in a low, bone-chilling voice. "I am Azarias, the keeper and leader of this small world."

Chadmight hesitated and stammered for a second, suddenly frightened by this creature. "I am Chadmight, and this is Agabio. We were brought from our home world of Binosia to Nazir, who just redeemed us. He gave us these molds and sent us here so they could be made into our armor and weapons."

"Splendid!" Azarias exclaimed, using his steel tongs to place his current project in a smaller, cooler oven, which sat between some shelves, to save it for later. "I shall start on them right away!" The cherub reached out his muscular hand to receive the molds. Chadmight immediately gave his, impatient to see how they'd end up. Agabio eventually gave his after a bit of hesitance and lack of trust in this new, threatening being.

Once Azarias had the molds, he set Agabio's aside and placed Chadmight's in the giant forge, which was already blazing.

"You wouldn't happen to have any food around here, would you?" Chadmight asked timidly.

"I'm afraid not," Azarias grinned. "I happen to be a creature that doesn't need food, and I have nothing here that I do not need. Your equipment will be done in no time, and I am certain you won't starve before then."

Chadmight groaned but complied, taking a seat nearby as he watched the forger work. Agabio stayed standing where he was, growing more and more in awe of what he saw. Since Panos wasn't there, he assumed no one here would understand his signs, so he said nothing for a while. After almost completing a few pieces of armor, Azarias took notice of this.

"I am sure you have questions, friend Agabio," the angel said. "Feel free to ask them; I understand your sign language."

Shocked that both this creature and the Vine understood him, he finally signed. *Thank you! So how old are you, exactly, and how long have you been here?*

"I have been here for over nine hundred years," Azarias replied. "Nazir has a millennial rotation of weaponsmiths who work here, so my tenure is close to being over. As for my age, my life began when the multiverse did. The Vine created the realms and the cherubim at the same time."

Agabio mouthed the word *wow*. *So you just don't die?* he signed.

"No, not really." Azarias smiled as he pounded Chadmight's greaves into shape. "Nazir made cherubim specifically to be immortal and undying, although some of us were still made to fight."

"Fight?" asked Chadmight, who didn't know Agabio's questions but regardless got to hear the answers. "What would you have to fight if you can't die?"

Azarias inhaled deeply. "That's a years-long story, but I think I have time to summarize it. There happens to exist a perverted division of us called dark cherubim. They go throughout the worlds attacking souls and minds, influencing and tempting everyone in their path. Not a single person is immune or exempt from their bombardments. They are led by a formerly elite cherub commander known as Marah. He is directly opposed to Nazir and is every Envoy's true enemy. Mind you, while he is quite cunning and mightier than I, he is no match for our multiversal King. He never has been and never will be. Marah once held high authority over the cherubim in Nazir's eternal home of *Paradeisos*, where you are now registered to live after death. But he wanted more power and authority and in fact wanted to become more powerful than Nazir himself. This, the Vine would not tolerate, and it was in fact impossible for Marah to do this. Nevertheless, he tried. Shortly after the multiverse was born, Marah had converted thousands of other cherubim to his cause and began an attempt to overthrow Nazir and replace him.

"I remember that battle well," Azarias continued as he started to pound on Chadmight's future horseshoes harder and harder. *Clang! Clang! Clang!*

Boom! Boom! Boom! Azarias, looking no younger or older, was being bombarded by the paws of a giant warrior beast, a breed of cherub created to plow down enemies. Little did Azarias know, he would be such an enemy.

"Dov!" Azarias cried between the creature's stomps, trying not to get trampled. "What are you doing? What has come over you? Why have you turned against our King?"

The fiend had no time to respond. Five more angels of varying sizes and shapes came to Azarias's aid, shoving the beast sideways. Once Azarias was free, he helped them shunt Dov until they came to the edge of the multicolored, gemlike ground they were on. This edge overlooked the expanse of the cosmos, at the bottom of which sat two circular portals next to each other. There was a giant white portal to the newly crafted multiverse called *Rôb Tĕbél*, as well as a black hole leading to *Pur*, the realm of everlasting death. The six proceeded to thrust Dov over the edge, watching him plummet into the black hole to *Pur*, where he was now doomed to be forever. All of them stared down for a moment, having lost a dear friend.

Azarias eventually turned around and looked in horror at his surroundings. This luxurious land that was teeming with life and joy was now a battlefield, although nothing of the environment was harmed. The trees still swayed gently, the golden streets remained flawless and transparent, and the streams flowed just as coolly as if nothing was going on at all. But something was definitely going on. This home that Azarias knew as *Paradeisos* was now riddled with skirmishes among friends he knew and had grown quite fond of. There was Abdiel diving over the flowing streams, and there was Tiras fighting three other cherubim at once. These two and tens of thousands of others had been convinced to aid in an audacious and horrendous effort to overthrow the Great Vine himself. Their objective was to attack the Vine directly, who was at the center of *Paradeisos*. Pulsating with deadly light, Nazir sat open and still, seemingly susceptible to any attack. But the King was never even touched, for the loyal angels were able to subdue the rebels before they got to him. But the revolutionaries were getting closer.

"Thank you, fellows," shouted Azarias amongst the frays. "Come on, we have many more rebels to cast down."

"Oh, that these rebels weren't our companions!" cried Oma, one of the five other loyalists with him. "I don't know how they succumbed to Marah's proposal, but I dearly wish they hadn't."

"Nevertheless, they did," Azarias replied. "And friends or not, they are perverted now, and our King and Creator is our top priority. We must follow his orders to stop this evil rebellion."

"Agreed," Oma said. "I see a squadron of mutineers on a side street ahead that isn't accounted for. Let's take them."

At that, the six drew their immortal swords, whose blades glowed yellowish-white like lightning. Their hair also turned to tongues of fire, and their eyes now glowed yellow. They opened their wings in a flurry and zoomed off to their new adversaries. As quick as a blink, their swords clashed as they darted to and fro around the tall, otherworldly buildings surrounding them. All of their strikes were too fast for a mortal to comprehend. These weapons would not kill either opponent no matter how much they were hit, but they would certainly weaken them. Azarias and Oma were the first to overcome, grab, and hurl all their enemies into the eternal dungeon, and they then helped their comrades do the same. This was no easy feat, since those on either side had very similar skill levels.

Suddenly, a larger being swooped down and crashed into the six triumphant soldiers. Azarias groaned as he got back up and saw the creature dart back and forth at a supersonic pace, gradually going for the Vine and giving powerful strikes to loyalists along the way. It finally stopped and hovered unnervingly close to the giant Vine's stalk. This being had six wings, using two of them to protect his lower body and the other four to fly (rather than using two to fly and two to protect his face, which was what they were made to do). It wore crimson, scale-like armor, and its body-long, flowing hair burned with passionate fire. This was the most beautiful and cunning of all the cherubim species. It was Marah.

"Nazir!" Marah echoed in a deafening, angry, yet silky smooth voice. His face was scowling and seething before the Vine. "Today is the day you lose your throne! Today is the day *Paradeisos* and *Rôb Têbêl* come under the rule of a greater k—"

Before Marah could even finish, he was smacked by one of the Vine's leaves, which had come even faster than he could anticipate. The enemy was knocked several yards sideways, where he crashed into one of Nazir's branches and landed on another leaf below. That leaf closed around him and squeezed him to the point where breathing was painfully impossible.

"Enough," Nazir echoed angrily. The whole cosmos heard his voice. "Because you have allowed your pride to overcome you, Marah, I hereby eternally banish you and your every follower to *Pur*, where you will ultimately reside in pain forever. Thus is your fate, your doom. I will not reverse it."

As the last of their opponents was thrust over the edge, the loyal cherubim watched in awe and terror as the Vine threw Marah like a ragdoll in front of him. Marah recovered and remained flying, daring to come face-to-face with his former King.

Marah raised his arms ragefully and pompously. "Do you not know who I am, what power and authority and influence I have accumulated? Who are *you* to banish *me*?"

Without a second of hesitation, Nazir bellowed in response for the multiverse to hear, "I AM!" That shout alone blew Marah away, screaming down the heavens' expanse and into the black hole as quick as a blink, with a trail of what looked like lightning behind him.

After taking several moments to grasp what had just happened, the loyalists turned to the Vine and broke out in victorious shouts of joy and honor and adoration. This lasted several minutes before they even started to die down.

Once they did, Oma asked, "So what happens now, my Liege?"

Nazir sighed. "Marah and his minions will not stay in *Pur* for very long. They are ultimately doomed there, but until I finally lock them in, they will find avenues to roam between there and the new multiverse I made. They will soon resolve to deceive the mortals whom I made to think, create, and love like me, with the goal of perverting them too and bringing as many creatures as possible with them to *Pur*. They will do everything in their power to thwart my perfect plan and overthrow my Kingdom in a new way—by deceiving and destroying its people. But my plan cannot be overturned. My Kingdom and my people will remain forever, even though it will cost me everything to make it possible. The people's only hinderance will be their own individual choice. You will understand all of this soon."

More cheers erupted from the Vine's armies, who were thankful and even giddy that their King's plan and love was inevitable, despite the uprising they just experienced.

Another angel then asked, "But how are you to still accomplish this if Marah is going to walk about and steal freely throughout each universe?"

"He won't be free," said Nazir. "He and his followers will be on a leash. That leash is my authority and commands . . . and you. You cherubim who are warriors and not my messengers or attendants are now responsible for ensuring Marah does not cross any boundary I set in place, and you know he will certainly try. You must unwaveringly guard every boundary set by either me or my people in my name. Is this clear to all of you?"

"Yes, my King!" said every cherub present.

────────

"And that is what we have been doing ever since," said Azarias as he ground Agabio's armor on a spinning stone. He had already finished Chadmight's at that point. The centaur was now clad in light gray armor and horseshoes. His weapons were a pair of rounded maces, whose heads could detach from the handles and were connected by chains that retracted into the handles. They were part mace, part flail. He was practicing a little with these new weapons but was also careful to continue listening to the forger.

Azarias continued. "Marah and his minions have wreaked havoc on the cosmos whenever they could, but every time they did, Nazir had to allow it. We angels are here to ensure that Marah never goes beyond what Nazir allows and that he stays away from the King's Envoys and future Envoys, namely when they resist Marah."

I see, Agabio signed in amazement. *So you have actually been to Paradeisos? What's it like?*

The cherub beamed. "It's beyond description, simply due to the fact that Nazir resides there in all his splendor. I could describe some things that mortals could understand, but not in the whole. All I can truly say about it other than what I did in the story of the battle is that it is more perfect and glorious and beautiful than you have ever hoped. It astounds me that some creatures wouldn't choose to live with the Vine there, but what astounds me more is the belief in something you haven't even seen yet—the belief you Envoy mortals possess. That is something I don't think I myself will ever comprehend."

Chadmight sighed with joy. "Well, after chasing pleasure and recognition for so long and only finding misery, that is something I can truly look forward to."

"And well you should, my friend," Azarias replied. "But I must warn you to not become so obsessed with it that you do nothing with the finite life you have right now. Make your every decision based on this reality of eternity, yes, but don't ever let it be an excuse for you to become stagnant. Envoys with this mindset quickly become useless to the Vine. Nazir still has a purpose for you on this side of temporal death. Which reminds me of something else I must tell you. The team you will be joining has a prophecy written about them and what Nazir will do through them. You two are included in that prophecy. Every Envoy has one, as Nazir has plans to use every creature he makes and loves, should they choose to accept him and those plans."

Azarius continued. "I cannot tell you the entire prophecy or that truly would spoil your whole lives. Besides, I do not know it all myself; only the Vine does. However, I am allowed to know and share this much: when Nazir chooses a score of diverse beings, and those beings choose him in return, he will, ultimately through these twenty, bring about an awakening like *Rôb Tĕbêl* has never before undergone. This will be the sign to confirm these individuals: the main leader will possess a great, blue sword, one will have a great bow, one will wield a thin, double-sided axe, one will bear the Envoys' flag with a spear, one will bear a giant hammer, one will have the ability to destroy weapons, one will be a shieldmaiden, one will fire arrows with an axe, one will have many knives, one will have flexible claws, one will wield a trident, one will have two retractable flails, one will carry a long pike, and one will have bladed whips. That is as much as Nazir told me."

"Very intriguing," Chadmight replied. "That is encouraging, and thank you for sharing that. But there are a few weapons that I don't remember seeing from this team."

"One of them is Agabio's, which you will soon see," replied the angel. "The rest of them you have yet to meet. There are also those whose weapons I did not mention. There is still much building to be done in your team, but that will come in time."

After saying this, Azarias got back to fully focusing on Agabio's equipment. As soon as his bright orange armor was finished, the cherub used his tongs to take from the forge a long spearhead with an axe head on one side and dip it in the oil tank. He coolly blew out the flames that appeared on it when he brought the piece out. He then proceeded to grind it to a perfect sharpness and fasten it to a five-foot-long dark, wooden pole.

Once he finished polishing the whole weapon, now recognizable as a pike, Azarias proudly stated, "The work is complete."

Agabio eagerly put everything on and tried out his new pike. Utmost confidence and satisfaction filled his face. *Thank you very much!* he signed. *I like this a lot!*

Azarias smiled. "Nazir does not make or tolerate bad work, and I daresay you two look fantastic. Now return to the Center to reunite with your team and receive the Vine's next instructions. Love and serve him as you have never loved and served before. You will learn just how infinitely worth it he is!"

At that bidding, the pair of new Envoys took their Daggers and created a portal, excited to see what their new lives would entail.

9

THE COMMITMENT

Amory stepped into the Center a bit more timidly than usual. He was slouching and his hands were subtly shaking. Within seconds, Theodore appeared as well. They both shook hands and hugged before approaching the Vine.

"I got your text," Theodore said. "You feeling all right?"

"Yeah, I'm OK," answered Amory. "That's about all I can say."

"Good morning, my sons!" Nazir chimed in.

"It is, indeed, Dad!" Theodore said. "You did a fabulous job in making today."

"Thank you, Theodore," said Nazir. "You look nervous, Amory. Is everything all right?"

Amory grinned slightly. "Truth be told, everything's going great. But yes, I'm nervous as heck."

"Might it have anything to do with the wedding tomorrow?" Nazir asked sarcastically.

"You know me well," chuckled Amory. "I just want to make sure it all goes right and that I don't mess up. Not just in the ceremony, although that contributes, but in the rest of my and Bernice's lives after that. I am stoked to marry her, and I get more excited the closer it gets, but also as it gets closer, the more inadequate I feel in being the man and husband she needs me to be. Financially I'm stable, otherwise I would've postponed the wedding date. But I still don't think I'm mentally or spiritually ready."

"Hey, let me tell you something," Theodore replied. "No one is ever ready for something as sacred as marriage. If anyone was, they'd be a perfect spouse and there would be no conflict ever. I personally am still not ready for it, as my wife can attest. But by Nazir's grace and strength, I give it my best shot every day because my bride deserves nothing less. My job is still to provide for, protect, and love my family. Do I do it perfectly? Of course not. But I rely on Nazir, and he makes it enough."

"He's right," Nazir added. "You must also remember that I've been guiding you every step of the way. I crossed Bernice's path with yours all those years ago in middle school. I made you to be attracted to her—and her to you—and led you to date her. I guided your relationship and showed you how to love and honor her, and all this time I've been preparing you to be the husband she specifically needs. Will you make mistakes? Yes. But if you keep leaning on me for forgiveness and endurance, then your marriage will flourish, as long as you both daily choose me first and then each other. This is the time I have appointed for you to marry Bernice, and that was no error."

Amory stood there for several moments, processing it all. "Thank you. I needed that, and I feel a little better and more confident about it now. I just don't want to do anything royally dumb that would affect her because she means so much to me, and I don't want to hurt her or make her think I don't love her."

"Therefore giving her a reason not to love you?" Nazir said.

Amory hesitated, then nodded.

"Amory, you can't control or deserve her love any more than you can Nazir's," Theodore replied. "You will do dumb things. Our human nature guarantees that. That's why it's so critical to remain close to the Vine, so he'll empower you to overcome your temptations and failures. When you do fail—in anything, really, not just marriage—it's crucial to get back up and turn away from the wrong you did."

"OK," Amory nodded. "I'll do my best to remember that."

"I know you will," Nazir smiled. "Now, in the presence of a witness, I commission you. Go and live, selflessly loving Bernice as I have selflessly loved you."

"Yes, my King!" Amory said, standing taller. "It would be my honor and pleasure!"

———

That evening, Bernice also entered Nazir's presence, breathing deeply. She didn't bring her flag and armor with her this time. She wore her blue after-work shirt and gray sweatpants and held her Dagger. She'd considered nothing else.

"Hey, Nazir," she said quietly.

"Hello, daughter!" Nazir replied kindly.

Edna and Twyla then came in behind her. Edna was also in her comfy clothes, and Twyla was dressed in her waitress attire.

"Oh, shoot, I forgot you were working tonight, Twyla," Bernice said in a shaky voice. "I'm sorry!"

"It is all right," said Twyla. "I am taking my break early, and I will stay as long as necessary. Your text seemed urgent. Are you well?"

"Yeah, I'm doing OK," Bernice answered. "I just can't believe it's all happening. I'm getting *married* tomorrow! I don't think I'll be able to sleep tonight."

"You're not excited, are you?" Edna grinned.

"No, of course not," Bernice answered. "I'm ecstatic! But I'm also afraid."

"Of what, child?" Nazir asked.

"Of the unknown. I mean, Amory and I have had a lot of conversations about our plans and hopes, and we've gone through all the marriage counseling, so I guess I'm as ready as I'll ever be. But somehow I still have no idea what I'm getting myself into. I'm going off of what other people have told me, but I don't personally know what marriage is like yet, and that scares me. I don't know what it's like to live under the same roof as the one man I love, to share every possession and secret, and to discover the differences in how we live in the minute details—

like how cold we leave the AC or how neat we are or aren't. I'm afraid that I'll do something wrong because I won't know what I'm doing, and I'll discover something about the way he lives that'll be hard to tolerate—or worse, vice versa."

"Tell me," Edna replied. "Have you ever heard of people divorcing over a room's temperature?"

Bernice snickered. "No, but many have over similar small things that they simply couldn't get over, and I don't want that to happen to us. But I also don't know how to prevent that."

"You prevent it by choosing him daily, whether you can stand him in the moment or not," Nazir said firmly. "You must embody my love, and you know that what makes my love surpass all other kinds of love is that it disregards feelings and remains constant whether the beloved is tolerable or not. This is what I do with you every day as you succeed and fail. Every divorce occurs because either or both spouses at some point think—truthfully or not—that it would be better for him or her to be alone than to be with their spouse. You know that Amory is a good man who is worth your commitment. If he sticks with me, he will remain so, so you need not worry about divorce being an option. If you find something in him that truly is evil and should not be tolerated, love him enough to bring it up gently, clearly, and honestly. I'll take care of the rest. By the way, the same is true of every relationship you have."

"I understand," said Bernice. "There's something else too. That HR job I kept pestering you about. Is this why you never let me land one? So I could marry Amory?"

"In a way, yes," Nazir answered. "You would be capable of handling both at the same time, but your attention would be divided, and you wouldn't be able to do your best in either. There might be times in the future when you are a wife and employee, but not now. I've been preparing you to marry Amory because that's the path that will bring me the most glory, but Marah used the possibility of working in HR to distract your thoughts and devotion. Thankfully you had good friends to redirect your gaze, and you've remained with me all this time."

"I have you three to thank for that," replied Bernice.

"We all love you, Bernice," said Twyla. "We see much potential in you. Remember what we discussed concerning our dreams and talents? Nazir still intends to use yours, but they might not turn out the way we initially want. However, it is the best way. For now, you must be willing to let go of this dream and fulfill the one that is right at your fingertips!"

Bernice hung her head and bit her lip. "It's so hard, though. I've had this dream since high school, and I've clung to it so tightly."

"So tightly that you have made an idol out of it?" Edna asked.

"Bernice, do you trust me?" asked Nazir gently. "Do you really trust that what I say is best, despite your desires?"

"Yes, Dad," Bernice said. "I do trust you."

"Then let go."

Bernice shook her head in hesitation, then knelt before her King. Twyla and Edna each put a hand on her shoulders. "OK, I lay it down now. I know that your plan's best, and I'm willing to let this go and no longer pursue this. This dream is no longer mine. It doesn't belong."

"Thank you, my daughter," Nazir smiled. "Now you are free from this weight and can focus on what lies ahead. I will take this dream from here and do with it what I wish, as long as you don't take it back."

"How do you feel?" Twyla asked.

Bernice sniffed. "A little freer but still sad."

"I understand that very well," grinned the elf.

"Thanks, Father," Bernice said as she got up. "Now I see that needed to happen before tomorrow."

"You're always welcome, Bernice!" said the Vine. "Now, in the presence of these witnesses, I commission you. Go and live, selflessly loving Amory as I have selflessly loved you."

"I would love nothing better!" Bernice replied.

"Come on," said Edna, side-hugging her best friend. "Let's get you home so you can rest. It's a big day tomorrow!"

April 15th turned out to be the host of Philadelphia's hardest downpour in years. Amory and Bernice had hoped for an outdoor wedding, but with one look at the horizon they immediately elected to move everything inside the venue they'd chosen. They had planned to hold the ceremony before lunch and eat lunch during the reception. However, it took all morning for the wedding party, the Banners, and whoever arrived early to set everything up inside. It took a lot for the dwarves to not swear as they carried speakers that seemed to weigh as much as the dwarves themselves. Amory ended up ordering pizza for everyone afterward, and once they all had eaten, they began the ceremony.

The hall, the edges of the chair columns, and the centerpiece were decorated with white and gold banners and flowers. The centerpiece itself was made of thick, rustic, wooden branches, intricately carved and woven together. On the right column of chairs (from a frontal view) was seated Bernice's family. Her parents, her two older brothers and their families, and all of her extended family were there. On the left sat Amory's coworkers, former classmates, and Envoy friends from his team and weekly gathering. King Eoin and Queen Fynballa, the elves Amory's team had helped a few years ago, were invited but had other pressing matters. Ambrose, however, managed to be there, along with Masato and his crew, Neisha, Chadmight, Panos, and Agabio and his parents. The non-Envoy humans present were rather at a loss upon seeing these different creatures, especially since they wore their armor over their wedding clothes.

Then, under the sound of rain pelting the roof came the music. It was classical music, Amory's favorite. (Since Bernice liked more upbeat genres, it was agreed that some of her favorites would play after the ceremony and during the reception.) Everyone looked behind them to see the approaching wedding party. Nels and Leona came out first, arm-in-arm. He wore a white uniform under his armor, and she wore a golden dress, with her breastplate overtop of it and her leg greaves and boots inside her skirt. They got to the end of the aisle and joined the officiator, who was the leader of their Envoy gathering. Next came Dilyn and Twyla in attire almost identical to those who came before them. Then came the best man and the maid of honor: Theodore and Edna, both wearing wide smiles. Instead of bouquets, the women and men both carried their weapons. Theodore's was a large, sharp, rectangular shield with wooden handles on every edge, the colors of which matched his maroon armor.

Amory came out next, escorting no one. He confidently strode to the front alone, wearing a gold-looking tuxedo under his armor, his sword at his side. He too joined the officiator, excessively beaming and sweating at the same time. He stood anxiously facing the doorway into the main room. The bridal tune came on, and everyone arose and turned. In came Bernice, bearing her armor underneath her white, silk dress, which was simple yet quite becoming for her. In one hand she held her father's arm, in the other she held her flagstaff high. Her hair was curled to perfection and adorned with a wreath of tiny yellow primroses. Second only to Nazir, Amory had never seen such a captivating sight. With the widest grin in the room, Bernice let go of her father and stepped forward, placing her spear in the middle of the centerpiece behind them. The whole party then looked at Bernice's parents.

"Who gives this woman to be with this man?" the officiator said.

"Her mother and I," said Bernice's father with a kind and sure smirk.

At that, the couple joined hands and looked up into each other's eyes, each beholding in the other a joy they had not yet seen. As the officiator gave his two cents' worth about each of them and how special and sacred this union was, it was hard for both of them to concentrate on him. They realized they were staring at each other probably too long and almost cracked up more than once.

Then they stated their vows to each other before their witnesses, vows similar to those made in an otherworldly wedding they'd attended awhile back.

"I, Amory, take you, Bernice, to be my wife. I vow to protect and lead our family, our team, and especially you to the utmost—whether or not you are able to care for yourself— during the good and bad seasons, and everywhere in between, even and especially if that means abandoning my life so that you will keep yours for decades to come until the Vine calls me home."

"I, Bernice, take you, Amory, to be my husband. I vow to fight for our union, our family and legacy, and our team to the utmost as you do the same, during the good and bad seasons, and everywhere in between, even if that means abandoning my life so that our legacy and Nazir's reign will remain for millennia to come until the Vine calls me home."

Theodore and Edna proceeded to give the bride and groom their respective rings. They matched in that the ring itself was made of golden, vine-like spirals all the way around. The only difference was the emerald-cut diamond on Bernice's.

After placing the rings on each other's fingers, they were finally allowed to kiss for the first time ever. This wasn't by choice, but it ended up that way, and they held that kiss for what seemed to be a solid minute as everyone in the room cheered.

Then, as Bernice retrieved her spear, the officiator declared, "I proudly present to you Mr. and Mrs. Amory Walters!"

As Bernice's favorite hit single began to play, the newlyweds jubilantly walked back down the aisle laughing. They made their way to the reception hall, and everyone else eventually followed.

After escorting Twyla, Dilyn tried to find Ambrose. He caught a glimpse of him walking out the door. Dilyn followed him outside but found no trace of him. He must've been teleported back to Ourrance. Disheartened, Dilyn returned inside and joined the others for the reception.

The food offered was a variety of sandwiches and fruit, along with a fruit punch bowl and the two-tier wedding cake. Panos had to keep Chadmight away from the table after he'd downed seven sandwiches and five glasses of punch. The centaur resisted a little but was beginning to understand the importance of holding back. He'd been learning a lot in the past three months. Leona also caught Masato disguising himself as different guests and going to congratulate the couple several times, just for laughs. She caught him in the form of Bernice's dad before he could approach them and scare Amory with some sarcastic criticisms.

After much laughing and eating, it was time for the couple to depart. Theodore pulled Amory's truck up into the awning, and everyone lined up in two rows and showered the Walters with rice and cheers as they got in the truck and sped off into the storm. As everyone went back inside and started cleaning up, Dilyn found Edna and helped her clear off the reception tables.

"So where are they headed?" Dilyn asked.

"To Amory's house to change, then straight to Hawaii for two weeks," Edna replied. "At some point after that comes our next mission."

"Good," said Dilyn. "I'll be able to graduate by then."

"Really? That was quick!"

Dilyn chuckled. "In trying to condense my schoolwork to make up for all the doctors appointments, I ended up ahead of schedule. Thank Nazir for private schools."

"How are you doing by the way?" said Edna. "Do you feel up to this coming mission, whatever it is?"

"Yeah, I'll be fine. I'm not getting the results I've been hoping for, but I'll make do. I have no idea if I'll survive this or not, but I'm going to make the most out of my life while I still can."

"I'm proud of you, dude," Edna said, patting him on the shoulder.

"Do Amory and Bernice know about the mission yet?" Dilyn asked.

"No, and Nazir said specifically not to tell them. He'll tell them himself in the right time. This is a special time for them. He said to let them enjoy it."

Thunder came in a deafening clap after an unignorable flash of lightning. That one hit something, and the Walters were afraid to guess what it was as they drove cautiously to the airport.

"Somehow this still doesn't compare to the storms in Hertengard," Bernice commented in the shotgun seat, looking out the window which was constantly being splashed. She now wore a t-shirt and jeans under her orange raincoat. Her garland was gone, though the curls in her hair remained.

"No, at least now we don't have walls of water and tornadic winds to worry about," replied Amory, who wore similar attire with his blue coat. His hair, however, was much wetter than hers. "This is still crazy, though! I've never driven in a storm this bad!"

"We're almost there, honey. We're good," Bernice said, Amory grinning at her. She changed the subject. "I can't believe this is real now! I'm finally your wife! We're actually married at last!"

"I know!" said Amory. "This is so surreal! I would never have imagined being your husband when we first met!"

Bernice smirked. "Really?"

"OK, the thought did occur to me once or twice back then, but I didn't think it would actually happen. I didn't think you'd have put up with me this long."

"Same here," said Bernice. "My family can attest to how much I can overthink."

"I know, and I still love you," said Amory. "They seemed surprisingly eager about all of this today."

"Surprisingly?" Bernice turned swiftly. "Dude, they might have been even more impatient than I was about you proposing! They've been excited about this possibility for a long time."

"Yeah, that right there surprises me!" Amory chortled. "I never thought that parents would be happy—though still sad, I know—about letting their only daughter go. And now this possibility is a reality!"

"I know! I can't believe it!" Bernice squealed. After a bit of silence, she said, "Sorry none of your family came."

Amory let out a singular laugh. "I'm not. I have absolutely no way of contacting them and therefore had no way to inform them about this, not that they'd care. They chose to not be involved with me when they left. I have no remorse."

"I know, and I wouldn't either if I were in your shoes," Bernice replied.

"However," Amory continued. "I am very grateful to have celebrated this with everyone who did come! All of them mean so much to me. Did you see that Ambrose made it there?"

"I did! I didn't see him at the reception, but I did during the ceremony. I'm glad he could come for at least that."

"Me too," said Amory. "He's a great friend when he chooses to be."

Bernice nodded. After a moment, she said, "This changes a lot with us and being Envoys. I mean, obviously we'll still be going on missions and training and being trained, but now we'll be together as one in it all!"

"Right?" Amory said. "I thought going on missions while dating you would be fun, but this is going to be so much more of an adventure that I can't wait for!"

"You don't have to wait anymore, dear," Bernice smiled. "This is finally happening now!"

PART III

THE FIRE EXPLODES

10
MULTIPLE SPLITS

A lone, Maewing sauntered along the hallways of the Self-Worthy Headquarters in Ourrance. The Sword of *Chârâsh* was at her side as always, along with a new twin-bladed sword to replace the one the wizard in Uchu had partially melted. Her human half wore a dark red sweatshirt, a gift from a human in her ranks. In her hand she held a glass of bright purple juice, which she sipped frequently. It tasted terribly bitter but gradually soothed every inch of her body. This was the rumored concoction that prolonged her life, which she managed to keep secret and unconfirmed all this time. Using ingredients from throughout the cosmos, she'd perfected it under the guidance of a dark cherub friend from her army. He'd said she only had to take it once a year, but now that she had lived so long, she began to age faster and recently bumped up the dosage to once a quarter. She chugged the last half of the glass, the final gulp followed by a groan.

There's still so much to be done, she thought. *I cannot stop living now!*

She then found herself at her destination: an open room next to her personal quarters. She came here often, namely on sleepless nights. Upon her entering, yellow triangles of light in the ceiling flashed on, illuminating the room. There were chairs and multicolored floor cushions (for those like Maewing who couldn't sit) throughout the expanse. They surrounded a wide, round table in the center, solid all the way through with no legs. On the surface was a map, apparently drawn into the table itself. It looked like an old, dark orange parchment, with black sketches of varying clusters of circles. Universes. Every world and its astronomy was recorded here, each with its corresponding name underneath. They were spread across the entire table, each connected with lines converging at an obscure center on the map.

Maewing pressed a button on the side of the table. As the lights dimmed, the colors on the map gradually switched; it was now a black map with orange drawings. Then those drawings were projected from the table's surface to form a three-dimensional hologram above it. Now the hollow orange worlds and cosmos were displayed as they were truly arranged in three dimensions. Maewing circumnavigated the table, gazing intently at every universe before her. She looked at every world the Self-Worthy had ever penetrated to any extent. Ourrance, Uchu, Hertengard, Binosia, even Earth. There was also the elemental world of Valico and the neighboring planets of the universe Wranity, both containing intelligent life.

"We've been to so many worlds," she said aloud, "but we still have so far to go. Why do we not have more influence in these places?"

I'll give you one guess as to why.

There came that strange voice again. Maewing didn't even flinch this time. She'd heard it so often lately that it ceased to startle her. She didn't intend her question to be for the voice, but now she welcomed its consultation.

"What you've been telling me all along: the Envoys," replied Maewing, not taking her eyes off of the holographic map.

In how many worlds have your ranks collided with theirs, even recently?

"Too many," Maewing murmured.

It won't stop. Not unless you make it stop. You will continue to come across Envoys in every world you visit unless you do something to prevent it.

"You mean kill every Envoy in sight," sighed the ponytaur. "I'm a warrior and a skilled killer, but I am not genocidal. Besides, I tried to fight off those Envoys in Uchu. They are unnaturally strong and daring. My troops and I were only able to kill a couple of them. What you suggest cannot be done."

Then neither can your dream. The voice paused to let it sink in. *If you are not willing to remove these obstacles, then there will be those who never find their true selves—all because the great Maewing backed down at one large barrier.*

"Enough!" Maewing shouted loudly, not caring if anyone heard. "My resolve is still firm, and we are almost ready for our next endeavor! My every ally is nearly prepared, and our target world was chosen months in advance. We will rescue people from oppression, and if we see any Envoys again, I will debate with them before attempting to kill them."

How did debating work out last time?

Maewing angrily punched the button on the table, which reverted back to normal, and she stormed out of the room. She stomped toward the main courtyard to gather her troops from throughout the multiverse.

Maewing!

She stopped short and turned around. This was a completely different voice, but again there was no one around. This one was loud and clear—and still male. She remembered hearing it before as a still and small voice, but this time it shouted, probably because Maewing had determined to tune it out.

"Who are you?" she shouted, still in a rage.

You know who I am.

Maewing grinned smugly. "What do you want?"

I want you. I want a relationship with you, time with you. I want to save you from this illusion. I love you.

Maewing hesitated. "Prove it."

I prove it every day. Open your eyes to see it.

"If you really loved me, I wouldn't have to look for proof. My eyes are wide open, and I see chaos in place of your love. If you truly were the King of the multiverse who controls everything, why is there so much plight in every single world?"

Much of it is a result of people's actions, independent ones at that. Our choices have consequences. Other dilemmas I still let happen, and I use it all to bring people to me . . . if they choose me. There is also justice for those who continue to live for self and don't choose me—who can give them true life and satisfaction.

"Why does everything have to be centered around you?" Maewing replied. "Why does anyone have to be the center of the multiverse? Why can't everyone simply be the center of his or her own lives?"

Mortals and cherubim alike have tried that since the beginning of time. That is precisely how all of this chaos began, and I've been healing it ever since.

"You have done a fantastic job," Maewing said sarcastically. "I am sorry. If you want me to trust you, you will need to give me more of a reason to trust you—such as protecting your Envoys from my wrath if I ever see any again!" She burst open her wings and darted out of the main entrance, flying speedily through the air in an attempt to escape this voice. It only came once more, more urgently now.

Maewing, do not run from me any further. I still love you.

Maewing only flew faster into the city of Laves, almost crashing into a skyscraper in the process.

The dusk sun shone blindingly through the windows of Theodore's warehouse office. He turned off his monitor, organized his papers (sister company synopses and promotion applications) in neat stacks on his stained oak desk. He had just gotten up to leave for the day when Amory knocked on the open door. Pleasantly surprised, Theodore continued to stand and greeted Amory with a handshake.

"Sorry for the timing of this," said Amory. "I know you're eager to get home."

"That's all right," Theodore replied as he sat back in his chair. "My wife doesn't mind when you're the reason I'm late. Come on in and take a seat. Welcome back, by the way! How was the honeymoon?"

"It was great!" Amory smiled. "The hotels and restaurants were nice, the beach was soothing, and the mountains were inspiring. It was one of the best times I've had with Bernice yet."

"I bet!" said Theodore. "Second only to fighting off goblins and evading military police, I'd imagine."

Amory snickered. "I just mean that wasn't the only good time we've had. It's definitely up there, though."

"Good. What brings you here?"

"The team's going on another mission tomorrow," Amory said somberly.

"I heard. Are you ready for it?"

"Sort of. I don't even know where we're going or what we're doing yet. I'm mostly used to that now. Honestly, I'm always ready to bring more people to Nazir. I just hope the Self-Worthy don't show up this time and ruin things. I asked Dilyn if he knew what their next stop was, but he left them before he could find out. So it's up in the air again, as it always has been."

"You're dwelling on this too much again, Amory," said Theodore. "You're still too wrapped up in them, and you need to let that go and trust that Nazir has planned this all along. Give that worry to him because he's the only one who can actually do anything worthwhile about it."

"I know, I know," Amory sighed. "That's why I'm over here, to talk through it again with you so you can talk me out of these thoughts. I seriously am trying, but it's hard when people's eternal destinies are at stake. I don't want anyone else to be deceived. I already have a good friend who's been taken in on their agenda for a while. I don't want there to be any more."

"Again, leave that to Nazir," Theodore said. "All you need to do is obey what you're commanded to do and leave the rest to your King. You're a leader, Amory, but you can't handle everything on your own. On a lighter note, what's the likelihood of you bumping into the Self-Worthy again in another world, when there are dozens of worlds out there?"

Amory nodded. "The chances are pretty slim, but it's already happened twice on two of our major missions."

Theodore paused for a second. "Then maybe Nazir has a reason for that. He must've crossed your paths on purpose—just as with everyone's paths—and he must have good reasons for it. That would be a good motivation for you to keep a level head in case they do show up again."

"I'll have to keep that in mind," Amory replied. "Man, I wish you were coming with us. I could use your voice on the field."

"Nazir's is the only one you need, and he hasn't made me a multiversal Envoy," said Theodore. "I'm meant to invest in my wife, my sons, my coworkers, you, and anyone else to whom Nazir leads me. I must be faithful in these areas."

"I know," grinned Amory. "One can hope, though."

"Good luck to you and the team," said Theodore. "May the Vine strengthen you in every way to accomplish this mission."

"Thank you, sir," said Amory as he got up, shook his hand, and hugged him. "I'll see you when and if I come back."

All twelve of Amory's team, bearing their armor and full backpacks, entered the Center one by one or in pairs. Excitement and nervousness were both displayed on each of their faces. The last to come was Chadmight, likely due to a big breakfast.

"Welcome, all of you!" Nazir exclaimed. "You all look splendid."

Thank you! signed Agabio, beaming. The others also extended their thanks.

"Congratulations to you, Dilyn, for graduating! That is a huge accomplishment, and you never gave up on it, even though you had excuses to recently. And congratulations to you, Mr. and Mrs. Walters! How was your honeymoon?"

"It was amazing!" said Bernice. "We got to spend time on the beach, which I enjoy, and the mountains, which Amory enjoys. It was super fun and relaxing, and I got to spend all that time with the love of my life."

"I couldn't have put it better," smiled Amory.

"Good. That is what I intended," said Nazir. "Now, about your mission. The world you will be entering, called Topiada, is on the brink of collapse. The two civilizations who live there have been in constant conflict with each other for millennia, and they've had many inconclusive wars. They have never made peace with each other, and despite my frequently sending other Envoys there, they refuse to turn to me or even consult me over this matter. Their warring has come to a head, and I have become livid with their stubbornness. If they do not turn to me soon, I myself will have that whole universe destroyed, as it would serve no other use to me. I have given them multiple chances to come to me, and they've taken none of them. By sending you twelve there, I am giving them one last chance. I am sending you to go to both cultures in my name and with my authority to make peace among them and to tell them my message of peace before it's too late. You will have pressuring distractions there, but you must stay focused on me, for a world's existence is at risk. I have equipped you with everything you need. You simply need to do the work and show my love. Is all of this clear?"

"I do have one question," Chadmight spoke up, "and this might only be because I'm new to all of this and I'm still learning about you. If you're the good King we believe you are, and you are indeed the source of goodness, how could it be possible for you to destroy a whole universe and everyone living in it?"

"A valid question, Chadmight," Nazir replied. "As loving and good as I am, I'm equally as just. This justice is not the opposite of love. In fact, they supplement each other, and justice is a very good thing as everyone knows. These people have rebelled against my authority and peace for millennia, and I've tried time and time again to snap them out of their twisted focus. They will not yield. Just as you deserved eternal torment before coming to me, so do they. The only difference between you and them is that you've actually submitted to me. They have not, and even though I love them just the same, my wrath must be satisfied on those who don't accept the alternative I've given. This is equally as good, as you will soon understand. This is not the first time I have done this. Many a portal in this Center has appeared and disappeared since time began, and more will follow."

"I think I understand," Chadmight said slowly.

"That alone should motivate us as we go!" said Amory. "Do you have any more instructions for us before we go, Dad?"

"Be watchful with each culture you enter," Nazir answered. "Although they are not shapeshifters like Masato, they will not be as they seem. Be discerning for the truth, and don't lose hope in or focus on me. I love these peoples, and I still want them to experience life fully. Now go and bring peace and unity and me to those who desperately need it."

"No pressure," Edna sighed.

"Yes, Father!" Amory smiled as he led the team through the portal Nazir had indicated. As she went through, Leona realized Dilyn wasn't with them and turned to see him lingering with the Vine. The portal's whiteness enveloped her, but she managed to hear what Dilyn said.

"This is my last mission, isn't it?"

She never heard the reply.

The Envoys suddenly found themselves in a thick, green forest. Unlike some worlds they'd been to, this one seemed to be teeming with life. The very air around them was luscious to breathe. And no wonder, for plants of all kinds surrounded them. They occasionally found a familiar bush or flower, but beyond that, every form of shrubbery here was grossly foreign to everyone present. They beheld plants of varying colors and forms which they thought were impossible. The trees, however, were much the same here as they were in every other world that had them: tall, strong trunks and branches with green leaves and different fruits or nuts. There were also several fallen trees and ruined logs.

Dilyn arrived a few minutes after the others, before most of them realized he wasn't there. He too took in all this life, wondering how this could be at the brink of destruction. Then again, they hadn't met its intelligent inhabitants yet.

"New vacation spot," Edna piped up.

"That is, if we can save it," Amory replied.

"Who are you jesting?" said Panos. "If the people will let Nazir save it. We are not the saviors of this world any more than we are that of our own."

"I know," Amory grinned. "My bad. Now to find the people. Do any directions stand out to any of you?"

"What directions?" Neisha answered. "There are no paths anywhere. Everything's too bustling with plant life."

"Honestly, I don't think it'd hurt to just pick a direction," said Masato. "I don't think it'll make that much of a difference."

"Yeah, let's just go the direction we were facing when we came in," said Dilyn.

"Good idea," Amory said. "Let's go."

The twelve set out, watching their steps as they sifted between trees and amidst frequent thorns. After a while, they realized that Agabio was lagging behind, minding his step and surroundings a little too much. Amory decided to slow everyone's pace and follow up at the back of the pack to make sure Agabio was all right. Since Chadmight was the largest, they let him lead the way and basically plow a path for them. He didn't mind a bit and was happy to be of use.

Masato also turned into a hawk, darting from tree to tree and looking out for anything that moved. For a couple of hours, nothing did, save themselves. However, they did hear the frequent crackling of branches on any given side. As time went on, the crackling happened more often. The Envoys gripped their weapons tighter, and Dilyn and Nels put arrows to their bows.

"Be alert, but stay your weapons," Amory said to them. "We have to show whoever's watching us that we mean them no harm, even if they mean the opposite."

"He is right," said Twyla, putting her knives back. "Besides, we do not know if they intend to harm us. Perhaps they are merely curious observers."

"Whatever they are, I just wish I could see them!" said Panos.

"You'll soon get your wish one way or another," said Nels.

"Hello!" Amory called out to whoever was listening. "Greetings! We mean you no harm. In fact, we bring peace. We're Envoys of Nazir, and we've come to tell you about his—"

Suddenly, several brown, croaking beings leaped at the Envoys from all sides, attacking them with various spiked weapons. The startled Envoys got out their weapons and fought back. After regaining their bearings and dealing some blows, they were better able to see the creatures that were ambushing them. They were humanoid tree-like beings with browned grass and leaves for hair, wood for skin, sap for blood, and bark for armor. Their heads were like most of the Envoys present, as were their arms (although some had more than two arms), which held widespread, multi-fingered branch "swords" that withstood clashing with the visitors' metal weapons. These creatures had no legs, only elongated torsos with roots that moved like tentacles underground, surfacing when the creatures jumped. The sounds they made were either low croaks or high creaks, depending on the gender.

"Please stop!" said Bernice, deflecting branches with her spear. "We don't want to hurt you! We come in peace, and we have a message for you!"

The tree people only roared in return as they continued to fight, apparently intent on killing their victims. However, they seemed to not know where to aim for fatal strikes, as their blows were very random. Out of the corner of his eye, Panos saw Agabio running from two assailants, dodging the normal trees as he sped around. The faun looked back at his pursuers only to crash into another tree. He cowered at its base as the tree people darted toward him. Panos had no time to think. He ran to his friend's aid.

"Panos, don't!" Amory shouted.

It was too late. Charging like a bull, Panos lethally headbutted one creature and impaled the other with his trident. He then reached a hand out to the faun.

"Have courage, my friend," Panos said as he brought Agabio to his hooves. "Nazir's given us all the training we need for this."

They looked and saw that the tree people were fighting more angrily now, and the duo were soon attacked by more.

"Don't kill any more of them!" Amory scolded. "We're supposed to bring these people to life, not death!"

"Then we will die instead!" said Masato, back in his normal form, as he almost stabbed one being's throat. "They won't stop until we're all dead."

"I don't care!" Amory replied. "Better to die in obedience to Nazir than to survive only by disobeying him!"

The rest of the team complied and avoided dealing deadly strikes. They switched to only defensive maneuvers, which seemed to work for the time being. Dilyn only fired his arrows at the creatures' hands to disarm them. He'd succeeded quite a few times before the creatures began to strategize and shot in more closely at Dilyn, preventing him from loading anymore arrows. He resorted to wielding his bow to block oncoming attacks. After a couple of swings, he found that he'd sliced halfway through one being's arm. He then realized just how sharp the spokes on his bow were and that they were meant to be blades. He used them more rapidly now.

Leona was having a harder time. A foursome of tree people had isolated her from the team and pinned her against a trunk. Everyone else was too occupied to notice, despite her calls for help. Leona was doing her best to keep up. While she used several martial arts kicks and punches (takedowns wouldn't work on them), it was hard to use her axe without getting dangerously close. It was even hard to block all the branches. At one point, one attacker sliced down at the top of her axe mid-swing with incredible strength, splitting the axe from top to bottom and cutting Leona's palm. She dropped the pieces and held her hand in pain. She looked in awe and anguish at her severed weapon, which she was so sure was indestructible because it came from her father and king. It was then that she noticed that each half looked exactly like a kama, a short scythe like those she used in her old dojo. Then she noticed the clips on the handles where it had split.

It was made to be split all along, she thought. *That's why the blades weren't symmetrical!*

Instinctively ducking from a creature's attempt at a stab, Leona quickly picked up her two kamas and stood poised to fight again, with a new style with which she was much more familiar. Two of the four tree people attacked her at once. She blocked both blows and used the curved blades to hook the branch swords and drag the creatures into each other. After that, she proceeded to block with one blade and strike with the other, gaining newfound confidence with each move. Suddenly, a fifth soldier snuck in behind her and grabbed her ankles with two of its roots. It yanked her to the ground and toward itself as it poised its jaw-like branch sword for a stab. Then it reeled back with a shriek and let go of her ankles. Leona quickly slid aside as it faceplanted to the ground, an unfamiliar throwing axe lodged in its back.

The tree people roared as more axes and arrows flew at them, killing a couple. The Envoys watched as a large squadron of red-clad warriors burst forth from the shrubbery and fell upon the tree people. Both sides fought with incredible skill and fury, but the tree people were outnumbered. After about a dozen were killed, they decided to retreat. The creatures scurried off and vanished into the forest within seconds. The warriors in red would've usually given chase, but for the sake of the visitors, they stayed. The Envoys soon realized that these warriors were human. One burlier man with a double-edged, sap-stained broadsword—who seemed to be the leader of the band—turned to the Envoys, who'd become fairly spread out.

"You are new to this world, yes?" asked the man with an old German accent, looking the Envoys over.

"Yes," heaved Amory. He noted that every man and woman in this squadron wore red armor and capes and white tunics and helmets.

The man continued to look around at all of them. "Some of you are human!" he exclaimed. "Others of you I have heard tales about. Still others I have never seen nor heard of until now. How came you here? Did you arrive through a whirlpool or a crevasse?"

"No, we came voluntarily," Amory answered, unsheathing his Dagger. "We use these to make portals in between worlds. We are Envoys of Nazir, who sends us to proclaim his peace to several worlds."

"I see," said the man with a slight frown. "In any case, we witnessed you all fighting the arborves. Therefore, you are their enemies and must be our allies. Welcome to the ranks of the New Topiadan army! Baron Rolle, at your service." Rolle gave a bow as he said this.

"Amory Walters," said Amory, doing his best to mimic the bow. "I'm the leader of our Envoy team, and I take orders from King Nazir himself."

"I am well aware of what Envoys do," Rolle said somberly. "Come, join us as we journey back to our village. Our princess is there gathering troops to hopefully end this accursed war we are in. She would be delighted to meet you."

"All right," said Amory. "Lead the way. We actually have a message for you, and I'm sure your princess will need to hear it."

"Indeed," replied the baron. "She would love to give ear to a message from her new allies. One way or another, it is best to save your message until we are in a safer atmosphere."

As the groups started off, Edna moved her way to the front where Rolle, Amory, and Bernice were. "So those tree people are called . . . what was it you said?"

"Arborves," Rolle answered. "Those beasts who have terrorized us since our ancestors first set foot in this world."

"Then I'm assuming they're the ones you're at war with," said Bernice, putting two and two together.

"Yes. Our strife with them has lingered for centuries, and we hope this attack we are planning will end it once and for all."

"This is not the first time I have heard those words," said a new voice, old yet clear.

Everyone turned to see something like an elf emerge from a nearby thicket. He had a five o'clock shadow and silver hair that reached his feet. He wore a leather belt and boots, a tan robe, a red bandana, and a battle-worn expression. He also had two transparent wings folded behind him. Rolle's band knew him, but none of the Envoys save Twyla and Nels knew who this was.

"You are Wybirt the Zealous!" Twyla exclaimed. "You are that great fairy warrior of old who wielded a sword with a bright flame for its blade!"

The fairy lowered his head and sighed. "Aye, I am he."

"Legend has it you disappeared in the Battle for Balterdane!" said Nels. "Everyone thought you were dead!"

"To them, I must remain so. I possessed such a reputation that everyone expected me to fight for them, to put on a good show. I knew not how to escape it without dishonor. During that battle—which, if you remember, was in a gorge—I fell into a crevasse that apparently transported me to this world. I knew not how to return, nor did I desire to. I have lived here ever since that day."

"I am sorry that you ended up here in the midst of this tumult," Rolle said. "Might I inquire the reason of your presence, Wybirt? Have you finally come to accept our several invitations over the decades to aid us in our conflict with the arborves?"

"Heavens, no," Wybirt said sternly. "I told you I prefer to avoid battles now. My house is nearby, as you should know, baron. I heard a commotion outside cluttered with voices of beings I'd never heard, so I came to see what it was about."

"It was merely another skirmish between the arborves and these new Envoy visitors who have become our allies," Rolle responded. "We swiftly put an end to it, you can rest assured."

"I see," said Wybirt. "Well, if this keeps occurring near to my residence, you can rest assured that I will swiftly put an end to all parties involved." The fairy proceeded to indicate a golden hilt attached to his belt. Then, he turned back the way he came.

"Well, that was quite a sight, wasn't it, sister?" said Nels, looking around for Neisha. After searching the group and calling several times, he realized she was missing. He hurried to tell Amory this.

"Come to think of it, where's Dilyn?" said Leona.

"And Agabio!" cried Panos. "He has also disappeared, and I regretfully have only now noticed!"

"Last I saw any of them, we were fighting the arborves," said Edna. "Do you think they took them? Or maybe . . . ."

"They had to have captured them," Bernice said. "Do arborves take prisoners, baron?"

"Yes, they do," Rolle said more angrily. "They usually keep their prisoners alive . . . for special purposes."

"We have to go back for them!" said Amory.

"We are too few in number and will be slain before we even get to where they are taking them. Believe me, we are already planning a rescue mission. Come with us so we can increase our numbers before we make that venture. I guarantee that your friends will survive until we get there."

Amory looked at his team who had all turned pale. They didn't want to take sides just yet, but this seemed like their only choice of saving their teammates. They decided to trek on with the humans.

11

A DISTORTED HISTORY

The nine remaining Envoys didn't realize how high the mountains here were until they had to climb them. Baron Rolle's squadron took them over about five peaks by Twyla's count. Every one of them was blanketed with trees and bushes of every kind. Everyone present kept an eye and an ear out for anything resembling an arborf but thankfully found nothing. They stopped only once to eat a quick lunch, much to the relief of a panting Nels and Chadmight. Throughout the whole journey, all the Envoys could do was worry about their absent teammates and about how this princess would receive their message.

At about dusk, they finally arrived at the encampment. It consisted of thirty log cabins, each large enough to house a hundred soldiers. Every cabin had a straw-thatched roof and a few small windows. All of it looked quite cozy and homely except for the restless troops and busy outdoor blacksmiths everywhere. The Envoys also noticed that there were very few trees in this area. Rolle's garrison led their guests further up the mountain to the end of the encampment, where sat a cabin larger than the rest. They went inside and saw that it was an enormous, two-story dining hall, each floor having three rows of long, wooden tables and benches complete with rugged candles. Attendants were busy preparing the tables for dinner, lighting the candles and dusting off the benches. The soldiers and Envoys walked past these to the end of the cabin where there were four wooden thrones painted red. In the furthest one on the right sat a young woman, no older than Edna. She had short, blonde hair and a frowning, battle-scarred face. She wore the same armor and garb as every other human here, except for a silver tiara instead of a helmet.

The baron stepped in front of the others and knelt before the woman, the other troops following suit. "Hail, Princess Valma," he said. "I return from our scouting endeavor with good reports and nine new recruits who come from several other worlds, including our ancestors' world."

At that, the Envoys knelt as well, quite intrigued by Rolle's last statement. The princess shifted in her seat, her expression remaining unchanged.

"Who are you, and what is your business here?" she asked grimly in Rolle's accent.

"I am Amory, and this is my wife, Bernice. These are Leona, Edna, Chadmight, Masato, Nels, Panos, and Twyla. We do hail from other worlds, but we do not yet claim to be recruits. We are Envoys of Nazir, and we have a message for you and your people as well as the arborves."

Valma's eyebrows furrowed. "I have heard stories like this. Nazir himself sent you, and you came voluntarily?"

"Yes, my lady," Bernice answered, unsheathing her Dagger. "We use these to get from one universe to another, wherever Nazir tells us to go."

"This is very fascinating," said Valma. "However you arrived here, I am grateful you did so that you may aid us in ending this brutal war. The top priority, though, is to hearken your message, as that was your initial purpose in coming." Then she stood up and faced Rolle's troops and the attendants. "Hark! Everyone present, come listen to these Envoys' message. No one leaves this room until they have finished. It must be critical if it brought otherworldly people here. Perhaps Nazir has some good fortune for us."

"Actually, your majesty, it's quite the opposite," Amory began. "Nazir says this to both you humans and the arborves: Both of your civilizations have been at war with each other long enough. There has been nothing but strife among you for millennia, and none of you over the years have sought to make peace. Your only goal seems to be to defeat or even eliminate the other, and you refuse to let go of your bitterness. This conflict has come to a head, and Nazir cannot stand to watch you tear each other apart any longer. He loves you and wants you to experience life with him, but you don't want it for yourselves. If you don't make peace with Nazir himself first, and also with the arborves, then Nazir will destroy all of Topiada, and no one will be spared."

The princess sat still and waited to see if Amory was finished. When she realized he was, she sat back on her throne, mouth open, deep in thought. All eyes were on her as she pondered this for what seemed like several minutes.

"There are so many factors that play into this," she finally said. "Everything we've ever known would be at stake if this is true. Then comes the question of whether or not it is true."

"Take it from us, your majesty," replied Nels, "whatever Nazir says, goes."

"Nazir made this plain and simple," added Leona. "Don't focus on all the *what ifs*. Just take him at his word and obey while you still can!"

"This is all assuming that Nazir is indeed real and that he is a man—or whatever he is—of his word," the princess replied. "But I will resolve this matter at another time, likely the next time I see my father, the king. Until then, I will consider this message as well as its gravity."

"Why would you delay something as grave as this?" Panos asked. "You have little to gain and everything to lose by waiting!"

"I told you my conclusion," Valma said sternly. "It will not change at this time. Discussing terms with Nazir, assuming he exists, might be possible, but I am afraid peace with the arborves is unachievable."

"Hold on," said Masato. "How did all of this conflict start? Perhaps we can help you come up with a solution."

Valma nodded. "It is nearly dinner time, and my troops are hungry. Let us wait until then. You all may sit with me, and as we sup, I will tell you our history."

The Envoys agreed to this and volunteered to help the attendants finish preparing. Once everything was cleaned off, they helped put wooden plates and chalices at every place at the tables. Each plate was filled with a variety of foreign vegetables and fruits cooked in various ways, including methods that the visitors had never thought of. Nels was quite disappointed that there was no meat, although he didn't remember seeing any animals on this world yet. Maybe there was nothing of the animal kingdom in Topiada save themselves.

Each chalice was filled with either water, juice, or wine. Chadmight voluntarily requested water, which impressed both Amory and Panos. Once everything was ready, Valma sent heralds outside to notify everyone that dinner was served. The three thousand men and women in this battalion gradually made their way inside and sat down, starting at the top story where Rolle was. The Envoys claimed their spots near the head of the center table downstairs where Valma sat. Everyone waited until all were seated before Valma arose from her seat at the table.

"Tonight we feast, and tomorrow we fight!" she shouted, and the soldiers repeated her statement. "May you bask in merriness today and in the glory of victory tomorrow!" Everyone cheered in return and dug in, and the Envoys followed along.

After a few bites into what looked like a pomegranate and tasted like cherries, Valma turned to her guests. "To keep my word that I gave you earlier, I shall now tell you how the strife between us and the arborves began. It started, as you have already said, a few millennia ago in another world, presumably the one from which you humans originate. In that world, our ancestors grew up in a nation riddled with war, as it is here. As mere youths, they joined up with thousands of other youths to retake from their enemies a sacred city in a faraway land, something their fathers had failed to do more than once. Unfortunately our ancestors also failed before they even arrived. The massive army of children was dispersed in various ways after several complications."

"The Children's Crusade," Leona thought aloud.

"I beg your pardon?" Valma said.

"You're talking about the Children's Crusade, something that happened on Earth hundreds of years ago exactly as you described. Time must move faster here if you already have thousands of years' worth of history."

"Yes, *crusade*," said Valma thoughtfully. "That was a word our people had sometimes used when telling this story."

"Then you really are from our world!" exclaimed Edna.

"How did you end up here?" asked Chadmight.

"After several factions occurred, our fathers hired a boat crew to sail them to the land of the sacred city, still determined to conquer it," Valma sad. "On the way, they came across an unnatural whirlpool at a time when the sea was calm. Unable to avoid it, the ship careened inside the tunnel of water. The ship began to break apart, and a handful of the crew and children were killed. To the survivors' surprise, they emerged from the surface after being underwater for only a few seconds. When they surfaced, they could instantly tell that they were in a completely different place. The air was richer and the water thicker. A hundred of them were adrift on what was left of the ship for a couple of hours before coming to a foggy shore filled with trees."

Valma continued. "Immediately after putting their feet on ground, arborves came out of a nearby thicket, and they met for the first time. It was not a pleasant meeting, however, as the arborves proceeded to kill all of the adult crew members and then started on the children. The first of countless battles ensued that day. Just when fear and dismay had overcome all our fathers, one boy, named Morrison, managed to start a fire on the land. He lit several loose branches and passed them to his friends and told them to do the same until every child had a flame to wield. Morrison was able to burn and kill the leader of that arborven band and sent every arborf left alive running.

"The children celebrated their first victory that day and made Morrison their new king, crowning him with a laurel of leaves from the fallen arborven leader. Morrison, from that day forward, would be called King Lauris, and his lineage would consist of all human rulers of Topiada, ending thus far with me and my absent brother. Since that day, we and the arborves have been in constant battle. My mother has died by their hands, and I will never forget that. We have not been able to technologically advance due to their constant raids, although we have plenty of ideas, as I am sure you do too. So tell me, do you see any way to make peace with those monsters other than by eliminating them?"

All of the Envoys thought long and hard. It was hard to deny the trickiness of the humans' circumstances. The fact was that peace needed to be made.

Bernice spoke up first. "Have you or your ancestors ever tried making a treaty or truce, or simply talking with them through the issues you have?"

"We have a few times over the ages," said the princess. "The arborves are aggressive by nature and know not the concept of peace talks."

"Have any of you heard of the concept of forgiveness?" Masato asked half-sarcastically.

Valma gave a sideways glare to the tanuki. "Yes, and we humans exercise it quite frequently amongst ourselves. However, it is difficult to forgive someone who refuses to change."

"That does not matter," said Panos. "The very meaning of forgiveness is to release someone from a debt they owe you. This pertains to money and other items and even apologies or a change of behavior. Trust in the debtor must still be earned, but forgiveness is not. It's a gift, and it's something Nazir gives freely to all who accept their pride and need of forgiveness from him. It's also a part of his character that he commands all of us to portray to those around us."

Valma paused to ponder this. "That will not change our dilemma with them."

"You would be surprised," said Twyla. "I beg of you, just do something that would prevent any further bloodshed!"

"I am afraid bloodshed is inevitable now," Valma replied. "You see, the arborves have recently captured my brother, Prince Valter, and imprisoned him in the arborven capital where their King Cosnoaldo resides. This is where the rest of your team will likely be taken, according to what Baron Rolle has told me. We have heard rumors that in that capital stands a mysterious tree whose sap, if touched by a human, can turn him or her into an arborf. If this is true, then that would mean Cosnoaldo, who has no offspring, will attempt to make my brother like him and therefore his suggestible heir. This cannot happen. I do not wish for my brother to be manipulated and controlled by anyone, especially an arborf. My father, King Hilmar, has rallied all ten thousand of his troops to march upon the arborven capital, take Valter back, and destroy the arborves, their leaders and legacy, and their city once and for all. On the morrow, my battalion will join his, and we will set out. Will you go with us? Baron Rolle tells me you all are incredible warriors, as he has witnessed."

Amory thought for a second and looked for his friends' concurrence. "We will go with you, if only to speak with your father. We cannot promise to fight alongside you. We were sent to help you make peace with the arborves, not try and find peace by taking them out of the picture."

"I agree, but what about Dilyn, Agabio, and Neisha?" asked Edna. "How are we going to get them out? If what her majesty says is true, won't the arborves try to turn them into their own kind too?"

"I don't know," Amory answered, rubbing his stressed face. "For now, we'll just have to hope they'll hold their own and give the arborves the same message until I can think of another option."

Neisha awoke to a constant pricking in her back. She found herself lying sideways in a thin ball of branches, formed and weaved by the arborf who carried her over its head. She tried to lift her head, but there was no room to. She then realized that her armor and shields were gone. She caught a glance of them being carried by another arborf behind her in what seemed to be a growing procession of arborves. Careful not to stab herself, she tried moving the branches around to find any loose spots. She found none.

"I already tried that," came Dilyn's voice. Neisha strained to turn and saw him getting carried in a similar cage in front of her. He was also devoid of his armor. "Best just to wait and see where they take us," he continued. "They'll likely want to learn more about us unless they end up being complete savages."

Neisha nodded. "Aye, good idea." She caught a glimpse of Agabio in front of them both. He was hunched up in his cage, fearing what would become of him and his friends.

"Agabio," Neisha called. He looked toward her slightly. "We'll be all right. If they wanted us dead, we would be by now. Nazir is protecting us. Keep asking him for courage; he hears you."

Agabio nodded and closed his eyes, talking to the Vine in his head. His body relaxed a little after doing this for a time. The ever-increasing band of arborves carried them through the forest for another half hour before their captives caught sight of an enormous, slanted tree at the edge of the thicket they were in. The tree's trunk alone stood as wide and tall as a skyscraper, reaching twenty stories high or more. Its redwood branches shaded acres of the forest and the nearby prairie below. The Envoys guessed correctly that this was their destination.

The arborves moved quicker now, making the rest of the journey to the massive tree in about forty minutes. They got to the base of the tree, where several guards kept watch. The visitors and the guards communicated in a language full of unutterable groans, creaks, and clicks. After a moment, the guards gave a low holler—something like a signal—and a large door opened vertically, perfectly camouflaged in bark. The arborven captors then carried the Envoys inside, which was engulfed in pitch black darkness. Dilyn supposed that these creatures must have good night vision. The Envoys couldn't even hear themselves breathe over the sounds of the hundreds of otherworldly voices around them.

At last they saw light. Daylight. As the procession emerged from the entry tunnel, the prisoners discovered that a giant chunk of the tree was gutted out, exposing a lot of it to some much-needed sunlight. (Like all plants, arborves lived on photosynthesis.) A city was built into the remaining wood of the tree, much like Glatinth was built from a carved-out cliff. Male and female arborves trudged to and fro amongst huts and stands on several floors connected by ramps and ladders. There were no buildings of any kind here. Apparently arborves worked and slept outside, which made sense if they were like trees. Additionally, every surface the arborves moved on was coated in a thick layer of rich dirt, nourishing them as they drank its moisture with the roots they crawled on.

Using ramps, the arborves took their captives all the way to the top of the tree, hidden by its branches but still exposed to some light. As they ascended, the Envoys noticed that almost all of the arborves had blonde hair and brown leaves and differing skin (wood) tones. There were a handful of exceptions who had green hair and leaves, and these seemed to be a lot more lively and aware. Agabio took note of this.

They finally reached the very top where sat amongst the shrouds of leaves a giant throne, which itself was part of the tree, surrounded by dozens of guards. Seated on it was an arborf much larger than the rest, reaching almost ten feet in height. His beard, hair, and leaves were brown and his skin beige. He also had three arms on either side of his torso; their thickness showed he'd lived many years. The arborves carrying the Envoys retracted into their hands the branches that made up the cages and threw their prisoners on the dirty floor before the larger creature. It and the visiting troopers talked in their own language for a second, likely talking about the skirmish and how the Envoys had arrived.

After they finished, the larger creature spoke to the captives in broken English (one must appreciate a tree's effort to speak as humans and dwarves do). "I am King Cosnoaldo of the arborves. You are human, but you wear different armor and clothing than the other humans here. Who are you?"

"We are Envoys of the Vine Nazir, King of the multiverse *Rôb Têbêl,*" said Neisha. "This faun and I are actually not human, and we all hail from other worlds on a mission to see you and the humans."

The arborven king lowered his head slowly. "This is just what we needed, more otherworldly intruders," he said sarcastically.

"What do you mean by that, your highness?" Dilyn asked.

"Topiada is the realm of the arborves, who are its original inhabitants," Cosnoaldo said. "Millennia ago, our kind was visited by alien humans who arrived on a vessel made of tree flesh. My father led a small band to investigate this unusual occurrence, and the sight of dead trees frightened them. My father grabbed one of the adult men to question him but apparently held him too tightly, not knowing that these creatures weren't as sturdy as we are. He killed the man instantly, which incited the other far younger humans to attack us. They used a weapon which was then new to us: fire." Uttering the word made Cosnoaldo growl. "They killed many arborves that day, including my father, whom I succeeded. I have been attempting vengeance on them ever since that dreadful day, and I will not stop until all of Lauris's heirs repay me with their lives."

"That was thousands of years ago, your majesty," said Neisha. "What has that cost you thus far, and what have you gained?"

"Oh, this conflict has cost my people dearly," the king replied. "Their zeal against the humans is as fierce as mine, and many have lost their lives in the countless battles we've encountered. At one point, my old palace was attacked and destroyed by fire, but I and a handful of others escaped. Xenia, the largest and firstborn of all still trees in Topiada, offered her life so that her trunk could be a fortress and sanctuary for us. Her remains are what we are standing on today, and for ages this Palace of Xenia has been a place of refuge for my people. The humans have not yet been able to lay siege to it.

"As for what I have gained from this grueling endeavor, my vengeance is almost quenched. I have come so close to extinguishing Lauris's dynasty, only for one or two heirs to escape. But now I have a plan to end it completely. My forces have captured the human prince and have made him touch the sap of our sacred tree beneath this palace. Anyone who touches that sap starts to become an arborf themselves. This true rumor will reach, threaten, and allure the current human king and princess here. Whether they come in stealth or numbers will not matter. I will use this trap to end their reign and finally avenge my father. Then and only then will there be peace, something which I have long yearned for."

"But that's why we've come, your majesty!" said Dilyn. "Nazir sent us to you with a message of how to obtain true peace that lasts longer than vengeance and indeed lasts forever!"

Cosnoaldo leaned in closely, holding up two of his hands to quiet his nearby subjects. "I am listening."

Dilyn took a breath. "Nazir says that your people and the humans have gone without peace long enough—peace primarily with him and with each other. This tumult has caused too much pain and death, which you yourself have admitted, O King. Nazir has stated that if you don't come to terms with him first, and then the humans, then Nazir will personally destroy all of Topiada, as it would serve no further purpose."

The king and his guards stood still for a moment, deep in thought . . . but only for a moment. "Many an Envoy have come and gone with similar messages over the centuries," he said. "They all came with threats and urges from the Vine, insisting that we make amends with the humans. None of them understood that humans are free thinking and flighty, and they cannot understand our ancient wisdom and insight. Coming to terms with them is impossible."

"Would you at least consider talking to the Vine?" Neisha asked. "I know he'd be delighted to see you."

Cosnoaldo growled. "Envoys in the past have taken me to him before, but I cannot trust him if he claims what he does while standing still in his own bubble. It is all foolishness to me."

But he does do everything he says, signed Agabio to his friends' surprise. They couldn't tell, but he was using a different sign language now, using slower, more rigid motions he knew the arborves understood. *Even though he doesn't move, he still controls things somehow. He redeemed me, he brought my friends to me, and he brought us to you.*

Cosnoaldo, shocked that this creature knew their sign language, signed back to him and said aloud, "My troops brought you to me, fool! How can you be so blind to such obvious things? My patience is draining, so I give you this final offer. See if you all can understand this: since you claim to bring peace, will you help me obtain it by extinguishing Topiada's wretched invaders?"

The trio didn't hesitate.

"We will not," Neisha said firmly.

"You have given the wrong answer," said the king, motioning for his guards to grab them. "Take them down to our sacred tree! Once they have all touched the sap, put them away with the prince until they are fully transformed. They will indeed fight with us."

The Envoys were quickly jostled back down the giant tree, hands bound by the guards' morphed arms. They had not gone far when they saw a shiny object shoot up from outside the foot of the tree. It took Dilyn a second to recognize it as a modern-day missile from Earth. It suddenly turned toward the open courtyard and shot straight into it, causing a massive explosion and several fires. Hundreds of heart-wrenching shrieks could be heard as the nearest surviving soldiers and townspeople immediately set to putting out the fires with whatever water they had. The Envoys, knocked over with their guards, then heard a smaller explosion at the base of the palace and saw from the aftermath and smoke several armored creatures emerging, killing everyone in sight.

"No," Dilyn mumbled. "They were coming here!"

A shadow brushed over the Envoys, and they beheld Maewing zipping everywhere around them, annihilating arborven troops and citizens. There was no hesitation in any of her movements, just pure determination. As the Self-Worthy made their way upward, the Envoys' captors got up and continued to smuggle them downward, trying to find alternate routes where the attackers wouldn't meet them.

"Did you know about this?" Neisha shouted at Dilyn as they hurried along.

"No!" Dilyn replied. "I left before I heard their next plans!"

They rounded a corner and came across two Self-Worthy bears with masks, indicating they were tanuki. Before they could pounce on the arborves, Cosnoaldo leaped from a nearby ledge and smashed one bear and kicked the other off the platform with his roots. He called in the arborven tongue, so the prisoners didn't understand him. "Every soldier to battle, and every able-bodied citizen tend to the fires! Protect Xenia from these wicked Envoys who deceived us!"

Someone nearby replied to him in the same language, but the king said nothing as he plunged into the battle below them.

Ambrose and Lisias helped lead the Self-Worthy legions at the foot of the palace. Neither of them had seen creatures like these arborves before. Their spiky branch swords and furious expressions daunted their attackers quite a bit.

"Be brave, friends!" called Ambrose. "Today we take the arborven king and take yet another step toward Topiada's liberation!"

They pressed forward, able to subdue and kill every foe who stood in their way. Ambrose thought he was getting pretty good with his cutlass. He confidently bobbed and weaved between enemy jabs and could slay an opponent with little more than a parry. He also frequently used his wrist-held crossbow for any enemies out of his sword's reach. He cared little for the allies beside him and never looked to see if they were faring well. Why should he? Everyone was supposed to look out for him or herself. Any help given would create dependence. He looked further ahead and saw a huge arborf charging at them from an above floor.

"That must be Cosnoaldo!" cried Lisias. "He is our primary target! Brace yourselves!"

The king wriggled his way toward his invaders with intense fury, deeply desiring to trample them all. Just before he reached them, Maewing swept down and kicked him aside with all four of her legs. The king fell on his side but quickly got back up and roared. Maewing came at him again in midair, trying to slice his arms, body, or head in any way she could. She darted to and fro with incredible awareness of Cosnoaldo's six arms. Ambrose was quite impressed by her finesse, which made him thankful she was their leader. It inspired him to fight harder against the foes in front of him while Maewing handled the king.

Then, out of the corner of his eye, he saw Cosnoaldo bait Maewing with one hand and grab her with two others. He then tossed her through a distant wall of the giant tree, and she didn't come back out. The king then started to charge at the troops again, forcing Ambrose to run for cover.

The Envoys and their captors picked up the pace even more and were close to the bottom of the tree when they encountered three more Self-Worthy members. The arborves made branch swords with their hands and started to fight off the intruders, still holding onto the Envoys. The Envoys were thrown back and forth as the arborves tried to keep the prisoners away from the attackers. They fought in a style very foreign to the Self-Worthy, and no one seemed to best the other for a while. In the scuffle, the Envoys gradually found themselves being peeled away from their captors and snatched by other branch hands. Before they knew it, they were being hauled further inside the bottom of the tree by a three-armed, female arborf quite eager to hide her new, still-struggling prizes.

12
THE SIMMERING

L et go of us!" Neisha screamed as the female arborf continued to pull her, Agabio, and Dilyn away from the fray. "We will not be turned against our king! We will not contribute to this war's horrors!"

"I certainly hope not," said the arborf in broken English.

The Envoys stopped struggling as the creature pulled them closer to one of the few natural lights in the hallway they were in. The Envoys could now see that this arborf was one of the handful who had green hair and leaves. She was also wearing a familiar badge and metal armor.

"My name is Malfreda," the arborf continued. "I am also an Envoy, and I believe every word you told our king. Far too long have our kinds been obsessed with war and vengeance, and I, too, am tired of it. I have tried to appeal to the king and tell him, but he has not listened to me, as he did not listen to you. They are all blinded by their desires and bitterness, and that is why there are so many whose leaves are brown. They refuse to let go of their old leaves—burdens and bitterness—as a still tree would let go of its leaves, and they cannot experience life and freedom and greenness without doing this."

"Oh," sighed Dilyn, taking all this in. "So is every green arborf we've seen an Envoy too?"

"Sadly, no," Malfreda answered. "Indeed, there are some Envoy arborves whom Nazir has redeemed, and they did let go of their burdens then. But just as still trees must release their foliage annually, so every arborf experiences new burdens in various cycles. Some have still refused to forgive the humans, and their leaves have turned brown again, having yet to be let go of."

"I think our kinds are similar in that way, just without the leaves," said Neisha.

"You would be surprised at how similar every creature is," said Malfreda. "Many are too stubborn or ignorant to see it. Come, let us get out of the palace while we are still hidden. This battle will distract my kin enough to keep them away from us. Our king thinks the attackers are all Envoys coming to rescue you, but I know they are not, and I tried to tell him a bit ago that Envoys would never do this. We Envoys are not meant to fight battles, only to keep the peace."

The trio hesitated at this statement. Agabio signed to her, *But you have armor like we do. Did Nazir not give you any weapons?*

In response, Malfreda grabbed from behind her back two urumi, or whip swords with a wooden-looking Damascus steel pattern on each blade, previously concealed by her long, grassy hair. Agabio recognized them from the prophecy but didn't have time to acknowledge it.

Malfreda said, "I have yet to use these, even against my doppelgänger, and I only would to defend myself or someone else."

"What about your homeland or another's homeland?" Neisha asked. "Your own world's existence is on the line as we speak, and you're saying you would rather passively watch it all die? Nazir has sent us to fight against people before, and when he commanded it, it was just. Granted, we have personally taken it too far a time or two, but there is a balance."

"I refuse to believe that violence is ever the right answer," the arborf replied. "But we can discuss this further another time. We have to get out of Xenia while we still can. I do not know whether she will fall or remain standing after such an assault, but I am not waiting to find out."

"Neither are we," Dilyn replied. "Lead on."

Malfreda quickly put back her urumi and led her new friends down several dark or dimly lit passageways in the palace's interior, descending closer and closer to the ground. They turned one corner and saw their missing armor and weapons lying on the ground. Malfreda revealed that she'd taken and stashed the trio's equipment before rescuing them.

Thanking her, they rearmed themselves and pressed on. It was obvious that they were getting further from the battle that still raged on. However, the smoke, clamor, and shrieks were unignorable. This was by far the most devastating attack on the Palace of Xenia in arborven history. In the occasional lights, Agabio caught glimpses of tears on Malfreda's face.

You're crying, the faun signed. Malfreda was thankful he didn't say it aloud. *Is this your home?*

It has been my home for several years, the arborf signed back. *The humans raided my original home decades ago, and I wandered for a while before coming here and finding Nazir. I have even been reunited with some family and friends here. I do not know what will become of them after today.*

That is sad! Agabio replied. *I'm sorry. I hope your family and home will still be all right.*

Malfreda signed *thank you* just before they came to a dead end, a solid wooden wall just like all the others. The Envoys decided to remain silent as Malfreda turned a disguised, hand-sized disc that was built into the wall to their left. After turning it completely, she watched the wall in front of them begin to rise. Twilight nearly blinded them as they emerged from the giant tree, which was becoming more engulfed in flames and terror.

"Do you know where the humans usually live?" Dilyn asked. "There were twelve of us who originally came here, and we got split up in a scuffle. I think the rest of them are with the humans who came into the fight we were in."

"That will complicate things," said the arborf. "I know your message was for both arborves and humans, but the humans will not take kindly to seeing me with you. I will take you to where our kind has tracked them before, but we will need to seriously think about how to approach them."

"We will," Neisha replied somberly. "After you."

Cosnoaldo's throne room had changed drastically within the past two hours. The canopies of leaves outlining it were in tatters, the throne was severed from its base and knocked on its side, and everything was shrouded in smoke. On a ledge from this area stood Maewing, overlooking the rest of the tree below. The battle was almost over. The remaining arborven inhabitants had all been taken prisoner, civilian and soldier alike. The fires remained, gradually destroying everything in its paths. Maewing gazed over it all with intention and ambition. Silent, still, and smiling, she basked in the glory of victory and the setting sun's orange beam. Soon, Ambrose ascended the ramp to the throne room and approached her.

"The last of the prisoners are being marched out of the palace, your highness," he said. "However, some arborves have escaped . . . including Cosnoaldo."

Neither Maewing's body nor her expression budged. "I would rather he be dead by now, Commander Brandt," she replied. "But I am partially to blame for his survival. I shouldn't have fallen for the trap he set, and I should've recovered faster afterward."

"It's also my fault, your majesty," Ambrose continued. "The moment he charged at us, I ran and hid until the coast was clear. I wasn't mentally prepared for him."

"It matters little," said Maewing. "Cosnoaldo's stronghold has fallen, and he is not as powerful as he used to be. He and the human leaders will soon be snuffed out to make way for the Self-Worthy to start over in this world. By making a fresh start, the Self-Worthy will be far more likely to establish and maintain our reign and influence here."

"Do you think their subjects will want to follow us after we've killed their leaders?" Ambrose asked. "This isn't like Liberdane where they'll just bow down to their king or queen's assassin."

"They will likely be tired of this ongoing war and of their leaders' blind passions," Maewing answered. "They have probably been wanting a new ruler and new order for decades."

"Perhaps you're right," said Ambrose. "Indeed you will make a wonderful ruler over this world, my lady. You've already led us for so long, and you've done a magnificent job. You've inspired me a lot."

"Thank you, Ambrose." The ponytaur cracked a happy grin. "I'm thankful to have you in our ranks. You've grown and contributed much since you first came to us. You've added so much to yourself and have discovered yourself, and it's been beautiful to see."

"That means a lot to me, my lady," Ambrose replied.

"Please, for the last time, just call me Maewing." She turned her head toward him, and they both smiled. "Once the prisoners are hidden away in the forest, give them the offer of joining us. Then remobilize our troops and prepare for a massive scouting party for the arborven king. The end is almost near."

"Yes, Maewing," Ambrose half-bowed. "Oh, one more thing I meant to ask. On our way here, Ives told me that it might be possible for the arborves to summon every kind of plant to their aid in battle if absolutely necessary. Is that true? If it is, maybe Cosnoaldo's still got some tricks up his sleeve."

"It is nothing more than an unconfirmed rumor, lad. Ives knows a great many otherworldly legends, but many of them are proven to be false, including this one. Rest assured that killing Cosnoaldo will be much easier this time."

"OK. Just making sure," Ambrose replied. "Thanks again." At that, Ambrose started back down the giant tree, which still stood as the fires began to fade.

Maewing turned again to the view of Topiada before her, so anxious to free this world from its strife. The sun was just barely over the horizon, and in a slight instant Maewing saw something reflect it with a flash. It was at the edge of the forest to her left. She took a spyglass from a sack on her horseback and looked around the area where she'd seen the glint. After a minute or two, she caught sight of four armored beings. One was an arborf wearing metal armor over its bark, which Maewing thought was curious. There was also an armored faun she didn't recognize. But seeing the other two made her heart stop. There was that Envoy dwarf she saw on the way to the wizard in Uchu! And there with them was Dilyn. She'd wondered how and why he'd disappeared all those months ago, and now she knew why. He was back with the Envoys. He betrayed her even further than he had in Uchu. Maewing's blood began to boil.

Dilyn will be the first of many to turn to the Envoys' side. That alluring voice came again. *Their cause is already gaining momentum.*

"You don't know that," Maewing said aloud, still watching them through the telescope.

It's clear that they're not finished here yet, otherwise they'd have left using their Daggers. Their mission isn't over yet. They are obviously running away from you, but they are also running toward somewhere.

"There can't merely be four of them," Maewing thought out loud. "They must be trying to reunite with the rest of their group."

And where do you suppose the rest of them are by now?

"One logical guess would be with the humans. But again, we don't know that. They could be hiding out on their own, waiting to pounce until the right moment."

That is not their way. They will either try and befriend a handful of potential converts or advocate to the masses. Either method—if executed well—brings plentiful results for them.

"I can't let that happen!" Maewing exclaimed. "I must send someone to follow them from a distance and to prevent them from making anymore converts! I don't need a third army to fight against."

As soon as the words were out of her mouth, the four Envoys disappeared. She looked a hundred yards in every direction but found no trace of them. They'd simply vanished from her sight. She brought the scope down from her face and slammed it shut.

What conversions they cause are inevitable now, said the voice, unfazed. *Your choice is not.*

"I cannot let what happened in Uchu happen again," said Maewing to herself. "They do not share my passion, but perhaps I can still persuade them to join me before any further violence ensues. I can predict that we will meet again. I will speak with them one last time. If I cannot bring them to see our side of things and they do not yield, then I will destroy them."

Night had finally fallen over Topiada. The creaking of trees was almost the only sound to be heard that night. There were no non-humanoid animals in this world. No roars or hoots or tweets. No scurrying paws, galloping hooves, or flapping wings. Only one pair of feet could be heard in this particular forest, and they belonged to Wybirt the Zealous. He'd been flying about all day, and now his wings were tired, so presently he moved on foot. He had just finished his evening venture of picking fruit, which he carried in a large clay pot. He'd always tried to respect the trees and not build or use anything made of wood—tree flesh, as the arborves called it. He used no baskets or barrels or anything wooden and was able to make things using only metal, stone, and dirt. He never really got used to living like a nomad. Still, there was an odd sense of peace in this simplicity.

After an hour of trudging, the fairy was finally home: a cave with an outer wall at the front, which he constructed. There was no door or window in the front. Wybirt's entrance was instead a hole in the roof of the cave. He also used this hole for a chimney, with a place for his cooking fire directly underneath. He landed inside and set the pot down. The cave inside was barely furnished. He used ledges and protrusions in the walls for shelves and late humans' clothing for sitting and sleeping mats. There was a pile of tools and weapons he'd collected near the front as well. Additionally, a small spring of water sat in a concave corner, which was formed naturally. All Wybirt had to do when he came across this cave was build a wall around the pool high enough to prevent overflow.

Wybirt immediately grabbed two rocks by his firepit filled with coal and set to lighting a fire. He could've easily used his flame sword, but igniting it brought too many traumatic memories. He only kept it on him for emergencies, and his standards for emergencies were high. Anything short of a life-or-death situation for him or the whole world didn't qualify. All else was none of his business.

A fire finally started, and Wybirt proceeded to draw water from a metal pot that he used for cooking. He set it in the fire and took one of many stone knives from a nearby shelf, eyeing his own Dagger amongst them. He sat down to slice his fruit.

Wybirt.

The fairy instantly recognized the voice as Nazir's. "No," he said aloud.

Come.

"I said no. I am done with you."

Come back to me, my child.

"I am no longer yours."

That is not in your power to decide. You could misplace your badge or throw away your Dagger, and you would still be my son. I am glad to see you have done neither of those things, though.

Wybirt glanced at his Dagger again and recalled where his badge was—with his armor under the pile of tools and weapons.

"They are merely keepsakes," he replied. "They are reminders of mistakes I have made."

You know better than to lie to me, Wybirt. You know full well that accepting and believing in me was not a mistake, and even now there is a small part of you that wishes that you were still fighting for and representing me because you have not known peace or hope or joy since the day you stopped.

Wybirt said nothing for a moment. How was that Vine always right? "That part of me is small and ever shrinking. I stopped because representing you became nothing more than a show."

You were not representing me when you sought to perform for and please others; you were making a name for yourself. Although you loathed it, you also enjoyed the attention just as much as you enjoy your privacy now. You made an idol out of yourself, and you constantly felt like you had to maintain your image, so much so that you forgot to advocate for mine. Following my lead doesn't require you to be someone I did not make you to be. It instead requires you to let go of yourself and your ego and to fight for something beyond yourself.

The fairy sighed, his jaw tensing. "What do you want of me?"

It is about time we catch up with each other. I also have a mission for you if you choose to obey. You have gone without a sense of purpose for centuries, and it has eaten at your soul. Come back to me.

Wybirt sat still for several moments, unable to deny anything the Vine had said. He stared at his Dagger for the longest time. He did not want to go. He just wanted to be left alone and leave everyone else alone. But he also knew that was not the destiny of an Envoy, and he knew that when he was redeemed. He didn't want to go, but he knew it was best. He stood up and grabbed only his Dagger. He didn't bother to put on his armor or badge, and he ignored his water pot, which was well beyond boiling point. He summoned a portal, sighed deeply, and walked through.

Absolutely nothing had changed about the Center or the Vine over the centuries. Nazir and everything around him were still as beautiful and fearsome as ever. Wybirt remembered to kneel, but he didn't just yet; he was still resistant.

"It's good to see you again, old friend," Nazir said. He kept his voice more somber this time, but there was still a hint of happiness in it.

"I would bet it is," the fairy replied. "Nothing much has changed here, I see."

"Should it?"

"Nay, I suppose everything is as perfect as you say it is. So how have affairs across the multiverse been?" There was slight sarcasm in Wybirt's tone.

"They have been fair," the Vine answered. "There is still strife and war and deception and pride, but I have advanced my Kingdom far through my Envoys, and more Envoys who have been dormant are starting to see the gravity of the fate of the unredeemed and are taking me more seriously. Everything is going as I have planned."

"Bravo," Wybirt nodded. "I am glad your dreams are still being realized."

"What about you, son? How have you been lately?"

"Did you not already tell me how I have been?"

"I want to hear what you think," said the Vine.

The fairy sighed. "Overall, I would say I have been fine. I have kept myself unstained by the world in which I now reside. I am not entangling myself in the militant affairs of the humans and arborves, and I have learned how to live with little, and I have experienced an eerie peace because of it."

"I see," Nazir replied. "But . . . ?"

Wybirt sighed deeper. "But that peace, I admit, has only been superficial. I have not had peace within myself for ages. I have tried everything, and nothing has satisfied that longing inside of me. There has been a void of tumult within me for centuries, and I have lately attempted to simply live with that void—to tough it out. That has been more challenging than I anticipated."

"Let me ask you something," said Nazir. "All that time, you knew I was your source of peace and rest and that I could give it to you if you would only let go of yourself and ask. You also knew how to find me. So why have you not come to see me since the day you fell in that wormhole and ended up in Topiada, even right after that happened? Did you not even want out, or at least answers, when you first arrived?" As always, Nazir knew the answer to this question. He simply wanted to hear it from Wybirt.

"I never came to you because it seemed so serene there, so starkly different from my life in Hertengard. There was no one to perform for and no one to please, save myself. I also assumed it was your plan for me to end up in Topiada, and I submitted to that. Which leads me to my own question: why did you not simply summon me and send me there personally?"

"Because you had stopped coming to me, and you were ignoring my voice," Nazir answered. "I did summon you, but you tuned your heart to ignore my voice. Besides, I wanted to do something different, and I meant for you to be in Topiada no matter how you arrived there. I did, however, want you to come to me after I moved you to at least ask me about it."

"I am sorry, the thought barely came to mind," replied Wybirt. "I admit that I was partially living for myself in Hertengard, and I did associate that with living for you. As such, after I was moved, I wanted to start over, to try a life without you. I only wanted to for a while, but the habits I formed stuck. I did not mean to hide from you this long, and I know you are my only source of lasting peace. I do still feel pain when I think about and see you, though."

"Why pain, my child?" Nazir asked.

"Because when I first accepted and believed in you, I thought life would gradually become easier. I thought that those around me would be quicker to accept you as well as I did and that I would not need to put on an act. I was wrong, and I discovered that the hard way."

"You were wrong about two of those three things," Nazir replied. "It is true that the life of an Envoy in fact gets harder rather than easier because of the very fact that people are not generally receptive to the truth. They can harden their hearts to it because it comes with acknowledging that they are in the wrong, that they cannot be good enough on their own, and that they are not as powerful as they think. You were initially right in that being an Envoy does not require you to put on an act. You need to candidly display the work I have done in you, not your own accomplishments or image. You lost sight of making much of me in trying to keep that good reputation you held so dearly."

"I see that a tad more clearly now." Wybirt finally brought himself to kneel. "I see that living for myself has served me no further purpose than living in seclusion in search of a rest that can only be found in you. Please forgive me for avoiding you for so long. I want your peace and purpose again, Father."

"All I freely give to you, son!" said Nazir, welcoming an embrace from the fairy. "As long as you forgive those who have wronged you over the years, even before you left Hertengard."

Wybirt paused a moment before entering the Vine's branches. "Aye, they are forgiven." Wybirt received Nazir's embrace after some hesitation. He felt that void gradually start to be filled, something which he had not felt in centuries. His body relaxed significantly. The pair finally released each other after a few well-enjoyed minutes.

"Now, I want you to return here with your armor," said Nazir happily. "I know it has not aged well over time, so I want you to take it to Azarias so he can mend and clean it."

"Understood, my Lord." Wybirt grinned, kneeling again. "Now what was this mission you had for me?"

Bernice had tossed and turned in bed all night long. Yesterday's battle and hike had worn her out, but anxiety overruled sleep tonight. Worry about her lost friends and the poor results of the mission thus far kept her body from relaxing. At last, she gave up trying after only getting a few hours of mild sleep. She opened one eye to the cabin window on her side of the borrowed room. It was still dark, but she could make out the scarce trees' silhouettes in the blue haze. The sun would rise soon.

She turned her head to the other side of the bed only to find that her husband wasn't there. This made her open both eyes and sit up slowly. She looked around the room and saw that his armor was also missing. Now quite curious and a tad concerned, she got up, put on her boots, and crept out of the bedroom belonging to one of the humans' thirty cabins. The main room of this cabin, almost identical to the other cabins, was quite homely. There were two fireplaces and several couches and cushions spread throughout. On two of these laid Chadmight and Panos, who were too large for the beds in the bunk rooms on either side of the cabin. Bernice wondered how Panos could sleep with Chadmight's incessant snoring. She tiptoed past them from the front of the cabin to the back, where the glow of a fire outside caught her eye. She opened the back door to see Amory, fully armed and ready for the day, sitting on one of three log benches surrounding a lit brick firepit, quite visible in the predawn darkness. His face was cold and stern as he tended the fire. He looked up to see his bride and relaxed only a little as he gave a slight grin.

"Did I toss and turn that much?" asked Bernice with a tired smirk as she sat beside him.

Amory chuckled inaudibly. "No, I did. I didn't want to wake you, and I wasn't getting a lot of sleep to begin with."

"That's OK, I wasn't either," Bernice replied, leaning her head on his shoulder. "How long have you been out here?"

Amory looked at his watch, unsure if Topiada revolved around its sun as fast as Earth did our sun. "About an hour, I think. Not too long. I've discovered that mornings here aren't as cold."

"We must've caught them at a good time, at least weather-wise," said Bernice.

Amory hummed in reply.

"Are you worried about the mission?"

"Tons," Amory answered. "No one seems to be taking us seriously, even if they say they are. Not the princess, not Baron Rolle, not anyone. Their whole world is at risk, and they don't even care. They are so blinded by this fleeting pursuit of fickle peace that nothing else matters to them. I'm afraid we're getting nowhere."

"I'm worried about that too," Bernice sighed. "I keep trying to tell myself that we just have to keep telling them the truth, and maybe they'll come around or at least compromise even a little bit. Maybe Nazir will tug at their hearts enough and they'll finally listen. It's just hard to see that happening right now."

"I agree," said Amory. "I don't intend on giving up until that happens."

"Neither will the rest of us," Bernice said, putting her arm around him as he did the same for her. "I just hope Neisha and Dilyn and Agabio don't either. I'm really worried about them, about what'll happen to them."

"They'll be OK," Amory replied. "Nazir's got them. Hopefully they were able to deliver the same message to the arborves who captured them and maybe even their king. Let's hope he's much more receptive."

Now Bernice hummed back. After a moment, she said, "That's another thing I kept thinking about last night. What if that king or the human king don't listen either? What if no one ever does? What if not a single person here turns to Nazir, and he actually does destroy this world like he said he would?"

"Then I would consider this mission failed," Amory answered. "I will not let that happen. I'll die before I see that."

"Would it be failed, though?" Bernice asked. "Nazir only sent us to give that message to both parties. Presumably, both have been done. I'm also determined to keep trying and delivering it to whoever we come across, but Nazir never said anyone would turn. It's not our job to see that through anyway; it's Nazir's. Our job is to just tell them the truth, and he'll handle the rest if people choose to listen to him. And remember what we were taught at our gathering a while back? Some people were told that if no one in an area or house they visited was receptive to this truth and hope no matter how hard those Envoys tried, then they were to leave that place to whatever doom would meet it and go to someone more welcome to them. Maybe the same is true for all of us Envoys."

"Maybe," said Amory after some thought. "But I'm not willing to leave this world without a fight, so to speak."

"Neither am I, hon," Bernice replied. "I'm just trying to keep my mind open to that possibility, sad though it is. I don't want to, though."

Amory turned to his wife. "Then let's do everything in our power to keep that from happening and trust that Nazir will play his part as he always does."

A couple hours of dawn passed, and soon everyone at the humans' camp was awake. Valma and her army hastily gobbled up breakfast, armed themselves, and broke up camp. The Envoys did their best to keep up, all of them still trying to awaken. By around six o'clock, the three thousand troops were fully prepared for battle and on the move, led by a princess who was very eager to meet up with her father and his armies. The Envoys continued to talk to her and Rolle about the urgency of Topiada's potential fate, but both of them would only say they would wait to hear King Hilmar's input. Neither Panos's passion nor Masato's persuasion skills hindered them.

They trekked all morning through a seemingly endless woodland. The Envoys began to wonder if there were any plains in Topiada that the humans didn't create. Shortly after noon had struck, they all began to hear rustlings to their left. Soon they could make out red figures stomping amongst the trees. Their paths soon crossed, and the Envoys deduced that this must be King Hilmar's battalion. These troops—far more numerous—were clad identically to Valma's, except these wore brass epaulettes. They were led by an older yet able-bodied man with white hair, a slender build, a scowling, scarred face, and a bronzed laurel on his head. The Envoys assumed that this was Hilmar himself and that the wreath he wore was the same one that his ancestor Lauris was given. The king greeted his daughter with a warm smile and hug.

"Valma, how happy I am to see you!" he said in a higher, rigid voice. "How do you fare?"

"I fare better with you and your legion before my eyes!" Valma grinned. "I am ready to fight alongside you again and take Valter back."

"As am I, my daughter. But first, we must pause and have lunch. My soldiers are tired, as I am sure yours are as well. We cannot rescue your brother if we lack our strength. Perhaps while we eat you could introduce me to these creatures who appear in your ranks with different armor."

Valma agreed, and everyone was ordered to sit on the ground and eat whatever they packed while keeping a rotation of guards going. The Envoys were then introduced to the king, and they were able to give Nazir's message to him. Hilmar pondered long and hard and had, in fact, stopped eating the blue citrus fruit he held.

"They told me the same message, father," said the princess. "But I needed your wisdom to know how to proceed, assuming these claims are true."

The king stroked his beardless jaw. "Several creatures have visited us from other worlds, talking of this Nazir. The fact that all of them intentionally came from other worlds to this one in his name helps prove his existence."

"So you are saying Nazir is real, and that what he says is valid?" asked Rolle. The Envoys held their breath for the king's answer.

"I have no reason not to believe in his existence or that these visitors follow him," Hilmar replied. "I do still hesitate to take what he says to heart. He seems out of touch with the worlds he claims to govern. Obviously what he says is irrelevant, as he apparently does not know that reconciling with the arborves is impossible at this stage. Too much is at stake to simply forgive them and make amends. I will not let my guard down and allow my son to be completely taken from me."

"All right, all right," said Amory, attempting a different angle. "Forget about making right with the arborves for just a moment. Will you at least consent to see Nazir?"

"Again, I am not sure if I could take him at his word if he does not know what he speaks of," said the king.

"How would you know that unless you actually meet him?" asked Chadmight.

"A person proves what he says by his actions," Hilmar replied. "I want to see Nazir prove his sovereignty."

"And how would you suggest he do that?" Masato asked probingly. "What kind of action are you looking for?"

"If he gives me back my son through or before our raid, I will consider meeting him," Hilmar answered, standing up. "I will not see Nazir before seeing my son again. My intentions to invade the arborven Palace of Xenia have not been swayed. Everyone to arms and move out!"

"But sire," Nels retorted, "you could die before then! No one is promised the survival of any battle. Do you not wish to confirm these claims one way or another before you put your life and the lives of your kin and soldiers at risk?"

The king had already tossed his fruit aside and started walking again. "Our lives have been at risk for centuries. That is not new to us. I believe achieving peace once and for all is worth dying for."

"We agree, and so does Nazir," said Leona as the thousands began to march on. "Nazir wants you to have this peace too, and this peace transcends our circumstances. It's a peace that you can have when you are surrounded by danger and turmoil and there's no escape. And you don't have to physically die to have it! Your highness, don't you want to simply enjoy a life with your son and daughter and not have to worry about their lives being at stake? Princess, don't you want to always have your father by your side, there for you? I sense that yearning in you because I have that same desire. Baron, don't you want the most of your worries to be your people's attitudes and welfare and not their safety?"

"Of course we want these things!" Valma said rather passionately. "That is why we are trying to end this war today!"

"More fighting will not make that happen," said Bernice. "Trust me, we've picked fights where we shouldn't have before, and it didn't end well."

"Nor did all of the peace talks we have attempted," Rolle put in. "We were always either turned away or attacked and killed. I am the sole survivor of our most recent treaty attempt.

I, too, desire peace, and I do not want to use my sword to attain it unless necessary. But the arborves will not heed us or compromise, so much so that they became enraged at us."

"All right, but again, what about simply focusing on making peace with the Vine first?" Panos asked.

"The Vine?" said the king, stopping suddenly. "What do you mean? Are you saying Nazir is a Vine?"

"Y—es," Amory answered slowly. "Haven't we said that before?"

"I would have noticed if you did," said Valma, appalled. "You are telling us that you follow and take orders from a talking plant?"

"We do," Twyla said. "Do you not believe that that is possible?"

"No, we do," said Hilmar. "Or have you already forgotten that we have lived in conflict with talking plants for millennia? Our trust for intelligent plant life has all but dwindled now."

"Again, how can you mistrust someone you haven't met yet?" asked Chadmight.

Just then, one of the officers shouted from behind them. "Sire! Is that smoke I see ahead?"

The leaders and Envoys looked up, and they did indeed see smoke rising in billows over the tree line. They pressed ahead until they came to a natural clearing that stretched for miles—a perfect battlefield (or a grounds for a massacre). At the end of it, northeast to the armies, stood a massive tree that towered over the rest—at least what remained of it. It looked completely barren and dead, and smoke rose steadily from inside it.

"The Palace of Xenia!" Valma exclaimed in a gasp. "It has already been besieged!"

"It looks thoroughly stripped of its inhabitants," said Twyla, who had keen elven eyesight. "It looks completely abandoned."

"Who could be able to do this?" Hilmar asked. "No one has ever been able to take that palace before, and most of my forces are here with me! It couldn't be Wybirt; he has been a pacifist for years."

Amory had a sneaking suspicion who it was, but he pushed the thought away with the hope that it wasn't true or likely.

"Perhaps the arborves are already annihilated," Rolle suggested. "Could the war finally be over?"

Suddenly, a patch of ground began to break open from the inside, a good distance from the Envoys on their right. Out of the hole that was made crawled a rather dirty Agabio, Neisha, and Dilyn, and a green female arborf. The humans noticed this immediately.

"It's an arborven survivor, come to spy on us!" Valma shouted. "Take her down!"

Soldiers were already charging at her when the three Envoys with her realized it. Neisha stepped right in front of her, positioning one of her shields above the other to fully protect her. Dilyn drew his bow, and Agabio readied his pike, both poised for defense. It took the rest of the Envoys stepping in front of them for the humans to finally stop. The nine Envoys were still wrapping their minds around the fact that their lost friends were alive and presumably safe.

"Is that how you treat every arborf you see, with aggression and assumptions?!" asked Edna. "These other three are our lost friends! I think she just brought them back to us! Spare her life and hear them out, for goodness' sake!"

"Thank you, fellow Envoys," whispered the arborf, whom the others now realized was clad like them.

"We've just escaped from the palace," said Neisha, talking to everyone. "The Self-Worthy attacked it, likely wanting to kill its king, Cosnoaldo. I have no idea what's happened to him or your prince. Malfreda here helped us escape and protected us overnight so we could come tell you."

Amory's blood boiled. This mission was going south fast now that the Self-Worthy was in the equation.

"Then we must go and find both of them!" declared Hilmar. "We will search the entirety of the ruins until we find a trace of them."

"If I know anything about King Cosnoaldo, he will have survived, as well as your son," said Malfreda. "I must warn you that he will continue to keep the prince alive until you reach him. My king is using your son as bait for a trap for you, your majesty, and it would be a mistake for you if you tried to gain him back with full force."

"Silence, fiend!" Hilmar hissed. "You are obviously trying to stop or stall my coming so they can transform my son into one of you monsters! I will never hearken to the likes of you." He then turned to his troops. "Move out! We march on to find my son and end this wickedness once and for all! If we come across this Self-Worthy band, we will happily join them."

As the humans started off again, Valma lingered with the Envoys. "None of you are permitted in our ranks anymore. Our trust in you is broken. You represent a Vine, and you now have an arborf amongst you. Your appeals are not in our best interests at all. Go now while I still allow you. Pray we do not meet again."

At that, the princess ran up to join her father. The now thirteen Envoys watched in horror as the humans marched on, their hearts further hardened against Nazir. The humans began to make formations and sharpen their swords, axes, and arrows. The Envoys looked ahead of the throngs and caught glimpses of arborves rallying at the edge of the shrubbery on the other side of the vast clearing. Many of them had survived and had amassed more support. Preparations for a battle were well underway.

Amory turned to his friends. "I'm beyond thankful that you three are back and you're OK, but we can celebrate the reunion later. There's no time to waste." He then turned to Malfreda. "Thank you so much for bringing them back safely . . . Malfreda, was it?"

"Yes," answered the arborf. "And I will eventually need to learn all of your names. My kind will not likely take me back because I helped you, so I will remain with you all. What are we to do now?"

"Our options are looking slim," said Edna. "The humans are determined to attack the arborves and maybe even us if we keep provoking them. How did things go with the arborves?"

"We were their prisoners, and they didn't intend to change that," Dilyn said. "We got to meet Cosnoaldo and give him

Nazir's message, but he didn't listen either. After he heard it, his plan was for us to suffer the same fate as the human prince. We were being taken to that mystical tree when the Self-Worthy attacked and Malfreda got us out."

"Did you know the Self-Worthy was coming here?" Masato asked, a bit ticked.

"No, I left them before I learned their next plans," Dilyn answered.

"I'm confused," Chadmight interrupted. "Who are the Self-Worthy?"

"They're an army of creatures from throughout the multiverse, promoting the idea of individualism and self-fulfillment," said Leona. "They've caused problems on two of our prior missions, and now this one."

"Their leader is Maewing, the ponytaur who led you astray," Amory added. Chadmight stood frozen with shock. Amory turned back to the freed Envoys. "Was she there during the attack?"

"Aye, and she seems as resilient and resolved as before," Neisha said.

"They are going to show up again," said Twyla. "What will we do then? We cannot stand against three adversary armies!"

"Now hold on!" said Amory. "Not one of these forces is our adversaries! They're all people Nazir wants to redeem and save from this destruction. We have to do our best to not fight them, no matter how tempting that may be."

"You're right," Panos replied. "What do we do then?"

"Time is running out, and both armies are getting in their battle positions," Amory said, stepping in front of everyone else, facing the plain. "Unless they're completely uncivilized—and at this point, I wouldn't doubt it—the leaders of both sides will meet in the middle to discuss the terms of the battle and maybe give one last chance for surrender or a truce. One way or another, we need to be there, in the center of the field, to meet them and continue to plead with them. We will be in the line of fire, and unless a miracle happens, I don't think either side will relent from trying to get us out of the way if our negotiations fail. But

Topiada's not gone yet, and we're still here, so our mission's not yet over. We cannot give up now, even if it means we go to our deaths. These people still have a chance, and we have to make sure they take it. Are you all still with me on this, even if it means we die?"

Bernice was the first to step forward and join her husband. "It'd be rather wrong if I wasn't," she grinned.

Dilyn was next, followed by Panos, Malfreda, Nels, Neisha, Leona, Twyla, Masato, Agabio, Edna, then Chadmight. They all took deep breaths.

"All right," Amory continued. "First things first: we need to ask Nazir for his intervention. Otherwise, this'll all be for nothing."

At that, the thirteen Envoys circled up, arm in arm, and closed their eyes. Panos said aloud, "Almighty Nazir, we thank you for uniting us again as a team and giving us all the same resolve. Thank you for equipping us with everything we need for this mission, and I ask that you do not stop now, at this most desperate hour. We are useless without you, and only you can soften the hearts of these stubborn people. As we go out and try to prevent this looming battle, I ask that you give us not merely protection from what might come but the strength and power to endure it. You sent us here for a reason; do not let it be in vain. Fill us with yourself as we seek to keep trying to represent you to these people who need you. Please let us return to you, one way or another, with someone else who otherwise would not have found you. Even if it is only one person, but I hope it is far more than that—even everyone in this world. Thank you again for hearing and answering us, Nazir! May you be seen and honored today."

Amory added in his head, *And please don't let the Self-Worthy interfere and mess things up any further.*

All the Envoys opened their eyes and smiled at each other, considering the possibility that this could be the last time they did so.

As they let go of each other, Amory said, "Now, we need to get to the center of the field before they do, preferably unseen. Anyone have any ideas?"

"Malfreda can burrow underground and sprint as fast as she wants without being noticed!" said Neisha. "That's how we got to you after getting out of the palace."

"Awesome," said Amory, turning to the arborf. "Are you good with doing it again?"

"It would be my pleasure." Malfreda smiled as she started to dig rapidly with her tentacle-like roots. A man-sized hole was formed within seconds. "Stay close," she warned.

Malfreda then tore off into the ground, digging with all her arms and roots as fast as she could. The others sprinted off after her, wondering what they would see when they surfaced again.

13

ESCALATION

B aron Rolle jogged from one end of the human armies to the forefront, where his king stood waiting, anxiously pacing. The princess then came from the other side.

"My troops are fully ready for battle, father," said Valma.

"As are the rest of your armies, my liege," Rolle added.

"Very good," Hilmar sighed. "Let us go and discuss the terms of battle, assuming those monsters will heed us. Be wary, for they might try something on us when we are there."

The three human leaders began the long walk to the center of the field, silent as they contemplated how this battle would turn out. Their mission was twofold: recover Prince Valter alive, and take out the arborves once and for all so no one would bother them again. Neither would be an easy feat, and they knew it would cost several lives—maybe even their own. Nevertheless, they saw this as achievable and worth it. As they got closer, they caught a glimpse of a handful of diverse figures already at the center, apparently waiting for them. They were the Envoys, including that arborf who brought more of them. The king's and princess's jaws tensed up.

"My, they truly are serious about this matter," said Rolle, half to himself.

"And equally as foolish and misguided," the king replied.

As they approached the Envoys, they saw Cosnoaldo do the same, flanked by two of his generals. One of them carried Valter by his back. When they all met in the middle, the prince was tossed to the ground. His face and half his body were now wooden, and bark began to form on his arm and under his torn red uniform. There were also patches of grass in his dark blond hair. He was breathing hard, not because breathing was difficult but because it seemed that oxygen was becoming less needed. He glanced up at the Envoys and the humans behind them.

"Father! Sister!" he cried. His voice sounded low and wheezy. "Do not listen to Cosnoaldo! Whatever he says, do not listen to him!" An arborven general struck the back of his head for that.

"Let my son go, you fiend!" Hilmar shouted.

"Come and take him, fool," Cosnoaldo replied.

Hilmar did not take the bait.

"Please!" Amory called between them. Both sides' attention were now fixed on the Envoys who stood firm and sure. "There doesn't have to be any more battling. You can all get what you want. You can all get the peace you yearn for!"

"So says the same people who laid waste to my palace and stronghold!" Cosnoaldo moaned.

"I told you, your majesty, they had nothing to do with that attack," Malfreda replied. "That was an entirely different assembly."

"Two otherworldly groups and agendas coming here at the same time?" said Cosnoaldo. "How unlikely. That has never happened before."

"Regardless, it is now," Amory continued. "We have appealed to both of your peoples to make peace with Nazir and each other, and none of you have listened thus far. It's not too late to think again. Please come see Nazir, all of you, and just see him for who he is, and listen to what he tells you! Please, while you still have a chance! You can still end this war without any more fighting or death. Nazir can save you from yourselves and from utter destruction, which is knocking at the door. What do you have to lose by simply pausing to see the Vine?"

"I would lose time as my son still turns into one of them!" said Hilmar, pointing to the arborven king.

"You are losing time now, young man," said Cosnoaldo, grinning.

Just then, everyone heard the sound of large, flapping wings. They looked to the east and saw Maewing swoop down and land amongst them, nearly trampling the Envoys in the process. She looked more stately and serious than ever, even though she was trying to appear friendly and welcoming.

"It's true then," Chadmight said under his breath. "She still lives!"

"Hail, people of Topiada!" Maewing began.

"I'm going to say this once, Maewing," Amory interrupted, keeping his temper steady yet forceful enough to show his passion. "Leave now. You've caused these people enough harm already."

"I remember you!" Cosnoaldo yelled. "You are one of the creatures who attacked us in Xenia! You must be their leader! It is a true shame that I did not kill you."

"Indeed, and the same is true of you, O king," said Maewing. "Your thirst for vengeance has led to nothing but suffering for your people, and I am here to end that suffering. However, I will give you one last chance to make things right. Give up your quest and join the comradery of the Self-Worthy, where you will find true fulfillment in yourself! You will find true freedom with us, and we want you to find it!"

"Excuse me," Valma said, only getting angrier. "Why do you extend this offer only to the arborves? What if we wanted to join you?"

Maewing's eyebrows furrowed. "Aren't you Envoys? Didn't the Envoys convince you to join them?"

"Heavens no," Hilmar answered. "Nor do we ever intend to join them."

Maewing couldn't help but smile. "Then in that case, I gladly welcome you to our ranks! I am happy to include anyone as my friend and partner."

"Then why did you ask if they were Envoys first?" Dilyn cut in, stepping toward her. "I thought you welcomed Envoys too, which is one major reason why I had joined you in the first place."

"I meant only Envoys who have forsaken the Vine," Maewing answered, her smile gradually fading. "Envoys who still follow him would become torn between two agendas, and they wouldn't be able to contribute to both of them faithfully. I do wonder, though, why you decided to leave us and rejoin the Vine, Dilyn. I thought you were happy and comfortable and felt seen with us. I thought you had become whole. I thought you were my friend."

Dilyn breathed deeply, also trying to use his words tactfully. "You wouldn't have known any better because, as time went on, your concern for my wellbeing diminished. I did as you told me, whether I was up to the task or not, which is not what you led me to believe would happen. The truth is that, except for the wholeness, I actually was all those things you said, but they didn't last. With Nazir, I am more than those things. I'm not just happy, I'm joyful. I'm not comfortable, but I'm strong—or strengthened, I should say. I'm not just seen, I'm known. Nazir's way is so much better, Maewing. His offer to come to him and hear him out extends to you too. I know you yourself also lack the peace and freedom you claim, and I'm here to tell you that Nazir will give it freely if you surrender to him!"

"Enough!" the ponytaur yelled, livid that Dilyn would affront her and her vision in front of these potential recruits. She looked at everyone before her. "This is your last chance to join me in seeking yourselves! I only want what's best for you, but if you don't want that for yourselves, then I won't let you stop others from finding fulfillment!"

Chadmight looked at the arborves and humans, wondering what they would say. They seemed partially convinced by Dilyn's words and questioned Maewing further, making her even madder. He then looked at his team and watched Amory and the others continue to advocate Nazir. As he watched, he noticed Agabio beside him who wasn't looking at any of them. Instead, he was staring into the sky.

"What are you looking at?" Chadmight murmured as he looked up and tried to see the reason for his friend's diverted gaze.

After a second of searching, he found three airborne objects circling the center of the field several hundred feet up.

"Good eye, my friend!" he whispered. He nudged Twyla subtly. "Can you see what those things are?" he asked.

Twyla peered hard at the objects once she caught sight of them. Her eyes widened when she recognized them.

"They are Self-Worthy archers astride winged creatures! They are aiming for the leaders of these three other groups!" Then she shouted, "Everyone, get down!"

She'd said it a moment too late. The instant after she yelled, Maewing opened her wings, and the archers fired. Having no time to think, Chadmight kicked Amory in front of him and skipped to where an arrow was heading. It ricocheted off the centaur's armor and thudded into the ground.

A very flabbergasted Amory got up from being kicked aside and realized that Chadmight had just saved his life. He looked around and saw that he was the lucky one. One of the arborven generals who had also seen the archers had taken a fiery arrow for his king and was burning and shrieking intensely as he died. Amory looked to the other side and saw Valma wailing over her now fallen father, who had an arrow through his chest. He was dead within seconds. Valter also began to weep. Dilyn and Nels quicky shot down the archers before they could kill anyone else, and Maewing consequently took flight and rushed back to the eastern edge of the forest.

Once he got his bearings, Cosnoaldo saw what happened to Hilmar. He chuckled. "Now you finally know how it feels."

Valma slowly looked up at him with rage in her tear-filled eyes.

Cosnoaldo quickly grabbed Valter and held a branch blade to his throat. Unfazed, the princess started to lunge at him, screaming. Rolle grabbed her and held her back, taking a few kicks in the process.

"Stop, your majesty, please!" the baron shouted. "For your own sake! He'll keep the prince alive as long as you're alive to take the bait. Going after him now will only get you both killed!"

The Envoys again stepped between the arborves and humans, very unsure of how to recover from this.

"This can end now," Bernice said sternly. "If you don't relent, then only more of those you all love and trust will die."

Cosnoaldo frowned harshly. "There is nothing you could say that will sway me now. Your thirst for others' death matches the rest of ours. My course of action is set, and it will not be undone." He then turned to his second general. "Go back to the soldiers and initiate our charge. We will plow straight through this field as if there is nothing in the way."

"No, it was the Self-Worthy who did this, not us!" Neisha cried. "We don't want to harm any of you while you still have a chance!"

Ignoring her, Cosnoaldo grasped Valter tighter as Valter continued to mourn his father, unable to attend to his sister. The general sped off to the north, and his king soon followed, carrying the prince high out of human reach.

Valma got up as Rolle picked up Hilmar's body. Her eyes tore into the Envoys' souls. "Today, my fury will be unleashed on the arborves and whoever stands in my way," she said. "Flee while you can, but rest assured that after today, I will hunt each of you down." At that, Valma and the baron turned south to go back to their armies and declare that their king was dead, and vengeance must be exacted. The Envoys looked at each other, all of them deathly pale.

"Nazir, what is happening?!" Panos cried.

"Absolutely everything is going wrong," Masato added. "What hope is there now?"

"Hon, what do we do?" asked Bernice.

Amory inhaled deeply. "While we and everything in Topiada still draw breath, there's still hope. We stand."

Maewing alighted in front of her legions, which now included several arborves, near the foot of the ruined palace. She wasted no time. "Our assassination attempt was only partially successful," she declared. "Some of the leaders survived, and they are rallying their forces to attack each other. We march out immediately to meet all our opponents in the middle. Take out their leaders and everyone who swings a blade at you. Spare as many as will join us."

The armies set out, chanting "All for one" after Maewing's lead.

Ives the elf, who was standing near the front with Ambrose and Lisias, called out, "Why do we not simply wait for the armies to tear each other apart and appeal to the remnant?"

"The accursed Envoys are out there," Maewing answered. "I will not let them claim another of our victories. Kill any and all of them in your sights."

"Is one of those 'accursed' Envoys my brother?" Ambrose asked.

"All for one!" Maewing shouted, ignoring him.

"Maewing, is Dilyn out there?" Ambrose urged, much more sternly.

"Yes, he's out there," Maewing said, facing him as she led her comrades out. "He has firmly made his choice, Commander. Now you must make yours."

Ambrose marched on, finally coming to terms with the fact that he couldn't please everyone.

The Envoys circled up, facing outward. They found the Self-Worthy army emerging from the eastern edge of the plain in vast numbers. The human armies in the south and the arborves in the north also began to approach. The west was still open, and the Envoys could still escape that way, but they didn't. They stood where they were, hoping their stubbornness would make something click in the minds of anyone coming toward them.

"Well, this will surely make a dramatic last stand," Edna exclaimed.

"Hey, if you have any other ideas, I'm all ears," Amory replied.

"Honestly, if this doesn't work, I don't know what will," said Leona. "It's too late to try anything else. We've done everything. This is our last resort."

"Nazir, protect us or bring us home!" Nels cried.

All three armies started charging toward the center now, each aware of and against the other two as well as the Envoys blocking their path. All the Envoys had their hands open, and none of them had their weapons out. Every army they faced was filled with ravenous fury, giving no sign of weakness or compromise. Amory and Bernice faced the Self-Worthy's side, watching Maewing primarily. Her eyes were wide, and her gaze was set. She was more determined than ever and sprinted the fastest out of all her troops. She and her comrades were about a hundred yards away from the Envoys when they suddenly stopped short and tried desperately to turn around. Maewing quickly took flight as a giant half-ring of fire spread out from above the Envoys' heads, descending on the forerunners of all three armies. The leaders all managed to escape in time, but not everyone was that lucky.

The Envoys stood in awe of what had just happened when they saw a winged humanoid creature land in front of them with a stomp of his fist, facing the Self-Worthy. It was Wybirt, fully equipped in his Envoy gear and wielding his flame sword. He swiftly turned to the Envoys.

"Quickly, to arms!" he shouted. "Defend yourselves and escape this madness! Nazir sent me to help you get out of the battle and back to the Center. We will make for the western forest's edge where we can make a portal in the safety of the trees."

"We're not done here!" Amory replied. "The world hasn't ended yet. These people still have a chance!"

"Not anymore," said Wybirt as the three armies began to regroup. "Nazir says their time is up, and they have spent all of their chances. This world has gone over its tipping point. He sent me to get you out before he has me destroy Topiada."

The others tried desperately to think of another option, coming to no success. With nods and tears, they drew their weapons—all except for Malfreda.

"I refuse to fight against any of these people," she said. "This is not the Envoy way."

"Yes it is," Dilyn replied. "Remind me to tell you some Envoy stories I've heard later if we survive this. And this is self-defense anyway. As much as I hate to admit it, this is just."

Malfreda relented and drew her urumi. Masato changed into a burly yellow dragon that would tower over the arborves. They began to run west, seeing that the humans and arborves had rerouted and were now charging at only each other between the Envoys and the forest. In a matter of minutes, the two armies clashed with utmost intensity. The Envoys hesitated for a moment now that their path was blocked, only to realize that the Self-Worthy were running toward them from behind, led by Lisias and Ives (Maewing was going to shoot in from the air, and Ambrose snuck further to the back of the masses). The Envoys were trapped.

"Quick, climb onto me, and I'll fly us out!" Masato roared.

The Self-Worthy heard that, and several flying creatures sped up and attacked him from all sides. He was able to bat away and incinerate most of them but not before they pulled one of his wings out of socket. He yelped in pain.

"I can't turn into another flying beast fast enough!" he cried. "We'll have to fight our way out."

The Envoys moaned as they got into fighting stances facing the Self-Worthy, bracing for impact. Wybirt and Masato sprayed fire on as many as they could reach, and Dilyn and Nels shot several soldiers down before the masses finally fell upon the Envoys. The Envoys were ready, and their weapons met with their opponents' with just as much power. Amory had both his swords out now, blocking and slashing with both of them at an incredible pace. Bernice blocked slash after stab with her flag and managed to rapidly strike her opponents with her pole and then impale them with her spearhead. Leona split her axe so she could have a kama in each hand, parrying and spinning with finesse. Dilyn gave up trying to shoot arrows and instead switched to using his bow's blades, surprised at how effective it was.

Agabio's courage only increased as he used his pike's length and range to his advantage, just as Panos had taught him. Panos himself fought with the most zeal out of everyone, spinning and swinging his trident with blinding speed and even headbutting his opponents when necessary. Chadmight opened his flails and ran about, swinging them madly in an unpredictable and effectual way, also trampling dozens. Malfreda whipped her urumi at dozens of enemies around her, slashing at them from several feet away and still having a free hand to fight in close quarters. She was surprised by her weapons' power, having never used them on live targets before now. Wybirt was almost untouchable as he threw several large waves of flames and melted every blade that met his sword.

As valiantly as the Envoys fought, fourteen could only do so much against tens of thousands. The Self-Worthy were soon pushing the Envoys back into the fray of the humans and arborves. Masato stomped on several of the troops behind them to ensure the Envoys wouldn't get killed instantly upon mixing with them. Before the Envoys knew it, the Self-Worthy had pushed them into the other battle, enveloping them and beginning to fight against the other two armies.

Thus, the Four-Way Battle of Topiada was underway. Twyla found herself fighting against a human, a Self-Worthy troll, and an arborf all at once, each wanting to kill the other. She killed the arborf while the human slayed the troll, and then Twyla turned around and stabbed the human. Then she tried to go further west as she found herself in another foursome, wondering how she would ever survive this. She and the other Envoys found themselves becoming more separated, unable to reunite.

A Self-Worthy kitsune found Cosnoaldo and assaulted him, managing to break Valter free from his grip. Cosnoaldo started to take him back but was then distracted by Maewing, who kicked him in the face as she'd swooped in. The kitsune grabbed a struggling Valter's arm and led him through the battle to Valma, who'd just slain an arborf. Before the kitsune could appeal to her, Valma quickly killed her and snatched Valter away, hugging him tightly. Valter's morphing stopped, but he wasn't cured.

"I thought I would never see you free again, brother!" Valma cried.

"Nor did I," said Valter, letting go of her and grabbing a dead soldier's sword. "But we are not free yet. Let us finish what our ancestors began and avenge Father."

Maewing was determined to defeat Cosnoaldo this time. She was more wary of his swings and baits, and she shot in and slashed him with her two swords several times. The king, knowing he wouldn't be able to keep up, called out in his own language for backup and for a trumpeter. Help soon arrived, and Maewing found herself dodging, batting, and kicking multiple branch swords and hands at once in midair. She kept up for a while, but then Cosnoaldo slashed her right wing's humerus, and she dropped to the ground. The king and those who flanked him then plowed through the battle (Maewing scooting out of their way) until they got to a safer standpoint with more of their own kind. A small, agile arborf holding a brass trumpet was there amongst them. Cosnoaldo leaned toward him.

"My strength is fading," he said. "I fear I might not have much left to give in this battle. Stand by for my order to sound the Forbidden Call so we can turn the tide if the need arises."

"Sire!" cried the trumpeter. "The Forbidden Call has never been given in all of Topiada's history! With all due respect, dare you defy our ancestors' warnings? It cannot be undone once it is initiated."

"I am aware," the king replied. "That is my desire. We have not needed it until now. Pray it does not come to that."

Maewing got up and looked for the arborven king, knowing his sheer height would betray him. She found him amidst dozens of regrouping arborves, and her path to him was blocked by the other three groups caught in various scuffles. She heard a familiar shout and looked to her left to see Ambrose struggling to fight against Rolle and two arborves. Ambrose and Rolle, between swings at each other, ended up killing the arborves, but the baron then took Ambrose down, swinging his broadsword with ease. He was about to run Ambrose through when Maewing charged in and kicked Rolle several yards away. She then glanced at Ambrose with a smile.

"Climb on!" she shouted.

"What?" said Ambrose, sure he misheard her.

"Climb onto my back! Between my wings and torso. I will protect you."

"Whatever happened to individuals holding their own?" Ambrose asked.

"You can't unlock your potential if you're dead," Maewing replied. "I can't afford to lose you, Ambrose. Climb on."

With hesitation, Ambrose heaved himself up onto his leader's back. He noticed her broken wing.

"You're bleeding . . . and injured!" he cried.

"I will live; it's not fatal," said Maewing.

"What's the plan now?" Ambrose asked. "Cosnoaldo's still alive."

"He is too reinforced at the moment. We will need to wait until he's more isolated. In the meantime, let us find and kill the human prince and princess!"

At that, she turned and started running through the human lines, trampling and slashing troopers as she went. Whatever enemies survived her were slain or shot by Ambrose. They went at this for several minutes, building momentum but failing to find the human rulers. A hint of blue caught her eye, and Maewing looked and saw Amory in the distance, fighting off three humans at once and inching further west. The ponytaur stopped in her tracks.

He is totally distracted! I can end this strife once and for all! she thought.

Maewing then turned toward Amory and began striding at him. Initially confused, Ambrose soon saw her reason and turned deathly pale. He didn't want Maewing to kill Amory, nor vice versa, for they were both his friends. Nor did he want to warn Amory, for that would make Maewing think he was taking the Envoys' side when he wasn't. He couldn't help both of them, so he decided to help neither of them. He said and did nothing.

Amory killed the last of the three humans and trudged closer to the forest, slowly but surely. Out of the corner of his eye, he saw something fast moving toward him. He turned, and his heart stopped as he beheld Maewing almost on top of him, swords poised, Ambrose riding on her back. Instantly, Amory closed his eyes and swung his main sword up diagonally, fleetingly hoping to block a strike. Instead, he felt it go through something, and he heard a painful cry. After a moment, he opened his eyes and saw Maewing collapse a ways past him, a deep wound between her human and horse body. She writhed for a moment and then relaxed, her face filled with fear. Ambrose had tumbled off of her, staring at her body and at Amory, trying to grasp the fact that the great and timeless Self-Worthy leader was now dead.

"What have you done?" Ambrose gasped to Amory. Amory was trying to take it in himself.

Ives found his way over to them and discovered what had happened. "No! My lady!" he cried. He looked at Ambrose. "Who did this? Who was powerful enough to kill our leader?"

Ambrose kept his gaze away from Amory, who was extremely nervous about what he would say.

"A random human whom I can't recognize or name," Ambrose answered. "There's no need for revenge. This world's already riddled with it."

Ives nodded, then saw the Sword of *Chârâsh* on the ground by Maewing's bleeding corpse. He picked it up and handed it to Ambrose, who hesitated to take it.

"You know how to use this," Ives said. "You take it." After a moment, Ambrose did. "What do we do now, Commander? Do we retreat?"

"And make Maewing's death be for nothing? No!" Ambrose exclaimed. "We can press on toward the humans and arborves and still try to take out their rulers. This conflict just has to end before it costs us any more."

At that, Ambrose gave one last look at Amory, then left with Ives to find Valma and Valter. Amory was stunned for a moment. He had actually killed Maewing. He stared at her lifeless body with neither gladness nor regret; he felt emotionally numb. He was also surprised that Ambrose didn't say that he'd done it and that he let him live and diverted the Self-Worthy's focus away from the Envoys. He came out of his thoughts when another arborf lunged at him. After several parries, he killed her with several strikes to her wooden neck. He then fought his way further west, trying to reunite with his team and escape the battle while they were hopefully still alive to.

Valma and Valter (who was still half-wooden) fought side by side for an hour or two, annihilating every arborf and Self-Worthy member in their path. They seemed to be empowered by each other's presence and unspoken empathy. Their opponents barely had time to swing or shoot at them before they were slain.

After a while, they finally came across Cosnoaldo himself, just after he had sent his last troops to deal with a large squadron of the Self-Worthy. All three of them were silent and solemn, stowing any fear they might have felt. No one tried to negotiate or talk their way out; it was too late for that. The human heirs circled the arborven king slowly, waiting to see who would make the next move. It was Valter. He stomped forward suddenly but went no further, distracting the king. Valma then sprinted at him with axe in hand. Cosnoaldo was able to kick her away with one of his roots, but Valter successfully jumped onto his trunk, hacking away at it with his sword. Groaning, Cosnoaldo grabbed him and took him off of himself as Valma swung at the shoulder of the arm that held her brother. She hit the mark, and Valter was instantly freed.

This bout of the king fighting one heir at a time and grabbing them before one freed the other lasted for a minute or two before Cosnoaldo became sick of it. Finally he grabbed Valma and then Valter when he tried to help her. He then made the branch fingers that held them grow longer and more intertwined, enveloping his victims almost entirely, excluding their eyes. He then started squeezing them, causing them to groan and gasp until they couldn't make any noise at all. Fear suddenly overtook both siblings as they rapidly lost breath.

Cosnoaldo grinned at them. "I have seen many of your ancestors make that same face, now including your father. You will be the last ones in your lineage to express it."

Without warning, tiny projectiles grazed underneath the king's eye, making him wince and loosen his grip on his enemies. He looked and saw a Self-Worthy human with a shotgun, accompanied by Ives with his sword, firing round after round at the king. Cosnoaldo roared and leaped on them both, and only Ives evaded him in time. Cosnoaldo hadn't realized that Ambrose had used this as a distraction and was now climbing up his trunk. He reached his upper back and ran the Sword of *Chârâsh* clean through it. Cosnoaldo shrieked as green rays glowed from his chest, and he let go of Valter and Valma. Everyone around watched as the king stooped over, heaving deeply. Ambrose didn't budge, although he should've. Cosnoaldo soon grabbed him with another arm and held him uncomfortably close to his seething face.

"My anatomy is unlike the other arborves'," he hissed. "You do not know where my heart is, do you?"

Then the king felt an axe in his neck, where Valma had thrown it. Ives then jumped high enough to grab it and strike the arm that held Ambrose. They both sprinted out of the king's reach.

"That is because you lack a heart!" Valter cried, partially kidding. He turned to Ambrose and Ives. "One must sever him at his base and cut him off from his roots. That is the only way a monster at this age will die."

Cosnoaldo now faced all four at once as they began to circle him again. He concluded that all of them would briefly rally together to take him out. He knew he didn't have the strength to take them all on. He bellowed for everyone on the field to hear, "Sound the call!"

After some hesitation, a low, almost inaudible trumpet blast was heard (if not felt) acres around the battle. For several moments, nothing happened or changed. Then, a multitude of rustlings occurred in the west. Ambrose looked to his left, and his spirit sank in terror. The western forest was slowly advancing toward the battle.

"It really is possible, then!" Ives gasped. "The still trees have been beckoned! The arborves have just gained the upper hand!"

14

THE MOST DARING MOVE

Amory saw the forest inching toward the battle, and he froze. He couldn't believe his eyes, although he had to. His team's way of escape had just become their biggest barrier. A fiery flash caught his eye, and he found Wybirt several yards away wreaking havoc on his foes. Amory made his way to him.

"What the heck is this?" Amory shouted, pointing his sheath at the western forest.

"The arborves have sounded the Forbidden Call, which enables every tree around them for miles to move and aid them in battle," the fairy answered. "I am just as surprised as you are. This has never happened before."

"Of course it would happen now!" Amory retorted. "Any suggestions on how to get to the Center now? We're practically out of the battle—or at least we were—and I'm not too keen on going back through to the other side."

"Nor am I, and trees are likely to start advancing from all sides anyway," said Wybirt. "They are still susceptible to fire, so we will use that to our advantage. Show me your swords."

Amory reached out his swords, coated in blood and sap, between him and the fairy. Wybirt touched the blades with the flame of his own and blew on them, and they instantly caught fire. Amory was startled before he realized that the fire on his swords stopped at the blades and never threatened the handles. The blades also stayed solid.

"Only *charisma* metal and cloth can stand against my fire," said the fairy. "Spread the flame. Let us find the rest of your team and touch their weapons as well. We should be able to get past these trees and deflect their jabs. Make haste!"

At that, they split up and went back into the battle to find their friends, which wasn't hard. All the Envoys had gotten near to the western edge of the fray by now. One by one, Amory and Wybirt found their friends, ignited their weapons, and gathered them all back together. Dilyn was the last to be found by Leona, Wybirt, and Nels. He only seemed half interested in them.

"Touch the fire on my blade with yours," Wybirt called. "We can still escape this madness."

"Not before I find my brother," Dilyn replied. "I'm not leaving without him. I've been looking for him, and I haven't had any luck yet."

"We're leaving now, lad," said Nels. "There's no time to search any longer."

"I can't just leave Ambrose to die!" Dilyn yelled.

"We don't have a choice, Dilyn," Leona retorted. "This world could be gone anytime now, and Ambrose has made his choice. Maybe Nazir will still spare him, since he said he has plans for him. All I know is that if Nazir wanted us to find him by now, we would've. The Vine gave us orders, Dilyn. We have to follow them now."

Beginning to bawl, Dilyn finally complied. As his bow was ignited, he murmured, "This isn't right." Then the four hurried to join the others.

After several minutes, everyone was reunited. Now Bernice's spearhead and flag, Chadmight's flails, Neisha's shields, Masato's claws, and everyone else's blades were in flames. They had all escaped from the now three-way battle and were several feet between it and the reach of the trees, which crawled toward them on their roots.

Wybirt twirled his sword. "Follow me! This forest is only a mile long, and we can make a portal once we break through the other side."

The fourteen then charged at the trees, yelling with all their might. Every tree around them swung or jabbed their countless branches brutally at them. The Envoys were able to block every strike that surrounded them and slash every trunk in their path, at least for the time being.

Cosnoaldo was doing his best to survive alone against his four foes. He used his every arm and root to his advantage to just hold the elf and three humans off until the forest arrived. He managed to inflict wounds on all four of them occasionally, but every cut they gave in return weakened him more.

Several bursts of fire could be seen in the distance, and Ives's curiosity finally conquered him as he looked for the origin. "The Envoys are heading into the forest!" he called. "They are leaving us!"

Remarkably, all five of them paused to see this. Cosnoaldo, Valma, and Valter all felt a brief yet undeniable sense of regret upon this sight. Ambrose was thankful they all escaped this chaos alive and hoped they would survive the trees. He also wondered how bad things really were getting if the Envoys were the first to leave.

After a moment, Valma thought to comment, "Good riddance."

"Indeed," Cosnoaldo snickered. "So much for that peace they proclaimed. What good did it do us?"

"Did you even try it out?" asked Ambrose.

"No, but it would not have done any good," Valter answered, stepping toward the arborven king again. "Only one thing will quench my thirst."

"You will die with that thirst!" Cosnoaldo roared.

So the five of them started fighting again, completely oblivious to their coming doom.

The Envoys were now racing through the forest, slashing trees left and right and ensuring no one was falling behind. Masato, still in dragon form, was the furthest ahead, simply crushing trees underfoot. The trees soon caught onto this, and the nearest ones to him in one moment grabbed all four of his ankles, pricking them everywhere as they locked on and pulled him down, careful not to touch his flaming claws. He could only breathe fire on those in front of him, and he yelped in pain. The other Envoys soon saw this and rushed to his aid. Edna, Malfreda, and Chadmight smashed away at the trees that held the dragon, eventually incinerating them.

As the trees' grip loosened, Masato decided to change from a dragon into a large leopard. Once free, he started jumping into the trees themselves, bounding from branch to branch, enflaming everything he touched with his claws. His ankles were still hurt, but he managed to fight through the pain with every leap.

Neisha and Agabio now led the way in addition to Wybirt, simply charging straight forward with their weapons poised, parrying when necessary. Everyone else attacked every trunk in their way and broke through every branch that threatened them. They fought against burly oaks, sharp birches, thick pines, shaggy evergreens, massive sequoias, and multiple fruit trees. Before long, they had cleared the forest and had come to a smaller clearing. After ensuring that no trees were chasing them from behind, Wybirt took out his Dagger and created a portal, ushering everyone through quickly.

Before she went through, Malfreda took one last look at her world. Topiada was up in smoke, and the sound of clashing metal and wood and screams was heard everywhere. She and Amory and Wybirt were the last to take their feet off of Topiada's earth before reaching the Center.

As soon as the team entered Nazir's presence, all of their weapons save Wybirt's ceased flaming. Immediately upon seeing the Vine, Amory moved to the front of the group and knelt low to the ground. His voice was shaky with remorse and fear.

"I'm sorry, Dad," he said as tears started to form. "I failed you, and I failed this mission. We didn't bring anyone to you except Malfreda here, who's already an Envoy. We told everyone possible about the message you gave us, and we tried to stop them from fighting, but we didn't succeed. You have every right to be mad at me."

"Amory," Nazir said gently, using one of his leaves to lift Amory's head by his chin, "you did well. You all did well. None of you gave up telling my message and calling for everyone to return to me, and you stood your ground even when it would've meant death. You did everything you could for this task. I pulled you out because despite me tugging at their hearts and sending you to them, none of the peoples—including the Self-Worthy—would budge. This was entirely their choice. All of them decided to stick to their grudges and pride instead of letting it go, lest they face me. And grudges are something of which you are not entirely innocent."

Amory sighed deeply. "I know you're talking about me and the Self-Worthy again, and I won't deny I do still have a little bitterness toward them. I'm trying to let it go, but if it weren't for the Self-Worthy's constant interference, everything would go so much smoother! Think of how many more people would've come to you if it wasn't for them!"

"They have free will just as you do," Nazir replied. "They chose to live the lie they do, and they chose every place they've ever travelled to. I also allowed them to go to the worlds they've been to, because it ultimately contributes to my plan. Don't forget that if it wasn't for the Self-Worthy, today you would be a pile of ashes in a fallen tower in Growan or slaves in King Ever's castle. Whether the Self-Worthy was in Topiada or not, the people there still would not have chosen me."

Amory nodded slowly. "I'm sorry for still letting my anger burn against them. I know it was wrong, no matter how much we conflict with each other. I'm also sorry for killing Maewing. I genuinely didn't mean to; I was just defending myself."

"Wait, what?" asked Bernice and Dilyn. The whole team was in shock.

"It's true," said Nazir somberly. "Maewing is dead. As with the others, I'd called to her several times and told her to come to me and find freedom, but she wouldn't listen. She decided to keep pursuing her vain dream, knowing full well her time was limited. I loved her the same as I love all of you, but she didn't love me, and it grieves me to say she died without loving me and therefore will spend eternity in suffering."

Nazir continued. "Amory, in Liberdane you learned that Envoys are not meant to bind with other groups and ideologies because their missions and values aren't all mine, however similar they might seem. But in learning this, you led your team down the other extreme, which is outright going against them. While your beliefs conflict, the Self-Worthy and any other group or culture are not the enemy. Our real enemy is much subtler, making anyone but himself seem like the real enemy, including me. But I do forgive you all, and I am not done using you yet."

"Thank you, Dad," said Amory, standing up to join the others.

Nazir turned to the fairy and sighed angrily. "Wybirt, it is time. Start summoning a fire wind and destroy Topiada and everyone on it until it no longer exists."

"Yes, my Lord," Wybirt answered, fully understanding but also mournful.

The fairy proceeded to wave his sword and empty hand around in different intentional motions, which made his sword and eyes brighter and created a ball of fire in front of him, starting out the size of a pea. It didn't look to be expanding just yet, but everyone knew it would.

As he watched this take place, Dilyn started shaking his head. He said aloud, "There has to be more to it than this." He then turned and boldly approached the Vine and dropped to one knee, bowing. "My King, I am requesting permission to return to Topiada to make one last appeal for everyone to come see you. No one there knows exactly what's coming. They might be keener on seeing you if they heard and saw their doom approaching. Could we give them a chance then?"

"Permission denied," Nazir said, unfazed. "These people have rejected me long enough. I delayed this punishment of their pride for millennia, and now the delay is over."

Dilyn was persistent. "But now that the punishment is coming, don't you think people would be keener to relent?"

"Dilyn, I have given these people innumerable chances to relent. This was their last, and they still refused. Their time is up."

"My Lord, may I ask how you would be glorified in that?" Dilyn asked.

"Dilyn—" Leona interrupted, trying not to let her friend make a fool out of himself.

Nazir eagerly answered anyway. "I will be glorified in that those who hear of this will fear me more and take me seriously, rather than thinking I am all love and no justice. Otherwise, they would assume I'll just forgive their unrepented evil deeds forever. I do indeed show immense and constant mercy, but it is limited by time for those who don't choose me. Justice must ultimately be done and their grievances atoned for, either by my blood or their own. I gave a free way out of their doom the same as I gave you, but they failed to see it."

"But what would people say of you afterward?" asked Dilyn, despite his friends' insistence on stopping. "Wouldn't they say that you send vine branches on pointless missions that produce no fruit, even though you said they would, which means you're going back on your word?"

"Dilyn, what are you saying?!" Amory gasped.

"Even though it's not true," Dilyn continued. "That's what people would think, and they would never come to you if they believed that. I've heard the Self-Worthy say several other bad and false things about you, Father. Why would you give them and other groups more ammo?"

The other Envoys stood silent and appalled. All of them, including Dilyn, waited to see how the already rageful Vine would react—what he would say, what he would do. He finally said in the same tone, yet now less angry, "I have heard you, and I will let you and whoever wishes to join you reenter Topiada and bring here as many people as will listen. But I will not stop my wrath from coming. You have five hours before Wybirt's fire wind is complete. Anyone still in the path of its destruction by that time will not be spared. Be back here before then."

"Yes, Father, thank you a million times for your mercy and justice," said Dilyn. He stood back up and turned to the team who was all as shocked as he was. He grinned. "Anyone else coming?"

Almost all of them stepped forward within seconds, smiling.

"We'd be fools if we didn't take this opportunity!" said Panos.

Then they realized that one of them was hesitating: Agabio. He was shaking his head repeatedly.

"Aren't you coming, friend?" Chadmight asked.

No, signed the faun. *I can't physically declare anything, so there is no point of me going. I'll just stay here and pray you bring many—no, everyone—here.*

"You'd be of more help than you apparently know," said Neisha, who was starting to comprehend his sign language. "You use a sign language that the arborves can understand."

Malfreda added, "And not all arborves speak in human tongues, which makes you and me the only ones who can communicate with them. I am going to need your help if we are to reach all of my kind. Please come with us."

After a little more thought, Agabio nodded and joined them. They all stepped closer to Topiada's entry portal, standing behind Wybirt.

Amory turned to face the others. "Everyone, synchronize your watches or put them in stopwatch mode."

"I will give you exactly five hours the second you hit Topiadan soil again," Nazir said.

Everyone complied. Even those who weren't from Earth had received watches upon arriving to Earth, excepting Malfreda of course, and Masato, who knew he wouldn't be able to keep one as long as he kept changing forms. Soon, everyone was ready. The time showed 6:58 p.m.

Amory breathed in deeply and put a hand on Dilyn's shoulder, shaking him firmly. "This is going to work," Amory said, smirking.

"Go and bring as many people to me as you can!" said Nazir. "You have my power and blessing. Be strong and courageous, and don't lose heart."

Wybirt stepped aside to let them through the portal, and the thirteen charged into Topiada once again, a refreshed zeal coming over them all.

7:02 p.m.

The Envoys found themselves on another smaller plain. The ground was very uneven and looked like a sloppily tilled garden. The Envoys assumed that a forest used to be here before being summoned to the battle. They wondered where the trees were now. Over to their left, they could hear the battle raging on, smoke rising likely from where the fourteen were earlier.

"All right," Amory began. "We have till midnight to gather everyone to the Center. To do that, we'll obviously need to split up. One team needs to go to the arborven habitats, one team needs to find the rest of the humans, and the last team needs to head back into the battle." Amory hesitated in thought. "And don't ignore the Self-Worthy. They need this hope and escape the same as everyone else. Any volunteers to any team?"

Malfreda crawled forward. "Agabio and I will take the arborves. I know where they all are."

"I will join you," said Panos.

"I'll go back to the battle," said Dilyn firmly. "We'll need to hurry before more people die."

"Agreed," Amory replied. "Bernice and I will go with you."

"I don't think that's a good idea," Bernice refuted. "Since you argued with and killed Maewing, I don't think the Self-Worthy will listen to us if you're there."

Amory sighed. "You're right, hon. We'll head the team going for the humans instead. Dilyn will lead the team heading to the battle. Who else will go with him?"

"I will," said Leona. Chadmight and the dwarves also stepped forward.

"I'll go with you guys to the humans," said Edna, and Twyla joined her.

"Which people is more widespread?" Masato asked. "I'll help that team get to everyone faster."

"The humans, actually," Malfreda answered. "They have multiplied a lot and have established many small villages and territories, including King Hilmar's castle. I can burrow, and I might be able to reach every arborven clan in time, so it would be good if you helped Amory's team."

"Very well," said Masato, proceeding to turn into another dragon. This time he was longer, sleeker, and blue, and could travel much faster now using four wings. As soon as the rest of his team mounted him, they all caught sight of a small, glowing yellow circle in the sky where the sun would've been at noon. It maintained its brightness even though the real sun was setting.

"The Midnight Sun!" Malfreda exclaimed. "An arborf in ancient times prophesied about this, saying that when it appears, the whole world will disappear! That prophecy is actually coming true! Only a select few believe in it, but we will use this regardless."

"It has to be Wybirt's fire wind being formed," said Amory. "Point to it for whomever you find. Time's running out. Let's go!"

7:20 p.m.

Dilyn's team finally got to the battle, managing to avoid the trees altogether. They were dismayed by the amount of corpses they saw. There were more dead now than living. Wasting no time, they plunged back into the fray.

"Are you winded at all, Dilyn?" Leona called. "Is the cancer hindering you?"

"Actually no!" Dilyn said, not looking back. "I don't feel the slightest bit weak. Not since we came back. I'll be able to make it."

They started to call out to everyone around them, having to block a few blows in the process. "Topiada's end is coming!" they all declared. "Nazir's wrath is going to fall on the world in a matter of hours, but he's extending his mercy one last time. You have one last chance to come with us to him and come to terms with him. Come to Nazir, so he might forgive you and spare you from the death and destruction to which this battle will pale in comparison!"

A handful of fighters from all three sides finally stopped to listen to them. They still doubted.

"How are we to know that this is true?" a woman asked.

"See that thing straight above us that looks like a sun?" Chadmight replied. "That is a ball of fire being formed by Wybirt the Zealous at Nazir's command. By midnight, it will be complete and unleashed on this whole universe. Are you willing to wait and see if this is true? It will be too late then."

The soldiers around them all thought for a few moments. Finally a male arborf asked, "How do we escape?"

Neisha immediately summoned a portal just outside the battle. "Go through here, and Nazir will be on the other side. Believe me, this is no trap," she said. "This is how we go between worlds. This is your only escape now."

A few of the troops started toward the portal, then saw each other and stopped. "I refuse to escape and let the humans escape too!" another arborf said.

"Are you willing to die with that hostility?" Nels retorted. "Or would you rather live, whether they live or not?"

After another moment, all three sides finally gave in and walked through the portal together. More soldiers saw this as the Envoys continued to call out to them.

"I'll stay here at this portal and call people from here," said Neisha. "I'll make sure it stays open. The rest of you, keep going!"

At that, the other four continued inward, shouting at the top of their lungs for all to hear.

8:00 p.m.

Masato and his riders finally spotted Hilmar's castle. They'd decided to start with the most populated human establishments to get to more people sooner. They figured the castle and capital would be a great place to start. This castle was mostly made of logs and a few cut boulders and sat on a rocky shore of an ocean stretching as far as the eye could see. The Envoys assumed this was the place where the humans' youthful ancestors had first landed and fought the arborves for the first time.

To avoid getting shot down, Masato landed at the entrance after swooping over the castle's courtyards and towers long enough for the people to see them. His friends dismounted him and ran toward the entrance—a closed and sealed wooden drawbridge that'd grant access across a jagged moat. The five got as close to the moat's edge as they could and shouted:

"Hail, humans of Topiada! We've come from other worlds to bring you urgent news about your own! Please let us in!"

Within a minute or two, the drawbridge was let down, revealing male and female guards, servants, and children, all confused and bewildered at these aliens. Bernice held her flag high as the Envoys sprinted across the bridge into the main courtyard where they knew they'd be heard from anywhere in the castle.

"Topiada's about to be destroyed!" Edna began, panting a little. "Your animosity with the arborves has gone on long enough. The Vine, Nazir, King of every world, has sent us to tell you that he's seen your ongoing war with the arborves and that neither side has come to him, who is the true source of life and peace and goodness. As King and creator of your world, he has deemed Topiada unfit for him now, since you care about nothing but vengeance. He is going to destroy this world in only a few hours."

"But he also sent us to extend his mercy to you," Twyla continued. "We are going to all of your villages and clans to urge you to come with us to the Vine so he can rid you of your pride and bitterness and save you from his anger."

Their audience had to take all of this in for several moments. Finally, a man asked, "Did you say this King of the multiverse was a vine? We were raised to distrust all intelligent plant life."

"I hate to say it, but you were raised wrong," Masato gurgled. "Not all plants are hostile, and Nazir is the epitome of good and decided to take the form of a vine. He is only hostile to those who are repeatedly and decidedly hostile to him. Yet even though we all were hostile to him, he loved us enough to bring us out of the way of his anger and adopt us into his eternal family. This invite is offered to you, and it is the last one you will ever receive. If you value your lives, please take it!"

"We must consult our king on this matter," said another man. "He would know what to do. We must wait for him to return from Xenia."

The Envoys lowered their heads. "We have already told King Hilmar about this," Bernice replied. "It did not sway him from going into battle anyway."

"So you have seen the battle take place?" a young girl asked. "How is it faring? Has it gone ill?"

"That battle should never have happened," Bernice said solemnly. "Many are already dead, including your king."

The now hundreds of humans gasped and wailed upon hearing this.

"This tumult has gone too far!" a woman yelled. "We must find a way to avenge our king!"

"No!" Amory bellowed. "That vengeful attitude is exactly what has gotten you this close to being destroyed in the first place! It's what drove your king to his death and possibly everyone else's still in that battle. Hopefully those who are still alive will accept the invite to escape Topiada's fate, but what matters is, will you?"

Edna then decided to make a portal in the center of the courtyard. "Enter here and see Nazir and be spared from your deaths. I will stay until the last minute and then join you. It's now or never."

The humans all thought for long moments. Finally, a little boy stepped forward, followed by a few others, who were in turn followed by a dozen. Soon, many started to come, but not everyone. Spouses came without their mates. Some siblings came alone. Children came without their parents and vice versa, all ignoring the calls of their stubborn loved ones. Other families came forward together.

"Go on in," said Bernice. "Nazir's waiting."

The few dozen who accepted started to go through, completely denying themselves and how they were raised to think. Several hundred still lingered.

Edna turned to her friends. "Go ahead to the next village. I'll stay here and keep the portal open. See you in a few hours!"

The remaining four were gone in a flash.

9:15 p.m.

During their journey to some of the arborves, Malfreda, Agabio, and Panos had to resurface from time to time to receive fresh air (carbon dioxide for Malfreda). Each time they came up, the sky was darker. By the time they finally arrived at the first larger arborven cluster, it was fully night. Agabio was banking on his assumption that arborves had perfect night vision. Otherwise his signs would be useless.

They surfaced in front of a new encampment, formed as Cosnoaldo's emergency retreat point. They were surrounded by another moving forest, headed in the direction of the fateful conflict. The trees sensed that the trio were not on Cosnoaldo's side, so they attacked them as they went. Panos was suddenly grabbed by an oak, and Agabio had to impale the branch that held him for the minotaur to be freed. Between jabs from the trees, Malfreda shouted in her own tongue that they meant the arborves no harm, but the trees wouldn't listen. The three had to get in the midst of the arborves for the trees to leave them alone. Arborven families, healers, and the wounded from the battle all stood or lay restless, waiting to hear the results of the fight.

One of the others present recognized Malfreda and spoke in the arborven tongue. "Malfreda, what are you doing here? Who are these alien intruders with you?"

Malfreda wasted no time. "These are fellow Envoys of the Vine, from whom we have just come. His anger with you has reached its peak. He is about to have Topiada destroyed, and he sent us to warn you and to give you a way of escape that will allow you to meet Nazir."

Several from the Envoys' audience shook their heads at each other. "This is fool's talk," one older, wounded soldier said. "Simply because a battle is occurring which these naysayers are against, they think the entire world is ending."

"This world is ending!" Panos shouted, with Agabio translating both ways through signs. "And this battle is merely one of many that brought us closer to this doom. Look to the heavens!"

The arborves glanced halfheartedly at the sky and quickly beheld a much larger yellow orb straight above them, dimly illuminating what was below it. Whispers were heard amongst them.

"That is the Midnight Sun!" Malfreda declared. "The long-foretold sign we were told we would see upon the demise of our universe. That sun will grow until it has matured, which now is less than three hours away. Once it is fully grown, it will be unleashed on this world until there is nothing left. There is no denying its reality."

"How do you know all of this?" one caretaker asked.

Nazir told us himself before we left, Agabio signed. *You have his word that his anger is coming and his forgiveness is waiting.*

Panos proceeded to open a portal before everyone present. "This is your only escape from death now," he said. "Are you willing to take the risk to wait and die, or take the risk to be momentarily ridiculed and yet live? I have been imprisoned for believing these things, and I would do it all over again in a heartbeat."

The arborves stared at the portal for a second. "This is the only home we know," said one of them despairingly.

I left the only home I knew to see the Vine too, replied Agabio. *I do miss my home, but what I found since I met Nazir has been so worth it. The Vine is worth leaving behind everything you know.*

"Your constant choices of your own satisfaction instead of your multiversal King and liberator brought you to this state," Panos added. "This is your last chance to undo that choice. I am so sorry it has come to this, but the fact is that it has. Who will come?"

A handful crawled forward, and then a few more. The Envoy trio was delighted but also determined to save more. Malfreda's eye fell on a short arborf carrying a trumpet. This was one of Cosnoaldo's many heralds and trumpeters, and this one had also stepped forward. Malfreda approached him.

"I have need of your skill, my friend. Every arborf on Topiada needs to know about this, and I now fear I won't be able to reach everyone in time. Please, could you sound the call that would summon every arborf alive to the call's source, so we can continue to appeal to them?"

"I am at your service, my lady," the herald replied. "I will warn you, though, that every arborf will hear the call, but it is still their choice of whether or not they come. I fear those on the battlefield will not come."

"As do I," replied Malfreda. "But there is hope for them yet."

9:30 p.m.

Dilyn and Chadmight were nearly blinded by the dark of night and almost muted by their sore throats. The Midnight Sun was their only source of light now, other than patches of fire here and there. They had both been bellowing as loud as they could for anyone to hear, and they had managed to convince some of those around them to walk through Neisha's portal. They would've made their own, but they had to keep moving and not have to gravitate away from any portals they had made. They had to be strategic about where they were and where they wanted the portals to be.

What voices they had left were suddenly drowned out by a loud and long multisyllabic horn, coming from the northern forest. Many of the arborves suddenly became a tad sidetracked and even disoriented. A few eventually left the battle and headed for the direction of the call. Dilyn and Chadmight didn't know what the sound meant, but they hoped for the best.

A familiar green glow behind some soldiers caught Dilyn's eye, and he and Chadmight went toward it. When they got to it, they found Ambrose wielding the Sword of *Chârâsh* once again, along with his cutlass of course. He and Ives had gotten separated from the others by the trees and were now trying to find their way back to the rulers. Ambrose had to look twice before he realized who had just come.

"You're back?" Ambrose exclaimed. "I thought you'd left!"

"We did, and then we asked Nazir to send us back," replied Dilyn. "He brought us out because his wrath is coming, and it won't stop before this whole universe is wiped out. He's going to destroy Topiada, Ambrose! That's why we're back—to tell everyone and to bring them to the Center so we can all escape this fate."

Chadmight had moved ahead while Ambrose stood there for several moments, looking around him and the slowly waning battle. "But I'm so close," he moaned. "I'm so close to finishing our goal."

"So is Nazir with his goal," Dilyn responded. "He won't bar his anger and judgment on these stubborn peoples much longer. As long as you're on Topiadan soil, you will face that judgment too. Chadmight, open a portal here!"

The centaur complied.

"Come with us, bro. What's keeping you from seeing him again?"

Ambrose paused, staring at the ground. Then, he used his Sword to create a portal of his own instead.

"Retreat!" Ambrose yelled to any of the Self-Worthy who could hear. "Fall back to Ourrance! Topiada's about to collapse!"

Dilyn watched in dismay as Ambrose found Lisias, who eagerly agreed to help him rally the others. A tear fell from Dilyn's face. This was not what he wanted to happen. He wanted Ambrose to finally come to terms with Nazir and become an Envoy himself, to find his true purpose and stop living a lie. This was not so, and Dilyn's heart sank. But as long as Ambrose escaped and was alive, he would still have a chance to surrender to the Vine later. Dilyn was OK with this thought. He then glanced over and saw several other Self-Worthy members hesitating, torn between which portal to go to. Ives was one of these creatures. Dilyn could see the confusion and disillusionment on their faces—the same that he had had several months ago.

"Nazir is waiting for you," Dilyn called to them. "You don't have to live these lies anymore."

Without another word, Ives and the others decided to walk through Chadmight's portal.

Thank you, Father, Dilyn thought.

10:20 p.m.

Only Amory and Bernice remained riding on Masato now. They had left Twyla at Princess Valma's encampment, where the Envoys had first been taken upon their arrival to Topiada. Several humans from there decided to go to the Center as well, which encouraged the Envoys to keep looking and calling. Now the remaining three looked for any and every human village or settlement in the world. They finally found one consisting of merely five houses in the thick of the woods. Masato landed in a nearby clearing, and the Walters bolted off toward the homes. The sight and sound of the dragon had awakened everyone. The couple gave the same warning and invitation as they had before and opened a portal. The families (lacking those who were able to fight) contemplated what they heard for a long time. Finally, one man too old for battle spoke up.

"If you claim that this Nazir is the source of goodness, then how could such a 'benevolent' King resort to such destruction?" he asked.

"Because our King is also the source of justice," Bernice answered. "He can only tolerate unrepentant evil for so long. He will forgive you of the ways you've gone against him if you acknowledge that you've done so and turn back to him, but not otherwise. All unforgiven evil still has to be punished, as I'm sure you're aware."

"If he was so good, why would he not simply purge all the evil in the multiverse and be rid of it once and for all?" one boy asked.

"What do you think he's doing now to your world?" asked Amory in reply. "All throughout the cosmos, he is indeed purging evil but in a way that he might spare us—those whom he loves more than we know. He's decided to do it gradually. Whether through destruction or mercy, he is ridding the multiverse of *our* wickedness, one soul at a time."

"Who do you think you are, coming to us as strangers and telling us that we're at fault and we're the reason the world will supposedly fall?" an older woman asked. "You have only just met us. You have no proof."

Amory was about to reply, but he and Bernice both heard Nazir's voice in their heads.

Leave them. They will not come.

"What? No! Not already!" Amory said loud enough for only Bernice to hear.

There's no time. Shake the dust off your feet and keep going. You've warned them and given them their only hope, but they will not yield. Don't waste your lessening time here when there are others elsewhere who will yield.

In tears, the couple backed away slowly.

"This is your last chance before we go to find someone else," Bernice declared.

"Good riddance!" said the first man. "I hope whomever else you intrude upon will be as sane as we are!"

At that, the Walters turned, wiped their boots on the ground, and headed for Masato. The portal closed behind them when Bernice got far enough away. The dragon was surprised when they both returned.

"None of them came?" he gurgled.

"No, and Nazir told us to move on," replied Amory. "Now to the next village."

"At the Vine's command," said Masato, and he took off again once the couple had mounted him.

After several minutes, they found another slightly larger settlement. This one sat in a clearing large enough for Masato to land in. Everyone here was asleep, and there were no candles or lanterns lit inside. Several lanterns and firepits were burning outside, however, to keep arborves away during the night.

Masato roared, "Wake up, humans! Topiada's about to fall, and time is short! We've come to help you escape!"

He didn't have to say it twice. Soon, every human there was outside, bewildered by the dragon, their other visitors, and their urgency.

"Is the world really ending?" one older woman asked.

"In a little over an hour," answered Bernice. "That sun you see in the middle of the night is a ball of fire that's going to be unleashed everywhere here."

"How will you help us escape that?" a little girl chimed in.

"Nazir, the good and loving and just King of every world, is fed up with the stubbornness and atrocities of both you humans and the arborves," Masato replied. "He's going to have this world destroyed because he cannot stand the evil here anymore. But he's sent us to bring you to him. If you choose to accept and turn from your pride and ask him personally to rid you of it, then he will gladly spare you and adopt you without hesitation."

The humans looked at each other, frightened. An old man said, "It is obvious that Topiada is mired in war and death. But we did not know that our world was one of dozens, or that there was a good king over them all. Are you sure that such a king would see us, a lowly and impure people?"

"Positive," said Amory. "We're just as lowly and impure as you are, and he joyfully adopted us when we accepted and believed in him."

"And you are sure that he will not hesitate to do the same for us?" another girl asked.

"Yes, we are," Bernice smiled.

"All right," said the second girl. "I will go see him." Her parents, brother, and several others agreed. Only one man remained unyielding.

The Envoys beamed, and Amory opened a portal. "Nazir is on the other side. I will join you soon," he said.

As the majority entered the portal, Amory eyed the man who was lingering. "I still have many questions," the man said.

Amory grinned tenderly. "I will stay and talk with you for a while, but we have a very short time before the end arrives." He then turned to Bernice and Masato. "Keep going further. Masato, drop Bernice off at the next village, and if they accept the invitation, leave on your own and find the rest. We're so close!"

Masato nodded. But Bernice, rather than mounting him, started toward her husband. Amory saw what was coming, and they both met and kissed passionately, hoping this wasn't their last one.

"I love you," Bernice said as she walked away smiling. She finally began to climb Masato again, who was rolling his eyes.

"You just had to get in one last one, didn't you?" the dragon groaned. "Oh, the multitude of reasons I'm a bachelor!"

Amory chuckled as the two whizzed away.

11:03 p.m.

The battle had decreased a lot in the past hour. Ambrose and what was left of the Self-Worthy had deserted the world, and now around a hundred humans and arborves remained, darting between the hostile trees. Neisha, Nels, and Chadmight fought to stay close to their portals, but once everyone around them had either left or died, they closed their portals and pursued remnants of the still skirmishing soldiers. They would not rest until everyone alive who they found at least heard about what was coming and the love that awaited.

Dilyn unexpectedly caught up with Leona, who'd been pleading with Cosnoaldo, Valma, and Valter. Their fighting had gotten far worse now that the trees had arrived. Cosnoaldo had two fewer arms, and the human heirs were not without scars and broken bones of their own. Leona herself could only hold her own for so long against so many foes. One tree had slashed and bloodied her side, and another had stabbed straight through her shin. When he got there, Dilyn had to dive and tackle her before another tree could run her through.

"Are you OK?" Dilyn asked.

"I will be," Leona heaved.

Dilyn then got up and created his portal, shooting the green ray directly through the trio so they would stop for at least a second. It worked. Even the trees shied away from the portal and left them all alone.

"Listen to us!" Dilyn shouted angrily. "Nazir is going to destroy your home within minutes because of your vengeful and stubborn attitudes, but at this rate, you'll all die even before then! Leona and I are here to give you all a chance to live. Are you so demented and set in your ways that you'll choose death over life? There is still time for you to escape this judgment and make things right between yourselves and Nazir."

The three stood there for only a moment. Valter, not breaking his gaze from the Envoys, yelled, "I will not go as long as the king does! I would rather die than live with my parents' killer!"

Cosnoaldo smirked. "I might go, but if these aliens go as well, I will still find a way to get back at them."

"Nazir won't accept that," Leona replied. "You must surrender yourself and your hostility to him. Your hostility is what angers him."

"Maybe we should listen to them!" A voice came from the darkness. In a moment, Baron Rolle emerged from the moving forest, also scarred by the nearby trees. "The Envoys might be right about this. Think about it: since they first arrived, they cared about nothing but our good!"

"From a superficial view, perhaps," Valma scoffed. "Are you really going to betray us too, Baron? I thought better of you."

"You may think as much or as little of me as you like, your majesties," Rolle replied, "but come to yourselves and think. Name one instance when these Envoys actually harmed us in any way. The assassins in the sky who killed our king were from the Self-Worthy, not the Vine."

"These two along with the others killed some arborven soldiers when they first arrived!" Cosnoaldo moaned.

"They attacked us first," Leona retorted. "We were simply defending ourselves."

"Time is running out fast," said Dilyn. "Please, choose life and see what lies in store on the other side!"

The baron added, "My lieges, my companions, after all of the risks of death you have taken as long as I have known you, why would you draw the line here? Come with me!"

After a moment, one of the rulers finally let down their arms. It was Valter. He dropped his sword and went with Rolle to the edge of the portal. He turned to Valma and reached out his hand.

"Join us, sister. Look around you. What more do we have to lose?"

Valma, at a loss for words and reason, glanced at her surroundings. The moving forest had passed entirely through the battlefield, exposing the thousands of corpses from all sides. The princess teared up as she saw all the human bodies, some of them belonging to close friends.

"So much blood," she finally cried. "This blood must be paid for."

"Nazir already paid for it with his own," Dilyn responded. "Anyone who stays behind will pay for themselves with their own."

Valma's gaze fell to the ground, and she tightened her lips and the grip on her axe. "Then I will be here to ensure it."

At that, she leaped onto Cosnoaldo again, who uttered a deep, malicious chuckle. The two began their ferocity again.

"No!" cried the others who watched.

11:55 p.m.

Malfreda, Agabio, and Panos were still ushering arborves through their portal. While many had ended up crawling away in scorn, many also gradually decided to take the Envoys at their word. There was a handful remaining now, still doubting. One of these Malfreda recognized as her mother, whom she hadn't seen in years. Suddenly, the wind started picking up at an exponentially increasing rate, swirling in every direction. To avoid getting whisked away, the arborves clenched their roots deeper into the ground, and Panos and Agabio held onto Malfreda.

Panos looked at his watch. "The end is upon us! Get inside quickly!"

Malfreda translated this, and without giving it a second thought, every arborf present sprinted into the portal, fighting the wind. After everyone else was through, Malfreda, pulling her two friends with her, trudged toward the portal. She took one last look at her dying homeland before stepping through.

12:00 a.m.

Leona looked at her watch as she tried not to go airborne in the wind. "Time's up!" she cried.

The whole world heard a large bang, and they looked above them to behold the Midnight Sun puffing out in an all-encompassing gust of fire, descending quickly toward them.

"Everyone, come here if you want to escape!" Dilyn called to anyone nearby. Some came at the last minute while others just fled.

Rolle and Valter grabbed Leona, and they all limped into the portal. As they did so, Valter looked back and shouted, "Sister!"

"Just a moment!" Valma yelled back without looking. She was hacking away at Cosnoaldo's base while clinging to him, ignoring his constant stabs and slashes.

Dilyn inched to the portal, not willing to give up. "Just let go and come on!" he cried.

His last call was void. He could feel the intense heat as he tearfully leapt into the white of the portal, glancing at the last second at Valma and Cosnoaldo, who looked terrified as they finally saw their judgment come before they were engulfed in red and orange . . . and then white.

15

SETTLEMENTS

D ilyn crawled into the Center to avoid Wybirt's fire and
found that he wasn't the only one doing so. All of his
friends as well as the handfuls of creatures with them were also
coming in at the last possible second. Surprisingly, there was
room for them all to come through. Dilyn beheld hundreds of
arborves, humans, and former Self-Worthy members all around
Nazir. The Center seemed to have enlarged to accommodate
them all. Everyone had paused to watch Wybirt finish the
punishment of Topiada.

The fairy stood still in a wide finished-striking stance. He
was out of breath from all of the buildup as well as the final
shout he'd uttered upon releasing the fire wind. Nothing could
be seen in the portal in front of him but a white, fiery light. After
a few minutes, the light inside started to fade, as did the portal
itself. Nazir retracted his branch that stretched inside the portal
until it was completely out, and the portal then disappeared as
though it had never been there. Only the backdrop of outer
space that covered the whole Center remained in the portal's
place. Topiada was no more.

Nazir then continued to speak with those who had already
come through—at the moment it was Ives and some of the Self-

Worthy with whom he'd come. What the Vine said to them, he extended to everyone.

"I was not going to stop my wrath," he said, talking about what had just taken place. "But I still love you enough to create a way for you to escape it and reconcile with me. Those who refused this love, for one reason or another, have now paid for their wickedness with their own lives, which you know is just. I am mourning those who are not here, but they made their own choices, and I cannot force them into anything. However, I am overjoyed at the sight of each of you here and that you decided to seek out a way other than death. This is that way. It is clear that you have all done evil things to me and each other, whether or not you knew it. Blood had to be paid for that evil, and it should be yours. But that would mean I would have no one to love, and no one to love me back. I would have no one to provide for, fight for, guide, correct, and give good gifts to. Therefore, I decided that I would pay the price with my own blood and then rise to life again so that whoever believes in this and accepts being adopted into my family would be pardoned and free. Those who do this I then make my Envoys so that those I put them around can also hear this news. My desire is that everyone would come to me and be freed from their bondage. But then again, that is each individual's choice."

Ives dared to step forward a little. "I speak for all of the former Self-Worthy present when I say that we have been deceived about you, O Nazir, because we had been relentlessly following Maewing, who told lies about you. Now we know that she, though seemingly right, was wrong and skewed, and we want to get to know the real you. I personally have seen you before, but now I want to trust you."

The Vine replied, "Maewing was right in that I created everyone uniquely and that each person has something to contribute to my Kingdom that no one else can. This is why I gave that to them. But she was wrong in thinking and teaching that anyone can be made worthy by their own right—worthy of acceptance, honor, or even life, let alone eternal life and the right to be with me forever."

"I know this to be true now," Ives responded. "I accept and believe."

The others with him said the same thing, as did the rest of the hundreds of creatures there. The surviving arborves and humans finally surrendered their conflict and hostility, ready to be free of it. Valter, Rolle, and Malfreda's mother were among them. Gradually, the arborves' brown leaves began dropping until every last one was gone. The Envoys outwardly rejoiced as they watched Nazir embrace the crowd all at once, purging their old blood, replacing it with his own, and filling the void in them that only he could fill. It was strange and delightful to see humans and arborves together in something other than a fight. It was just as delightful to see people from the Self-Worthy come to see the truth as well. As the adoption was completed, some of the new converts were crying and even laughing.

"Now," said Nazir, "I have some gifts for you all." He proceeded to give them all Daggers and molds for their weapons and armor. A couple of them even received flags. "Go to the portal behind me on the right, and the forgers there will assemble your Envoy armor and weapons. I love you, and I am so thankful you each came to me!"

"Thank you and praise you, Nazir!" the throng said in spurts. They then sifted through the portal to *Chârâsh*.

When the last of the new recruits were through, Nazir turned to Amory's team and Wybirt. "They won't be long in there. I gave Azarias help today because I knew there would be a great harvest. Well done, all of you, for being bent on bringing all these souls to me and persisting until the very last moment. You all set an example that many Envoys in the future would do well to follow because you followed my own example. Your mission is not quite over, though, as these people now need new homes. The former Self-Worthy must return to their old homes and loved ones to tell those around them about their change. The arborves will be led to Liberdane and the surrounding Hertengardian realms by Wybirt—yes, son, you must return there—Ives, Malfreda, who is to join Amory's team for good, and Dilyn. The arborves will do well in that atmosphere and climate. Everyone else will lead the humans back to Earth to get settled into the U.S."

"Wait," said Edna. "Why is Dilyn going to Hertengard and not Earth?"

This was news to Dilyn too, but he was at peace with it. He answered, "Because that's apparently where Nazir's sending me to finish my mission . . . my final mission."

"What?" asked Nels in disbelief.

Dilyn sighed and looked at his friends. "The cancer's spread too far. It's overtaking me even now, and my time in this life is running out. That's why I pushed so hard to go back into Topiada, because this was my last mission, and I wanted to make it count. Nazir's sending me to Hertengard so I can follow up with it and cultivate the seeds that have now been planted in the lives Nazir just saved. I will not be returning to Earth." This last part he said with a gulp. "This is goodbye . . . for now."

"No!" cried Leona. "Why can't Twyla or the dwarves go instead of you? This can't be the last time I see you!"

Dilyn put a hand on her shoulder. "Because that's Nazir's will for me, and we all have to submit to it. This is how it has to be, and there's no use arguing, although I also want to. Evidently this is the way that Nazir gets the most glory and conquered hearts. I probably wouldn't have even wanted to reenter Topiada if this wasn't my last mission! And this won't be the last time I see you ever. After death is *Paradeisos*, and we'll all eventually be together again there!"

The new recruits gradually began to return from the forge. They lingered with the Vine while Dilyn said his goodbyes. He started with Chadmight, Agabio, and Panos, all of them tearfully placing their right fists on their chests in salute.

Panos stated, "No honor trumps that of suffering for the Vine, but a close second is the honor of serving alongside an audacious and compassionate Envoy such as you. You will be dearly missed, my brother."

Agabio then instantaneously lunged to give Dilyn the tightest hug he'd ever given. Dilyn chuckled between breaths, "You are stronger than you know, man! I can't wait to see you again."

When they let go, he turned to Masato in his original form, who simply shook his hand. The tanuki wasn't even close to crying, but his beady eyes did show deep care.

"It's been fun serving with you," Masato said swiftly. "Things won't be the same without you."

Dilyn grinned. "Things haven't been the same since you joined! Hey, do me a favor and teach these guys how to live a little on your next missions. Our leader tends to get a bit of a no-nonsense attitude at times." This he said smirking at Amory, who smiled back.

A grin broke out on Masato's face. "Oh, don't worry. I got you," he winked.

Dilyn giggled and proceeded to face Twyla, Neisha, and Nels. Each of them embraced him individually, Nels for the longest.

"I wish we had more time together, lad," Nels sighed, "not so I could teach you more but so you could teach me more, as you did today!"

"I wish we did too," said Dilyn. "All three of you have taught me so much through your example and words, and you guys have given up far more than I have to this day! I hope you guys train up more Envoys to be like Nazir in that way."

"As long as the Vine permits," Twyla curtsied.

Then Dilyn turned to his four human friends. Before he could say anything, they engulfed him in their collective embrace, no one holding back their tears except Amory. Dilyn himself got choked up a bit.

"Thanks for never giving up on me," he finally said after several moments.

"Thanks for not giving up, period!" Edna replied. "You've gone from being a quitter to being the last one to quit. Nazir's done a lot in you, man!"

"I just hope Nazir makes me half as good a leader as you were today," said Amory.

"Just keep loving and trusting him," Dilyn responded. "He'll get you there and so much further. I'm happy I got to serve under you."

At last, they all let go. As they stepped back, Bernice added, "Just don't go near any spiders." All five of them laughed, including Edna, who was told that story shortly after joining them.

Still crying and smiling, Leona went in for one last hug. Dilyn hugged her tightly in return.

"It's gonna be OK," Dilyn whispered in her ear.

"What's it gonna be like without you?" Leona exclaimed.

"I can ask you the same thing!" Dilyn smirked. "I honestly can't answer that."

Leona pulled herself back and grinned, hands still on his shoulders. "What will I tell your parents when you don't come back . . . and our gathering?"

"Eh, you'll think of something snarky yet true," Dilyn answered. "You always do. They will be all right." After a sigh, he said, "I love you, my friend. You've been the best companion one could hope for. Don't limit that to just me."

Leona's lips tightened. "I won't. I love you too, Dilyn."

At that, they let each other go. Leona limped toward her team and the humans while Dilyn made his way to the arborves and other creatures. As he passed Nazir, he put his hand on his stalk. "See ya soon, Father!" he exclaimed.

"I love you, my son!" Nazir replied joyfully. As the last few recruits reentered the Center, Nazir turned to the humans' side. "When I redeemed you today and replaced your blood with mine, I also healed all of your battle scars. But there is one here who is wounded whom I haven't healed yet. Leona, do you want to be healed?"

Leona's jaw dropped. "Are you kidding me?! You want to heal *my* wounds, which I can live with, while you let Dilyn die of his? How could you ask me that? Why aren't you even asking Agabio, or someone else who could use it more?"

The Vine sighed patiently. "My daughter, you don't get to choose who I heal and who I don't yet. Every healing does happen, but according to my timing and plan. This is how I can advance my Kingdom the furthest through Dilyn, and how I can through you requires healing now. You won't be able to get far in your future missions with those deep cuts and with a hole in your leg. Do you want to be healed?"

"Why does it always have to be about *your* kingdom?" Leona asked. "Don't you care about each individual's best interests?"

"Leona, you know I do," the Vine answered. "I see each and every creature, and I see where they end up and what it takes for them to get to me to become whole. Do you not want them to taste and live in my love and redemption?"

Neisha chimed in, "You know full well where we all would be if not for Nazir's progressing Kingdom reaching us. People desperately need a loving and righteous and perfect kingdom to be a part of, and Nazir's is the only one that truly is that."

Appalled, Leona looked at Dilyn, raising her arm toward the Vine to indicate his audacity. Dilyn's only response was a firm and assuring nod. Leona looked to the ground and shook her head, her fists clenched. Without looking up, she limped toward her Father and closed her eyes.

"Fine," she sighed. "Have it your way."

Without another word, Nazir reached out and placed a leaf on her side. The gash that was there was soon gone, as well as the hole in her leg and every wound she'd accumulated on every prior mission. Not a single scab could now be found on her.

"Thank you," she said begrudgingly as she made her way back to the team.

Nazir then declared, "It is time for all of you to find new homes. To you who were previously part of the Self-Worthy, I want you to return to your home worlds and your families so you can give a testimony of the change they will see in you. I will show you which portals to go through. Arborves, I am sending you with Dilyn, Wybirt, Malfreda, and now Ives to find homes in Hertengard. The land is ready for you now. Humans, I am sending you with the rest of Amory's team back to Earth. Much has changed there since your ancestors left, and it will take time for you to acclimate to the differences. But you will be in good hands, and I will be with you—and everyone here—always. The peoples you will each be aligning with will be very curious as to what you're doing in their worlds. Do not hesitate to tell them your stories and about me. Go and be fruitful in your new lives."

"Yes, my King," the hundreds replied jubilantly, and they followed their leaders to the respective portals. Dilyn, Malfreda, and the rest of their team exchanged one last glance through the crowds before entering the white.

The Self-Worthy-turned-Envoys had mixed experiences upon returning home. Some of their families and friends eagerly welcomed them back after hearing that Nazir had redeemed them. Others were treated with mild concern or contempt and were subtly outcast. Others met direct opposition and started to be persecuted because of what they were saying. In every case, though, Nazir provided each of them with fellow Envoys to train, strengthen, and walk beside them, and none of their faith in the Vine wavered.

The Topiadan humans were baffled and amazed at how technologically advanced Earth had become. It took them months to get accustomed to it all, including the American culture. Their Envoy leaders assured them that the European cultures from which their ancestors originated had changed a lot too and that none of the cultures were perfect.

After deep searches for small and medium towns that could hold the newcomers, Amory's team finally found homes for everyone, mostly on the east coast, as well as other places Edna recommended from her family's travels. Having lived medieval lifestyles, the new visitors were no strangers to manual labor and eagerly attained work wherever they could find it. Over their first several weeks, Nazir had provided them with everything they needed. Thanks to him, they had also become far more merciful and understanding, talking to others about him whenever they got the chance.

The arborves were taken to Liberdane to see about finding some territories to live in. Dilyn, Wybirt, and Ives were shocked by the differences they saw in this once barren and dying country. They went directly to Liberdane's rulers, King Eoin and Queen Fynballa Vyctor, who hadn't aged a bit but were far more wonderful than Dilyn and Ives remembered them when they'd last seen them. Their majesties were delighted to see all of them and to help in any way. Soon, the arborves had acres upon acres on which to populate and thrive, and whatever land the monarchs couldn't provide, they successfully petitioned other nations to. Within weeks, every arborf had new sets of fresh, green, flourishing leaves to replace their old, brown ones. They were now freer than their kind had ever been before.

All the elves soon heard and were astounded by the news that Wybirt the Zealous had returned, and the fairy told them all about his whereabouts in the past centuries and how he returned to the Vine. He went on to resume his duty as a peacemaker, aiding in battles, treaties, and law enforcement wherever Nazir guided him. This time, though, he was careful to be faithful to the Vine with his recovered celebrity. Malfreda, once her kind was well established in their new world, went to Earth to join Amory's team and grow alongside them. Ives settled in a small, remote elven village and took a break from fighting to learn more about Nazir and the truths he'd been deceived from. After much urging from Eoin and Nazir, however, he got back to battling, now for his country and the Vine. Even so, he led a peaceful and quiet life, other than talking about his redemption. Dilyn fell more and more ill as time went on, and as the last arborves were getting settled, he was finally put on hospice in the Diamond Culet, the king and queen's pentagonal castle and home.

From back in the Self-Worthy's fortress in Ourrance, Ambrose heard where Dilyn was and why. Immediately upon hearing the news, he took the Sword of *Chârâsh* and went straight to Hertengard, bringing only Esorbma with him. They agreed to look as non-threatening as possible, armed with the basics and wearing t-shirts and jeans. They, too, were stunned by how Liberdane had changed and flourished. There was barely a dead or dying thing to be seen, save themselves. After a bit of asking around, they finally found the Diamond Culet, which was also far more beautiful yet less fortified than the ruined crucible they remembered it being. They reached the portcullis entrance before being stopped by two guards in indigo armor. These guards were goblins-turned-elves who were survivors of Ambrose's raid on this castle a few years ago. They recognized him and his Sword and doppelgänger.

"We cannot permit you to enter," they said firmly.

"My brother is in there," pleaded Ambrose. "I heard he's dying, and I want to see him before it's too late. Please don't deny me this!"

"I am sorry, sir," said one of the guards, unfazed. "Even if that were true, we cannot grant you access. With that Sword, you have a high potential for hostile intent. We cannot let that intent inside these walls."

Ambrose was about to unstrap and put down the Sword to prove his peacefulness until he heard a female voice call out, "Rhys. Osian."

Instantly, the two guards stood erect and turned to face each other so they could see their visitors and the person who called them at the same time. On the other side of the portcullis, a radiant elven lady approached them. She wore a long, indigo dress that was stunning yet didn't hinder her mobility. On her head was a crown of diamond and gold with two thin wings on either side. From underneath the crown fell a wavy brown cape of hair. Ambrose barely recognized her as the scrawny vagabond who was with Amory's team when they were last in Hertengard. It was Queen Fynballa herself.

"Let this man inside," she said gently yet succinctly. "This truly is Envoy Brandt's brother, and he poses no threat to us anymore. He comes alone and in peace this time. Let in only him, however. His doppelgänger must remain outside."

"Thank you," Ambrose exclaimed. He complied, happy he didn't have to leave his Sword.

"But what will you do without me?" Esorbma protested.

"Plenty," answered Ambrose firmly. "Just stay here and keep quiet."

Esorbma snickered. "I literally can't keep quiet . . . because you can't."

Ambrose ignored this last comment as the guards let him in a side door. He bowed to the queen when he got to her.

"Thank you again, your majesty. You've changed a lot since I last saw you, and I'm shocked you recognize me. It's been like three or four years!"

Fynballa chuckled. "Your Sword gives you away, plus it is difficult to forget your zeal. As for me, you can thank Nazir for any good changes you find."

Ambrose nodded as they started strolling down the open courtyard. "If you don't mind my asking, how is it that you came to rule?"

"The Vine himself appointed me and Eoin, who is now my husband. He is attending a peace talk with another elven nation," replied the queen. "Nazir ordered all the events that took place so that he could fairly put us on the throne. I suppose I have you to thank for partially contributing to that."

Ambrose only tightened his lips and hummed in reply. He glanced at her shoulder to find an Envoy badge pinned to her dress. He then observed his surroundings: the repaired castle, the fruitful plants and animals in the courtyard, the content people. It was all that he and Maewing had wanted for this world yet couldn't achieve.

"Well, it looks like you've done a good job in restoring the land. I'm genuinely impressed," Ambrose finally said before stopping and turning to the queen. "How is Dilyn?"

Fynballa's countenance changed. "Not good, which is why I am glad you are here. While he has been in Hertengard, we have given him every fruit, meat, and herb we have access to, but all it has done is relieve his pain. If the healers on Earth cannot save him, neither can the elves. He said this was the Vine's plan, though, and he has much peace about it."

Ambrose sighed deeply. "How long does he have to live?"

"From a few days to a few hours," Fynballa gulped. "I shall show you where he lies."

The queen personally escorted Ambrose inside one of the castle walls to a bedroom overlooking a new arborven territory. She then left as he opened the door. This room was neatly kept, furnished only with a window, a stand holding Dilyn's armor, a nightstand with a vase of gem flowers and Dilyn's Dagger, and a twin-sized bed that held Dilyn himself. His skin was almost as white as the clouds outside or the tunic he wore. His sunken eyes brightened when he beheld his brother, and he struggled to sit up.

"I thought I wouldn't see you again before I go!" Dilyn moaned excitedly. "You don't know how happy I am that you're here."

"Of course!" said Ambrose shakily, hurt that Dilyn barely had any strength to move. "Anything for my little brother. How're you feeling?"

Dilyn grinned. "Honestly I feel fine. I don't feel any pain at all. I just wish I wasn't as weak so you and I could have one last tennis match or something. I'm gonna miss that a lot."

Any efforts Ambrose made to fight back tears were in vain. He let them roll now. "Nah," he said. "You're not weak. You're stronger than I'll ever be."

Dilyn rolled his eyes. "Well, thanks anyway. How are you? I see you got the Sword back. I take it you're still part of the Self-Worthy?"

Ambrose sighed and raised his eyebrows. "Yeah, I am. Not only that, but I took Maewing's spot as their leader. Topiada cost us dearly, though, so we're taking a long breather."

"Huh," said Dilyn, his lower lip perched. "After you all get the rest you need, then what?"

"The Self-Worthy is done fighting," Ambrose answered. "We'll be going from world to world speaking peacefully now, appealing to the individual. No more convincing by force."

Dilyn sat back. "You do know you're not gonna convince everyone, right? Whether by force or not. I have to ask you, bro, what is the point? Why are you still doing this?"

Ambrose was prepared for the conversation to turn in this direction. "Because working to fulfill my own potential is finally succeeding, and I'm now the leader of the group that helped me seek to reach it. I'm happier than I ever was, Dilyn."

Dilyn chuckled a tad. "I can see right through you, bro. You're still yearning for something to fill you, and the fact is you always will. There's a better way, Ambrose. The only way. A way that leads others to the one and only truth that saves them from eternal death, which is something you still must face, even if you conquer every world."

"Is that way really worth all the scorn and toil you've been through?" Ambrose asked.

Dilyn slowly turned his head toward the window, through which he saw arborven children playing in an open field with some dwarves. He beamed. "It's exceedingly worth it."

Ambrose glanced at the same scene and shook his head. "I'm honestly not super sure about that, or about eternity being real. I've just never heard any solid proof for it."

Dilyn looked back at his brother. "Then why are you here?"

Ambrose started fully crying now. "Because my brother is about to be gone forever, and I won't forgive myself if we don't depart on good terms!"

Dilyn smiled. "It won't be forever. If you accept and believe in Nazir once and for all, then we will see each other again. That's the only way, though. And we're already on good terms, Ambrose. Anything you've done against me is forgiven, and I hope you forgive me for what I've done as well." Dilyn then caught sight of a small vine branch in the upper corner of the room behind Ambrose that wasn't there moments ago. He smiled even more as he said, "Stop running from him, bro. He won't wait forever."

Dilyn then lay still, continuing to eye the vine branch. It took Ambrose a moment or two to realize his brother was now gone. He began to bawl as he knelt beside the bed, touching the cold face and bringing the lifeless hand to his forehead. All the memories he had with Dilyn, good and bad, came to his mind in throngs. He couldn't bring himself to believe that making those memories had come to a screeching halt.

"Why, Nazir?" he finally bellowed. "Why would you do this to me?"

Ambrose sat in that room crying for a whole hour. Eventually, he brought himself to get up and leave. People needed to know. He slowly inched his way back to the courtyard, his knees feeling barely strong enough to stand. The elves took the hint immediately and rushed to take and care for the body.

The queen approached Ambrose with deep concern, knowing exactly how he felt. "Are you all right?"

"No, and I won't be for a long while," Ambrose replied without looking at her. After a minute, he asked, "What will you do with him?"

"Eoin will return as soon as he hears what has happened," Fynballa answered. "He and I will personally take the body to Earth for the funeral." She swallowed hard as she said this. "We will ensure he is properly honored and his body well cared for."

Ambrose nodded slightly. "Then I guess I will see you there. I have to return home."

"Aye," said Fynballa. "May the Vine give you the peace you desire."

Ambrose came out the same side door that he entered in, his doppelgänger awaiting him. No sooner had the door shut behind him than Esorbma declared, "Now, you are finally free of that burden!"

Without a second thought, Ambrose grabbed his Sword and stabbed Esorbma in the chest. He then created a portal inside his body, and the screaming doppelgänger folded and disappeared into the portal, teleported to oblivion. Ambrose knew that somehow Esorbma would find a way to come back, but he didn't care. He had had enough, and he wished there was a way to get rid of him for good. He then made a new portal in front of him, weeping as he entered to tell his parents that they just lost their son.

16

RESOLUTIONS

C raghill actually had decent weather on this bittersweet day, considering it was mid-September. The sun beamed through the cloudless sky and gradually brought the temperature to almost fifty degrees Fahrenheit. The memorial service for Dilyn Brandt could be held outside. It took place at Craghill's main cemetery, right at Dilyn's burial site. Canopies and outdoor heaters were provided.

Along with Amory and his team and mentor, Ambrose had come with his parents and some Self-Worthy members who were closer to Dilyn. Dilyn's old friends and extended family were also there, rather flummoxed by all the aliens around them. Eoin, Fynballa, and Ives were there, as well as several elves and dwarves from Hertengard, including Ida and some of the orphans from the town of Growan. Masato, his crew, and a few other creatures from Uchu also made it there, all in human form. Also among the attendees were Valter, Rolle, and as many arborves and Topiadan humans as could come. There were not enough seats to accommodate the hundreds that were present. Everyone wore black—whether formal or not—as was American human tradition.

Standing on a podium behind the painted steel casket, the leader of Amory's team's gathering officiated the ceremony and allowed anyone to come to the front to honor Dilyn by sharing some memories about him. At least a dozen participated, but the most notable orations were those of Valter, Ambrose, and Leona.

Valter began by summarizing the whole tale of the Final Battle of Topiada and how Dilyn and the others brought them out and to the Vine. "My ego was invaded by Nazir through Dilyn," he said. "I am only sorry that it took a world's destruction and the fall of my entire family to wake me up. I knew not about Dilyn's disease until the rescue was complete, but I was deeply inspired by his ability to fight it, the battle in Topiada, and the battle to bring people to Nazir all at the same time. If it were not for Dilyn's courage, determination, and selflessness, I and thousands of other creatures would not be alive today."

Ambrose went next to last, the Sword still at his side, though concealed. In his hand was a piece of parchment, which he unrolled when he got to the pulpit. He started to speak, then began to tear up and shake his head. After a minute, he leaned over and took a deep breath, still struggling for words. "For those of you who don't know, I had the undeserved honor of being Dilyn's brother. Since I was older than him, I often looked down on and even neglected him for most of his life. Dilyn originally was just more timid and less confident in himself. We'd compete over everything, and unless it had to do with math or logic, I would almost always shamelessly win. Regretfully, I loved asserting that I was, or at least thought I was, flat-out better than Dilyn, which made him hang around me more so he could be more like me, which honestly just annoyed me."

Ambrose took another deep breath. "All that changed after a certain misadventure where I almost lost Dilyn." At this, Ambrose eyed Amory and Leona. "After that, I began to value him more and actually wanted to be around him. We did get to be together a lot these past couple of years, but during that time I got distracted from him and his needs. By the time I realized that, it was too late." Ambrose took another pause. "I could've been such a better brother to Dilyn. I could've been more present for him . . . to see him more often. When I finally came to my senses and truly saw him again, he was saving countless lives in the most self-denying way I've ever known. I am unworthy of having the same blood as a man and warrior like Dilyn, and there's nothing I can do now to make it right. But for once, I'm gonna turn the tables. Before, Dilyn aspired to become like me. Now I am aspiring to be more like my little brother: selfless, noble, and loyal. These are a few of many qualities in Dilyn that I could adopt."

Ambrose lifted the parchment a little for his audience to see. "I received this parchment from the elves who brought Dilyn's body. They said he wrote the song that's on it on the day he passed and wished it to be read for his ceremony. Now, I'm not going to fool you or myself in thinking that I'm gonna be able to get through reading it, so I've asked my close friend Leona Ferris to do it."

Leona stood up and took Ambrose's place, patting him on the back as she passed by him. She cleared her throat, determined to get through without crying. "Before I read this, I want to quickly share something about Dilyn. I've gotten to watch him grow up from his high school years and beyond. I watched him go from a nobody to a little punk to one of the most kindhearted friends I have ever had. This last change was only possible through the best Friend and Father there ever was and ever will be. Like Ambrose said, Dilyn wanted this song he wrote to be read aloud at this time, so that every eye present would look to the one who planned this all along for the benefit of the multiverse. The one who saves, then redeems countless times afterward. The one whose justice and mercy are equally unwavering. This song is entitled 'You Have Won.'"

Then, she read off the words in prose.

[Verse 1]
The night was strong and eminent
Its voidness could have crushed a soul
I pursued what I thought was good
Sprinting further in the black hole

[Pre-chorus 1]
But in the chasing, a light burst through
Directed straight toward my heart

Exquisite and unignorable
With it I could not depart

[Chorus]
Now you are my King forever
You made this rebel a loyal son
Your conquest of love has drawn me in
This war, these worlds, this soul you have won

[Verse 2]
I'm now part of your family
That doesn't mean life won't be hard
I go through trials that I can't bear
Always being chased back toward the dark

[Pre-chorus 2]
But in the chasing, a light bursts through
Directed straight toward my heart
Exquisite and unignorable
With it I cannot depart

[Bridge]
You changed a sealed fate
And sealed it for yourself
You fixed my smashed pieces
put on your perfect shelf
And each time I crash and burn
You're ready for my return

This song touched the hearts of everyone there, and after the ceremony had ended, Dilyn's body had been buried, and the customary meal had been shared, they all went home pondering it and Nazir's redemption.

A couple of weeks later, the elves put music to it, and the song gradually spread throughout the entire multiverse as one of many songs passed down to remind its listeners of their great King and Redeemer. Many more in several worlds became Envoys after hearing it a few times, including Dilyn and Ambrose's parents. Since the day Nazir adopted them, they never tired of talking about him, their son, and his story.

All was quiet in Amory and Bernice's wooded cottage except for the sound of sizzling in the kitchen. Amory was teaching Bernice how to make homemade chicken and waffles with honey barbecue sauce and green beans. Amory was more of the cook in the relationship, while Bernice would usually just eat whatever her parents cooked or what was premade at the store. She wanted to learn more scratch-made recipes though, especially Amory's. He was happy to oblige.

"Then we'll add some paprika to the batter for a little kick," Amory said.

"Which batter, the one for the chicken or the waffles?" Bernice asked.

"Hmm," replied Amory, "I never thought of putting it in the waffles before, but that might be good too! Let's put it in both."

"Might be?" Bernice cracked up. "Dear, we have a guest coming. I don't think now's the time for experiments."

"Eh, I really don't think it'll be bad." Amory smiled. "Let's put it in."

"All right. Are we ready to dredge the chicken now?" asked Bernice.

"Yes!" Amory answered. "Once we put them in the egg wash and the batter, they'll be good for the air fryer."

"How is it you know so many recipes, hon?"

"Way too much time on my hands as a kid," laughed Amory. "Once I heard of a new dish, I'd experiment with it until I came up with something decent, then I'd dabble on improvements. I was still unsupervised, and I've almost burned the house down more than once."

"Now that I believe," Bernice giggled.

The waffles were almost ready by the time their guest drove up in his truck. It was Theodore, complete with his armor and bladed shield. The three of them gave their greetings.

"It smells terrific in here!" Theodore exclaimed. "Anything I can do to help?"

"Only in making yourself at home," answered Bernice. "We're almost done . . . aren't we?"

Amory chuckled. "Yeah, we are. Lunch will be right out."

And so it was. All of them thoroughly enjoyed this new dish, and the paprika in the waffles was a success. They caught up on a lot as they ate.

"How's your family?" Bernice asked Theodore.

"They're doing well. My wife just got us a new dining table, which she's excited about, and our boys are growing up fast. Two of them are already teenagers. Nazir's given me a lot to be thankful for and a lot to learn. How's the team?"

"They're doing well," Amory replied. "It's been a month since Dilyn passed, and there's hurt still in all of us. But Nazir's been faithful, nonetheless. Edna got a gig as a consultant at a small fashion store, and she's been enjoying that a lot. Leona's teaching is going well, and she says she's been more dedicated and involved with her students as people and not just names on a paper. Everyone else who isn't human is doing well in adapting to this world, or at least as well as one can expect. It's harder now for Malfreda to find soil to walk in and get nourished by, and Masato is having a hard time staying in human form at his new construction job. Other than that, things are good. Nels started to mentor Chadmight a few weeks ago, and Panos is continuing to train Agabio, and all of them have grown a lot. Also, I heard that Neisha and Twyla are now dating some guys they've gotten to know!"

"That's awesome!" Theodore responded. "I'm very happy to hear that! How's the married life so far for you?"

Bernice nodded. "It's going OK so far. There have already been some speed bumps and conflicts as we expected, but we're prepared and are working through them, and we continue choosing each other. We're just thankful we get to do all of this together and that every battle in the cosmos and at home we can fight side by side now."

"I'm ecstatic for both of you." Theodore grinned.

Amory added, "Also, since our last mission with Dilyn, I'm learning to be a more assertive and radical leader, going against the grain of culture and not just going with the flow of however I feel or fear. At the same time, I'm going to Nazir constantly to make sure I'm on the right track and I'm not going out of line. It's been a learning curve for sure."

"And it always will be," said Theodore. "*Rôb Tĕbêl* needs more leaders like that, especially nowadays. Marah's starting to lose ground, and he's going to do his very best to gain more and more as the end draws near. We must be ready for however he attacks us." Then Theodore proceeded to get up and pick up his shield. "With that being said, are you ready to take me on after we clean up lunch?"

Amory smirked as he picked up all three plates. "I've been waiting so long for a match with you! Would you like to join me, hon?"

"Oh, don't worry," Bernice beamed, "I wouldn't miss this for the world."

EPILOGUE

I n his apartment two stories up, Ambrose stared out of his living room window at the world outside. He didn't have the luxury of a country view, but he liked the cityscape better anyway. It was a Saturday afternoon, and there were people in abundance on the streets and in traffic. Whether each of them was going to work, shopping, browsing, meeting with someone, or seeking to stir up trouble was unknown. It was irrelevant to Ambrose. All he saw was the sheer number of them and the subtle despair and lostness in their faces. He knew that everyone down there was still in dire need of fulfillment, and he still believed that they could quench that need themselves.

After people-watching a little longer, Ambrose glanced at the Sword of *Chârâsh* on his kitchen table and decided to return to Ourrance to lead the Self-Worthy in preparing for more movements, this time on Earth. Just as he picked up the Sword, he heard a whisper in his head as clearly as if it were right outside his ear.

There are a lot of lost worlds in Rôb Têbêl, said the voice, *but Earth is one of the most lost. It is so close to realizing the truth, yet it has still missed the mark.*

Ambrose lifted the Sword higher in a battle-ready position. That voice wasn't his. It wasn't Nazir's, and it definitely wasn't Dilyn's. It was cunning and very pleasant to the ear, but Ambrose still wasn't keen on hearing voices in his head.

"Who's there?" he asked, slowly and hesitantly looking all around him, positive he was the only one in his apartment. "Are you coming from the Sword?"

No, but like it, I have great power and can take you places that you cannot get to on your own. If you'll have me, I can be your guide in achieving not only your potential but that of everyone with whom you interact.

"I don't need anyone else to help me achieve that," Ambrose replied. "I am self-fulfilling."

Tell that to everyone who helped you get where you are now, everyone who taught you that you could indeed fulfill yourself.

This voice seemed to know Ambrose and appeared to have watched his life play out. This threatened Ambrose more, but he saw there was little to no point arguing with it.

"All right, I'll play along," Ambrose said. "You said that Earth is one of the most lost universes. How am I to help them then?"

I know you intend to appeal to them through peaceful and nonviolent campaigns. Verbal appeals have been attempted and failed over the centuries here, and you know that. As difficult as it is to accept, something more might still be necessary.

Ambrose chortled. "Are you serious? More violence and force? This is my home. I'm not gonna bring about more death and ruin than there already is! That has failed over the centuries too."

Your home is indeed falling apart every day. Something must be done.

"Tearing it apart more is not the answer!" Ambrose shouted. "Thanks a lot for nothing. You can go ahead and leave now, and don't bother trying that stunt on me again, whoever you are!" Ambrose immediately dropped the Sword and stomped outside to get some fresh air. He had to clear his mind and regain his focus before returning to Ourrance. But the proposed thought never left his head.